Another Summer

JUNE BARRACLOUGH

Another Summer

ROBERT HALE · LONDON

© June Barraclough 1998
First published in Great Britain 1998

ISBN 0 7090 6323 7

Robert Hale Limited
Clerkenwell House
Clerkenwell Green
London EC1R 0HT

2 4 6 8 10 9 7 5 3 1

To Frances and Michael

Typeset in North Wales by
Derek Doyle & Associates, Mold, Flintshire.
Printed in Great Britain by
St Edmundsbury Press, Bury St Edmunds, Suffolk.
Bound by WBC Book Manufacturers Limited, Bridgend.

CONTENTS

PRELUDE

London
1994

Whatever anyone tells you, even thirty years ago teaching was hard work, and in those days I never managed to save any of my hard-earned salary. I remember thinking in my twenties that life resolved itself into problems of Work, Men, and Money, with never enough leisure for reading, which in my case meant reading novels.

I was however much concerned with love. I say 'love' rather than 'sex' deliberately, though sex also preoccupied us in those pre-pill days. Sex in those days usually came wrapped up for women in the clothes – or rags – of romantic love.

One day in the distant future I wanted to have a baby, or rather, a child. People always talked as if babies lasted for ever. I was not frightfully interested in babies but I was in favour of carrying on the human race.

Alas, I never achieved my desire, probably because I did not marry until I was almost forty.

I wasted my twenties on a long affair with Peter Richardson, a married man twenty years older than me. Peter certainly loved me, but it may have been for this very reason that I didn't feel as romantic about him as he felt about me.

Before Peter I had often indulged myself in unrequited love, so it had been a bit of a surprise to find someone in love with *me*. I knew however that it would be impossible to have Peter's baby without hurting other people.

After Peter I still felt strongly attracted to men. Too often. I'm sure my frequent infatuations arose from my botched relationship with Peter. I thought that I was a 'romantic' woman, falling in love with artists and writers, the kind of men who did not or could not reciprocate. The wrong sort of men to settle down with in any case, as I was often told. I thought that I was an 'idealist', destined for unhappiness in that love into and out of which I frequently fell. Mother Nature however went on giving me an almighty push, often towards the wrong men. On the other hand I was not reckless, disliked living on the edge, as several of my friends did at that time. I suppose I was much more conventional than I imagined I was, and in the end, I married Roland, and became the respectable Mrs Wilson.

Roland was a surprising choice: at least that's what everybody thought, even if they didn't say. It's true he was a journalist, but he was an agricultural correspondent for some West Country papers and at the time I met him he was working in London. We got on well, were well-suited, and I liked and respected him. I believe I added something good to his life, though I didn't have for him those feelings of crazy infatuation I had earlier gone in for.

For some reason I've always looked back to 1964 as the real watershed in my life. It was that summer – eight years before my marriage to Roland – that I went on holiday to northern Italy with

Liz Grove. I had got over Peter two years before and I suppose I was ready to fall in love again. I learned in Cusio the usual lesson: that I could not have what I thought I wanted. That I still hankered for excitement was, I thought, an example of the defects of my character. It was Roland later who showed me that I might have needed something quite different at that time.

Roland died in 1984 after we had been married for twelve years. For a time I was all at sea. Not just on account of my grief over his death, but because I had to readjust to a completely different way of life. All the little things, like the time you get up and go to bed, put the cat out, decide who will water the garden and when to go shopping. As we had no children – the tragedy of my life, and I think Roland's too – I had nobody really with whom to share my mourning. Roland's parents were dead and he'd been an only child. When I say it was a tragedy I don't mean that it was the only thing I ever thought about or wanted from life, but I'd always dreamed of a daughter.

A few months after Roland died, I went back to teaching, thinking it was the best thing to do in the circumstances. I'm glad now that I did. By the time that I retired for the second time four years ago, however, I was very relieved to go. It has taken me those four years to adjust myself to my second new life, and to decide what I want to do with it.

Most, if not all, women take their husband's name when they marry. When I married Roland and became Mrs Wilson it was quite a wrench to lose my old name.

I was christened Beryl Vivien Butterworth, always known as Vivien. When I was a child, my class mates used to call me Butterfingers, and my own pupils did the same before I was married. I didn't mind; they didn't intend any malice and as a matter of fact I have always been a bit of a butterfingers, never having had the slightest talent for ball games.

I had a Northern surname because my grandfather went from Bolton to Dorset in the 1890s when the bank he worked for opened a branch in Weymouth. I was born in 1932 into the respectable Butterworth family in a village not far from Dorchester. My mother's male relatives, the Hodges, had all worked on the land from the year dot. But even years before Mother was born the way for girls to escape peasanthood was to go to a training college and emerge as elementary school teachers. This is what my mother, Hilda, did. In this she was like both Thomas Hardy's sisters, and many other intelligent girls who were not 'ladies'.

I went myself to a local grammar school and then to London University, where I studied English. It was quite a feat in those days not to go to Exeter or Southampton, but I was determined to hit the bright lights. Eventually, however, I too ended up working in schools, as many women graduates of my generation did, teaching for a salary the subject we once studied for love. In my twenties and thirties I taught in all sorts of schools, and had a busy London life with many friends, frequent visits to the theatre and cinema, and summer holidays abroad to recover from the year's exhausting efforts.

It was about a year after Roland died that I heard that Peter Richardson had also died. By now I'd returned to teaching, and was keeping myself busy, but at that time I did not think much about my pre-marriage years, found it difficult to remember my long-ago years with Peter in much detail, or to grieve for him properly.

Our memories seem to operate in circular fashion; we remember things when we are ready to remember them, and I suppose as you grow older you begin to remember further back. I often wish I had met Roland earlier, though I have never regretted my late marriage. So many people arrive in one's life at the wrong time. Either you are not ready for them and they are wasted on you, or it is too late and you are no longer what you once were.

It was after my second retirement from teaching, this time for good, that the memory of our long-ago Italian summer holiday began to come into my thoughts, I'm not sure why. It may have been because I had begun to see it as the end of my early youth, of the time of illusions, though I suppose that at thirty-two, which was the age I went to Italy for the first time, I ought to have been grown up.

I believe I once mentioned Cusio to Roland when we were telling each other about our pasts, but it hadn't seemed important then. Liz Grove and I had gone to this little town – more of a village really – by Lake Cusio, and during the holiday we had met some young Italians. One of them was Sandro Montani, a painter. Sandro seems to me now a sort of emblem of my many minor unrequited passions. Not the great love of my life, for I did not even have an affair with him. Nor really even the man I'd have liked to marry, but the man I imagined then – and later – as an ideal father for my imaginary daughter. Perhaps that was the real reason he'd remained in my mind. I expect I began to remember him and the little town where we stayed with such nostalgia, because when we'd gone there I'd been poised to find myself a lifelong partner.

I didn't find him there in Cusio. I'd still been romantic then about painters and writers – as well as a sucker for good looks – and Sandro Montani had both the looks and the talent. I hope I never embarrassed him with a lovesick manner. I must say straight away that the feeling was all on my side. My memory of Sandro, submerged for so long, and my memory of that lovely little place, has probably become sanctified by time. Now when I see Sandro's face in my mind's eye it is the epitome of Italian charm, though I know that he did not really look what people think of as typically Italian. Anyway, when I finally retired from my job teaching English in a rather old-fashioned girls' school, the thought was already vaguely in my mind that I'd like to return, just once, to Cusio.

I often thought too how freedom comes to most people too late, but I had a reasonable pension, along with what Roland had left me, and I was one of the luckier ones. At last I could spend my time as I wanted, even if I was now both widowed and retired – in the wrong order. Before he died Roland had been considering his own retirement. When the time was ripe we planned eventually to leave our London suburb. My husband was a country man at heart and we were dreaming of going back home to live in Dorset.

Later, it seemed that I had always known I would return to Cusio one day, but in spite of all the reasons I have given I'm still not sure why I wanted so urgently to go back. It certainly wasn't to look for Sandro Montani, though I had kept up an interest in modern Italian painting. I didn't think Sandro would still be living on the shores of the lake. Even if he was, he'd probably be a grandfather several times over. Maybe it was just that idea of a watershed, and of leaving something of myself unfinished there, a part of my life that, in spite of my marriage, remained incomplete. I didn't want to go back to 'find myself', as they say nowadays. I thought I knew myself too well. I may have wanted to experience again the old feel-ings of happiness, or response to a beautiful place that I remembered from my youth, feelings that had been smothered under the sadness of my widowhood or the weariness of my work.

What I was to find, which was much more important, was a completely new perspective on what had happened there during that hot summer of 1964.

In my twenties and early thirties, I had many friends, most of whom I still know: Helena, and Polly, and Liz, and Joanna, and my oldest friend, Eleanor Edwards. Roland always used to say how women kept up their friendships so much better than men. He still saw his old friend Oliver Fairfax but others had slipped away from his ken. Oliver is now a friend of mine. He is what we used to call 'queer', so there is no constraint between us. Roland never alluded to it. He wasn't in any way 'queer' himself, but he liked Oliver, with whom he had been to school. They got teased a lot because of their two names.

Helena, with whom I used to teach years ago, was a true bohemian if ever there was one, but her drug, apart from nicotine, was sex. She has worn well, however. She has never married, but she has lived with Joe Philips for fifteen years now. Another friend is Polly who once racketed round with Helena. For all I know she's happy living alone. She goes on long Alpine walks, and plays the organ, and does all the things I have no talent for. She's exactly my age and continually reminds me of the fact. I find that people all measure themselves surreptitiously one against the other for signs of old age.

Joanna Fielding, whom I met about twenty years ago, is another good friend. She was always a marvellous cook, used to live with her husband Robin in the house next to ours. At that time she was a journalist on our local rag. Actually, she once presented me with the prize for a crossword puzzle I'd sent in. Then suddenly Joanna became a cookery writer, which made me quite afraid of her. I'd always been a bit worried about inviting her to eat *chez nous*, but now she might expect me to follow the advice she dispensed in magazines, and then in a book. She was on to a good thing.

Long before I knew Joanna I used to enjoy trying out Elizabeth David recipes – it was before everyone else did – but then everyone else caught up with me, and I had been at no time a brilliant cook. It was in the seventies that people went in for elaborate dinner parties, and we decided not to compete. For the last ten years or so even the married women I know have stopped being martyrs. Joanna once asked me for my favourite standby meal and all I could think of was the herrings and marjoram that I used to cook on a small gas ring when I lived in a bedsitter. Before we gave up dinner parties, my favourite dish was *paupiettes de veau*. It turned out that after I had stopped bothering I would soon not have been able in any case to buy veal. After the calves' transportation scandals, my local butcher was picketed. That's the sort of suburb it is.

Apart from Jo and Robin, and Oliver and Helena and Polly, my closest friends are those whom I've known from childhood or from work. My best friend is still Eleanor Edwards. We go back a long way, to early childhood, when we grew up together in Dorset. Eleanor was divorced five years ago and, like me, has no children. During my second autumn of freedom in 1993 I went to stay with her in Dorset for a little holiday. She lives in a village only a few miles away from my old home. Neither of my parents are there any longer. My father has been dead for years and my mother was by then – at her own request – in a Birmingham nursing home near where my brother Roger lives.

During that holiday it rained a good deal and I wished I'd persuaded Eleanor to accompany me somewhere sunnier. She, however, seemed perfectly content, and I realized the dissatisfaction arose from myself, not just the weather.

When I retired, it had been both with the intention of enjoying myself and having the time to learn something new. I can honestly say that it has always been unusual for me to be bored, yet once I had time to myself, why had I so far done so little with my new freedom? It had satisfied me only partially. It's true that my existence wasn't then and isn't now a completely selfish one: I contribute to various charities, collect for the Red Cross in my South London suburb, help 'reluctant readers' at a local school when they need me, and have plenty other interests.

When I moved to the flat I brought everything personal with me from the house Roland and I had lived in. I couldn't bring all the furniture but I brought all my own possessions in large boxes and cases because I couldn't bear at the time to go through them all. It was enough that I'd had to dispose of Roland's clothes and golf-clubs and maps. I'd intended to sort through my own stuff when I retired, and now was the time. The flat was not poky – in fact it was better organized than our old house – but the whole detritus of my life was beginning to depress me. On returning home from Eleanor's I decided that it was now the time for a really good clear out. Then I would make positive plans for the future.

I tidied my collection of compact discs, and did my best to sort out my books, of which I have many. I also made a long list of all the books I wanted to read, but did not possess, and managed to get round to reserving some of them at various libraries. I amused myself watching a few videos of the kind of French films I'd always loved, one of those with a plangent piano soundtrack, often by Rachmaninov, or one of Chopin's preludes. I looked for and found my old sketch books, thinking I might try to use my oil crayons or even paint in oils again, but I couldn't seem to produce anything decent. I had my piano tuned and threw away the tattier remnants of my old sheet music, and got hold of prospectuses for local adult education courses – but could find nothing that really attracted me. I sorted, or tried to sort, all the many photographs I'd taken, especially those after I'd bought my new camera on my honeymoon.

I turned out cupboards and found boxes of notebooks devoted to preparation for even longer-ago lessons, and in the drawers of my old desk I discovered letters from other friends, some from more than thirty years back, to whom I was no longer as close as I still was to Eleanor or Lizzie, my other long-established friend: Elizabeth Hill née Grove, with whom I went on that holiday to Cusio.

I spent several days reading the letters, not sure whether I wanted to throw them away. Many of my friends had left London, and some of them had swung away completely from my orbit. Now they wrote only at Christmas. There were even people whom I had almost forgotten. Without this written proof they would have eventually become completely so. I decided that as I had kept these stacks of letters for so long I would continue to keep just a few from each person. I hated to think of the passage of time, scything down all that had once been important to me. My life had been rich and many-layered, though to someone who didn't know me well it must have seemed a little boring and ordinary. None of us however is ordinary to ourselves. How much one forgets! I hate forgetting, now that my life is less busy.

At night I seem always to enter another world. Sleep and dreams have always been important to me. Each morning, when I have to get up I lie in the half light from my thick curtains, deliciously half asleep, pursued by fragments of dreams and ideas. I enjoy my own thoughts and look forward to the inner life of the night.

I don't *live* in a dream though. I am a methodical person who likes a daily routine with nothing too unpredictable. I get up, clean my teeth, wash, dress, decide which jewellery I shall wear and go through to my kitchen for breakfast where I read the newspapers and the letters that happily still arrive. I make up my face before I tidy my flat and do any necessary housework. I suppose I shouldn't bother with my face, but it's a habit. When I have made the bed and done some washing I make a cup of coffee, and then write a shopping list, considering what I shall have for lunch. I check in my fridge that there is a bottle of cold white wine, for I allow myself a glass at lunch time and a glass or two in the evening. By about eleven o'clock I am ready to walk to the shops. I don't run a car so I get enough exercise. All the tenants of the flats, which are in a big old Victorian house – modernized inside – have a small patch of garden. Here I plant bulbs and have my special rose bushes.

If I'm not going to meet anyone for lunch I usually stay in for the afternoon, though I sometimes walk to the library, or do a bit of what I will not dignify with the name of gardening. I read a lot and listen to music and write long letters to friends and never have television on until the Channel 4 News at seven o'clock. Every Friday morning I do my big shop at the supermarket. I often see acquaintances there, as well as the local characters who haunt the place.

A few days after my discovering the cache of letters, I decided to clean out a cupboard, and I found at the bottom some old shoe boxes full of picture postcards, a collection of scent bottles and even some tails of pink knitting.

Whenever had I found time to knit? It must have been years ago when the Hills' daughter Emma was a baby. We girls all used to knit a lot during the war – for what we called 'the duration' –

chiefly wool squares for blankets. My own childish knitting was not very successful, and judging by the bits I found in my cupboard, baby Emma would probably never have worn any of my efforts. I had been teaching in Bromley by the time Emma was born, and in suburban commuter trains I used to see the nimble fingers of self-satisfied-looking women wielding their needles, busy on complicated patterns. I must have imagined I might emulate them. (I have noticed that there are fewer of those women now – though I try to avoid public transport in rush hours.)

Emma's mother, Lizzie Hill, who went with me to Cusio, was still Liz Grove then. We had got to know each other at the London school where we both taught, Liz mathematics and myself English. I suppose we never had a great deal in common but I do remember it was because Eleanor could not go to Italy that summer that Liz offered to accompany me. In the staffroom I'd mentioned the already-booked ten days, saying there was a place going for anyone who hadn't made any other arrangements. I'd already paid the deposit and Eleanor was frightfully guilty about pulling out, but her mother was ill and she felt she ought to stay in England.

Anyway, Liz said she really needed a change. In the coming autumn she was to be married, but her fiancé was very preoccupied with all the work he had to do before that. She was exhausted from teaching – which she did not enjoy – and her mother was sending her mad, fussing around organizing the wedding in the autumn. Even Mrs Grove said Liz needed a good rest or she'd have a nervous breakdown and start her married life on the wrong foot. That's how it came about that it was Liz who accompanied me to Cusio all those years ago.

Lizzie has been married now for over thirty years to Adrian, an architect, and they are still happily married, with three grown up children. I used to envy her marriage, less so perhaps after I married myself, but I always envied her the children, especially Emma, the baby for who I had done the knitting, my goddaughter, a lovely girl.

I devoted a few days to throwing things away – or rather *not* throwing them away. I'm afraid I am an inveterate hoarder, but I did get rid of the knitting. Even old registers from my early days of teaching were evocative. I remembered the girls I'd taught, in the 1950s, when I had been not much older than my pupils, all the Carols and Valeries and Lindas, later to change into Jackies and Debbies and Karens.

One morning I was turning out a bottom drawer I'd left till the end because it stuck a bit and the knob was broken. I managed to open it, took it out completely, and found a bag of old photographs that had never been stuck in albums. Colour photographs had only just come in at the beginning of the 1960s, and there were various envelopes, in one of them some pictures of a lake, and of Liz Grove sitting at a café table, and one or two of young men at a similar table: Sandro and his friends Mario and Marco, taken, I seemed to remember, on our last evening in Cusio. I put them aside and then searched in vain in more envelopes full of stray snaps for further photographs of the two men, or of another friend, Raffaelo. I thought I might have taken others of Sandro at a café table on the Sacro Monte, or in Stresa, but if I had, they had disappeared. It is probably more sensible to have memories in one's mind's eye rather than some frozen moment from the past, but I have often thought how differently our memories must operate since the invention of photography, which in my humble opinion is the best invention of the last two hundred years.

Over the next few days I began to see my life, despite my late but happy marriage, and my later adjustment to solitude, as a story with no real progression in it.

Was it because I had never had a child? I knew that having a family had not always made some of my friends very contented. I'd had friends divorced in middle age and left with teenage children, and I knew that a long marriage was sometimes a façade. it can be a sort of a backdrop held together only for as long as the younger characters in the play are on the stage, and sometimes not even then. In Eleanor's case, her husband had not had to wait for any children to grow up – he'd found a younger woman and left. I thought of Peter's wife and realized that Peter had behaved towards her better than Eleanor's Clive.

Roland hadn't been that sort of a man; he was a good, loyal person who was only in his early fifties when he died. There was no point thinking about might-have-beens. At least I had been married to a faithful man – I wasn't the superannuated spinster career woman I so easily might have been. Marriage had changed my old preoccupations, as it probably does for most women unless they are very poor, or married to the wrong man. I hadn't had to worry too much about money; I'd even stopped earning my living for a time; I hadn't been concerned with the future; I'd lived in the present.

And some marriages do last – Liz Hill's, for example. Was that luck or good management?

I return to the winter of my second year of freedom, after all my clearings out. I had already had my bus pass birthday but I still felt young inside, though I was also feeling increasingly unsettled. Not exactly unhappy, just that there was something else I wanted to be doing but was not sure exactly what. Hard to put my finger on the exact nature and order of my feelings. They took some time to surface, and even longer for me to realize what it was I definitely wanted to do before I became too decrepit. In the February of 1994 I was still thinking I might move back home to Dorset, near Eleanor. Yet I knew I no longer really belonged there, however much I loved the place. Then I found myself thinking of those solitary, not quite young, but not quite old, women whose favourite season is autumn and who stay in European hotels in the kind of novels I enjoy reading.

I am older now than most of those, and I went back to Cusio in the winter. Snow lay on the ground the day of my return … but I must not run on ahead.

Reading has always been my favourite way of spending my time, but I also enjoy visiting art exhibitions, and listening to music. I'm not so keen now on going out at night to theatres but I often go to matinées, sometimes with Oliver, sometimes even alone.

Whenever I go to the Royal Academy to an exhibition, or to the National Gallery, I like to observe other people, especially in the restaurants. On weekdays it is predominantly women who greet each other cheerfully over their teetering lunch trays. A few are quite young, but the average must be nearer mine. Some of them are tall, some short, some thin, some dumpy, some married, some widowed, some never married, but they have all had similar lives, a similar education – and they are all recently retired. In the distance they all look alike – intelligent, purposeful, with predominantly grey polls. They probably look a bit like myself, although I must confess my own hair is not quite the colour nature intended it to be at my age and I make sure that it is well cut. Not that you could mistake my friends for the sort of 'Senior Citizens', invariably sporting identical white perms, who attend bingo halls or go regularly on coach tours, though doubtless, like ourselves, they still think of themselves as unique.

All young people think they are unique. It seems though that when you are middle-aged, or, that awful word, elderly, you are no longer unique. Then you wear your past like a badge.

That you *have* a past is the point.

Sometimes in the restaurant I catch sight of a woman I know who might be a year or two younger than myself, and I realize with a start that she too has joined the club of the retired, as I must have done. Quite often, though, I look up from my lunch – they have an excellent menu in both places – and see across the tables, and occasionally even smile at, some woman I take to be a friend before I realize she is nobody I know. She might change places very easily with my friend, and nobody would notice. We often go around in small groups, and you could interchange these groups too. They would absorb newcomers with no difficulty. Whether we know each other or not, we have a lot in common – but then women have always had something in common.

These slightly gloomy realizations set me thinking once more that I needed a change before it was too late. It might be just that I needed new faces, another garden to look at through the window? I didn't want life to come to a full stop. I felt occasionally that meaning seemed to have drained away from the world, now that all that was familiar to people of my generation seemed so utterly changed. I knew it was the advent of age that was bothering me but I didn't really want to go back to being thirty-five, though I'd settle for forty-five, just married to Roland and both of us looking young for our age, as we were often told.

Neither Roland nor I had ever wanted to have holidays away in

Europe. In fact I think Roland really preferred England. Doubtless we lacked the spirit of adventure, but neither of us could be bothered to travel long distances. We had however, been all over France, and Catalonia and Austria, and Switzerland, and to Florence and Venice and Tuscany and the Italian riviera and Emilia Romagna – and of course Lombardy and Piedmont. In fact one summer we were not very far from Cusio but I somehow never connected it with the earlier holiday.

I kept one of the old photographs of Sandro and his friends propped up on a bookshelf and sometimes mocked myself for doing so.

I knew now that I wanted to return to Cusio, but I needed an extra push. Sometimes I managed to put the idea out of my head, feeling vaguely guilty that I might be planning a nostalgia trip ... until I received a message from an unexpected quarter.

It was in the February of 1994, after a visit to an exhibition at the Royal Academy, that I was walking along one of those streets near Cork Street where several smart art galleries are to be found.

My attention was suddenly caught by a painting in the window of a small gallery, and I was stopped in my tracks.

The painting was of a lake with a small island.

I went in, but I found I was looking instead at a superb exhibition of *photographs*. When I studied them more carefully, I realized that they were all of Lake Cusio and the island. In winter. In the snow. The gardens near the lake were all white; roofs had white icing on them; footsteps made patterns on white paths; lacy wrought-iron gates stood with a thin layer of snow or ice on their ledges. I remembered Sandro saying something once about painting 'all the whitenesses'. His English was not always too good but I had known what he meant.

'Out of season': I liked that phrase. A summer holiday resort in the winter snow is, like the windswept beach of some seaside town in autumn in England, the kind of place to which I have always been attracted.

These black-and-white photographs, like the old colour snaps I had found in the drawer, were definitely telling me to go back to Cusio. That February afternoon I knew there was nothing to stop me from returning to that backdrop for one of my unrequited passions. Not that I expected to see anyone there whom I knew. It was more a matter of drawing a line under one of the stories of my life, before I returned home to resign myself to growing old.

When Lizzie Hill, who was then Liz Grove, and I went to Lake Cusio in the summer of 1964 I'd been wanting to spend a holiday in such a place for ages.

Somewhere unspoilt, a small gem of a village. The place I found had only two hotels, both by the lake, wonderful walks, and an island you could reach in five minutes in a little boat. The steep ascent behind the village led to an old cemetery and behind that, on the top of the hill, there was a large, strange park, called the *Sacro Monte*. Here, spread over several acres, in woods, hidden from view, stood twenty baroque chapels, all built between the sixteenth and the early eighteenth centuries. I was told that they were monuments to the Counter-Reformation. They housed – and this was the weirdest part – not the figures of crucified Christs but of the ordinary people of those centuries, standing in lively tableaux dedicated to the life of St Francis of Assisi. I was always to remember them and they still entered my dreams long after I returned to England.

The houses in Cusio were also extremely old; some might

already have been there when the chapels were being built. They were constructed right on the narrow cobbled, main – and only – street that led to the market place. Many were already converted to flats, with different families living on different levels.

The first time I looked inside the open entrance of one of the houses, I wondered what it would be like to live in them. If you ventured inside the outer door, you saw a stone-flagged floor and an inner door, and a narrow twisty stone stair leading up to the next two, or sometimes three storeys. Greenery grew around the inner ground floor door, as if the garden had colonized the house like an indoor patio, and there were gaudy flowers in big pots crowded around the entrances on all floors – I saw them when one day I tiptoed up the stairs out of curiosity. Each door had an electric bell. I imagined the plumbing would be primitive and the flats would be terrible to heat in winter.

Several artists always stayed for the summer in Cusio, and there were one or two art shops that sold their paintings, or hoped to sell them. The less expensive pictures were sold chiefly to tourists, but the artists always hoped to find rich Milanese businessmen who might be willing to pay more and become their permanent patrons. The painters, along with the sellers of pots and silk and jewellery, settled in Cusio only for the season, returning to their home towns or cities in the autumn. They came back again to the village in May to open up their shops or galleries.

Sandro Montani exhibited in one of these shops-cum-galleries. He told us he intended to stay all winter in Cusio that year. 'If the good sisters on the island are hardy enough to stay in their convent throughout the winter, I reckon I can stay here,' he once said. He said that in Italian, but he also liked to practise his English on us.

The convent on the tiny island of San Rocco, only a short boat-ride away from the jetty, was housed in a building that had originally been a medieval monastery, then a seminary. In the nineteenth century it had been built on, altered and improved. There were stories of seventeen-year-old girls arriving with their parents and being rowed across to the island. Later, the parents would return without their daughter, and clutching an empty suitcase. Only thirty or forty years ago, quite a few girls decided to become novices. I wonder if there are any would-be nuns now. I'd wager the average age of the good sisters is at present nearer seventy than twenty.

I had always wished I could see the village in winter. Cusio was a summer place and I could hardly believe it existed in any other season . . . .

Unfortunately, it happened that after my visit to the little gallery I had other things to think about during the next few months than dwelling on the distant past.

Like many members of my family, my mother, as I have said, had once been a teacher and had taken a lively interest in the world. She had been failing for months and I'd had to spend a good deal of time visiting her in her nursing home. In one year she had been diminished from a still powerful character to a confused shadow of herself. After she died in the autumn of 1994, I knew that if I was to continue to go abroad on holiday, never mind return to Cusio, I had better make arrangements very soon, or I'd be contemplating a sort of nothingness. It wouldn't make any difference to my life; my youth was all over and done with, had been for years, but paradoxically my mother's death, which ought perhaps to have made me see myself at last as the oldest generation, urged me to consider myself still not quite yet old. Death had truly been a happy release for my mother, but when the last parent dies you really do feel alone. I had been spared for so long because she had lived on into her nineties.

There were other matters that needed attention too, matters that I dreaded bothering with: repairs and repainting needing to be done to my flat. I knew that I could spend my life putting off what I really wanted to do. I needed a change.

My brother had agreed to take over the administration of Mother's estate. She had not left much; her nursing home had swallowed up most of the capital she had left from the sale of the house that she and my father had bought together in the Sixties. He had died shortly afterwards. In his retirement he had made a bit of money in property and had given us some of it when we married, one of the reasons for my being more comfortable now.

After the funeral it was Roger who urged me to go away and enjoy myself, have a winter break. There's be enough money for a winter cruise – he could lend it to me in advance, until probate was granted. I refused his offer; I had savings of my own, but I took his advice, though not to go on a cruise.

It was now or never, and I decided to ask Lizzie if she'd like to accompany me to Cusio, just as she had done over thirty years before. I knew Eleanor wouldn't want to go – she prefers to stay in her country hide-out, but Lizzie was always saying she wanted a rest from family life. Her husband Adrian is perpetually busy with his architectural practice, and for many years she has grumbled about 'doing Christmas' and tried to persuade him to go abroad with her at that time, or even to a hotel in England for the festive season, away from chores. Adrian always claimed it was his busiest time of the year – once he had 'enjoyed Christmas' with his family, which he insisted upon doing.

Lizzie however said, no, she didn't fancy Cusio in the winter. What about somewhere warmer? Naples, Sorrento, Positano – she might consider one of those. Since my whole idea had been to return to Cusio, I suppressed any expression of disappointment but realized that this trip was one I would be taking alone. I saw Lizzie was puzzled why I wanted to go to the place again, why my thoughts – as I had told her – kept dwelling on a summer in Piedmont over thirty years ago.

Was I, an elderly woman, still fascinated by what love really meant? Was I just gifted – or cursed – with an enormous propensity for nostalgia?

Lizzie isn't the sort of friend you talk to about your inner emotional adventures, just as she wasn't the friend with whom I had shared my feelings on Roland's death.

'Oh, that summer I was still dreaming of Mr Right,' I said to her lightly. 'According to my mood I can still feel sorry for wasting my youth, though often I am irritated by my old self.' She looked at me sceptically. 'We were only thirty-two,' I went on. 'It was just before I went to work in Croydon. Thirty-two was still young enough to dream of Mr Right!'

'Women always seem to be young enough to dream of *him*,' said Lizzie.

I thought of those white-haired ladies I have mentioned, older than myself or Lizzie, exchanging their romances at the public library. Married for years; even, like me, widowed, and still hoping?

When I got back home after this conversation with Lizzie I was remembering colleagues from years ago who had been resigned to spinsterhood. In those days there were plenty of youngish women who were like that, though the word feminism was never mentioned, not even in a whisper. These women filled the staffrooms of the 'better' girls' schools, and they were all well-educated. Not very well off, but always intent upon Abroad for their holidays. Ours must have been the very last generation of women who ever used the word 'spinster' about themselves. Now that I'm what people call 'quite comfortably off,' I could go abroad for months instead of weeks, and in the winter not the summer. Roland and I had owned our house, having paid off the mortgage the year before Roland died, and I bought my flat when I sold the house at the height of the 1988 boom. I am attached to my flat and a bit reluctant to stay away from it for too long. Why should I go on a wild goose chase without even knowing what I was looking for?

The next time I saw Lizzie I said perhaps we could go away together somewhere warm in the spring or autumn, but after Christmas I intended to travel to Cusio.

'I still can't understand why,' she said. 'I didn't know you were *so* keen on the place – I thought it was slightly boring, really.'

'Well, of course, when we were there you were thinking of your wedding,' I answered.

Lizzie had only gone away with me for a short period of calm before the wedding her mother had planned for Adrian and her. Almost as soon as we returned, she would get married. Liz was always a little difficult for me to understand. I used to puzzle over her character, so very unlike my own. Some people called her stand-offish. It was true she could be quite sharp and critical, but I knew she was also capable of kindness for she had been extremely good to a pupil whose father had died. She told me her own father had died when she was fourteen.

My friend did not suffer fools gladly. Sometimes I used to think she thought I was a bit of a fool and she often teased me. Usually I joined in the laughter: I was as aware of my own faults as anyone else. I think she is more tolerant nowadays, but she often used to puncture my wildest flights of romance or fantasy. She was probably good for me. Lizzie never gives – in the sense of never bending like a tree in the wind; she's not flexible, but keeps to her own chosen path. Neither is she overtly generous, in that other sense of giving, but she is amusing, and pleasant to be with. She is popular too; people enjoy her dinner parties and I must say she is an admirable hostess, always cool and collected. She is a good cook, and the Hills live in some style.

Cusio seemed, and was, a long time ago, and obviously my old friend didn't have my golden memories. I wished I hadn't said so much to her about it, for when I looked dispassionately at myself my desire seemed once more quixotic. An elderly widow-woman travelling on a sort of pilgrimage to her youth? Roland would have understood, but it was not strange that I had never wanted to go back to Cusio whilst he was alive.

My goddaughter Emma understands me, I think. I have always got on well with her. Her mother used to say she was difficult but I have never found her so. She must be nearly thirty, and she works off the Charing Cross Road, administering the arts. According to her, during her first year in the place this consisted in daily reducing a tottering pile of files to a position half way down, only to find the mountain had grown again by the next morning. Then she had been permitted to draft replies to various bodies, and even later to sit in on decisions about grants and to help in the arranging of exhibitions. She thought she might be about to be elevated to taking the minutes at committee meetings – of which there were many. It had taken ages for a word processor to be delivered to the office but when it eventually arrived it was to be Emma who proved her value, since nobody else knew how to use it. By the time I decided to revisit Cusio, she had worked five years in the place.

'Vivien just wants to retrace her steps,' she said to her mother, as I sat drinking a glass of wine and talking to Lizzie after an early supper in her vast kitchen. Emma had called in after work.

'I can't understand why,' said Lizzie with some asperity. 'I might understand it if you wanted to go somewhere you were happy with Roland – but there are lots of places in Italy that are more beautiful—'

'My mother lives in the present,' said Emma, smiling at me.

Elizabeth is a chic woman. She has a straight nose and a full mouth and pale skin and the most incredible hair. When she was younger she had tiny tight curls of the purest silvery gold. She is still fair, her hair that silvery-fair colour that takes so easily to a blond colorant. I think she does colour it now from time to time. Lizzie always had a good figure and she's as tall as her husband Adrian who has a chunky look about him. He used to have thick mousy hair but now it's a shock of grey.

Emma has her mother's nose and her good taste but is not so tall, nor so fair. Of their two other offspring, both boys, young men now, one of them – Simon – still lives at home whilst he finishes his Bar studies and the other, Andrew, is already a fully fledged accountant. Simon takes after his mother and is well over six feet with fair hair. Andrew resembles his father more.

I still envy Lizzie her family: well, mainly her daughter, I suppose I mean. I never find much to say to very young men, and Adrian talks about buildings when he talks at all.

'I think you should go by yourself and take lots of lovely photos,' Emma went on. 'I wouldn't mind coming with you if you'd have me, but there's a lot on at the office at present and I can't get away till March.'

It was kindly meant, but she had many friends she could go on holiday with and I wouldn't dream of inflicting myself on a young woman. Emma had recovered from some long relationship the previous year, that her mother had called 'unsuitable'. Lizzie had been both worried about her and cross with her.

Before I went away I threw a little party that I believe was a success. All my friends were there except for Eleanor. Joanna was full of her ideas for a new book. She had decided that cookery had become too popular and said she couldn't decide between two new topics: 'Remedies' and 'Superstitions'. She went round with a notebook to all my guests collecting ideas. I was surprised she was going to abandon her cookery books as they were a nice little money-spinner, but I supposed she knew what she was doing.

Lizzie and Adrian arrived a little late. Adrian had received a telephone message from a client just as they were about to leave, and in a continuing recession you can't afford to neglect someone who wants to pay you for doing what you enjoy. I was thinking, as I talked to his wife about my holiday plans, that Lizzie didn't look her age. Since she married she has never worked out of the house. I suppose my generation of wives was the last generation to be expected to stay at home with the children. Lizzie had been a sort of secretary to her husband once the children had been old enough to go to school.

She told me at the party that she suspected Emma had been seeing a new boyfriend for some time and she had great hopes that this time he might be 'The One'. She wouldn't even mind his being a partner rather than a husband – which for Lizzie was saying a lot.

Her marriage to Adrian had been such a success. No wonder she'd always wanted Emma to marry.

'You've decided to return to the haunts of your youth – go down memory lane? A winter holiday will be a nice change,' said her husband, coming up to us. 'Send us one of your postcards, won't you.'

I believe I am notorious for my long-winded postcards. 'I've never forgotten the lake and that island and those strange chapels on the hill behind,' I replied, a little drunk with my own wine. 'I have the feeling there is still something there for me to discover.'

Lizzie looked at me somewhat sceptically but said nothing.

In the end it had taken me almost a year to make up my mind to go, but – at last – at the very beginning of 1995, so many years since my first visit to Cusio, I flew back there.

I had no travelling-companion this time but I was used by now to being alone. All the way to Milan I was thinking about my magical summer holiday of 1964. I knew I'd probably forgotten most of the details, even if I'd always remembered the beauty of the place and my own reactions to it. My feelings about the place itself were so fresh they might have happened yesterday. Had it been enough then to be young and still full of hope? Was that where the 'magic' had come from?

Falling in love had marked my life until then but Cusio had finally made me realize I might be looking for the wrong thing. Sandro might have been only one of a long string of infatuations, but he had marked the end of my being unselfconscious about them. Roland had been quite a different kettle of fish, but by then I was almost middle-aged.

In Cusio I had been *young*!

Not *too* young, not with the soon-to-vanish sheen of one's early twenties, but still, young – and reasonably attractive.

In 1964 I had been waiting for love, ready for my life to take off.

And Cusio had been so beautiful that it had probably seduced me as much, if not more, than any young man I met could have done.

PART ONE

PART ONE

CUSIO

Summer 1964

One hot summer afternoon two young women, of whom I was one, arrived at Lake Cusio from London via Milan. The travel company we were travelling with was a new upmarket one, trying to become fashionable with young professionals, but this was the first time they had sent any of their clients to Cusio. Most holiday-makers were catered for about fifteen miles away in Stresa on Lake Maggiore or even further away to the east on Como or Garda. Our company coach had deposited most of its occupants in Stresa before continuing its journey to this much smaller lake. Cusio was barely seven miles long, a 'small jewel', and 'almost unknown', if you went by the brochures.

'In fact,' I was saying to Liz. 'I read that in the last century the English used to come here quite a lot – intellectuals, and painters, and clergymen who collected wild flowers. Rock climbers too, who wanted a rest.'

'Trust you to have done your homework!' said Liz, not unpleasantly.

I had found the office of Amy's Elite Tours tucked away in a side street in Earls Court, not far from the small flat I was sharing at the time with my brother Roger. I had been immediately captivated by the picture of a village – you could not call it a town – on the edge of a lake, a clear blue sky above and the high Alps in the distance. There was also a small island that looked anchored in the lake like a cruiser. I had suggested to Roger that we go on holiday together, but he had other ideas, wanted to go to New York. 'The States are the *only* place to go nowadays!' he said.

It was Liz Grove with whom I was to find myself unpacking in a large double room on the first floor of this small hotel by the lakeside. Liz was, I suppose, at that time the closest to a friend I had on the school staff, but we were not really close, just found ourselves occasionally raising our eyebrows at the antics of our 'progressive' headmistress. We'd have to get to know each other better during the next ten days. We only found ourselves together because at the last moment my friend Eleanor had been unable, because of family responsibilities, to accompany me to Italy, so I was grateful to Liz. I didn't know her very well, though we were colleagues, saw each other every day in the staff room, and rubbed along quite pleasantly. We were different sorts of people.

Even with the window open it was very quiet. 'Unusual for Italy,' said Liz. 'I do hope something is going on – I can't see myself sitting fishing all day.'

I was always prepared to be enchanted, and I was already under the spell of the place, with its cobbled streets and ochre-coloured houses, geraniums and petunias spilling over their balconies. I asked for nothing more than to sit and dream by the lake for a day or two, taking a little rest from the weariness that followed upon

the teaching of adolescents. I also hoped to meet some local inhabitants, for I snobbishly avoided my compatriots on foreign
holidays.

'Don't worry – we can go over to Switzerland – they're laying on
a trip there and over to Lake Maggiore if this is too quiet for you,'
I now said soothingly.

The holiday had been my idea, so I felt responsible for my
friend's impressions. Liz was engaged to be married; the wedding
was to take place in September shortly after our return. She had
confided to me that she was already irritated by her mother's fussy
arrangements and would actually welcome a little hen holiday
before she entered the state of matrimony. She had known her
fiancé, Adrian Hill, an architect, for ages, and her being away for a
bit would give him a breathing space to complete a difficult work
assignment before they went off on their honeymoon.

'I expect it will be all right,' she replied now, carefully unfolding
her clothes from layers of tissue paper. Like all the people of my
acquaintance who taught maths or science she was very neat and
tidy. I was already worrying lest my own haphazard ways might
annoy.

'We can eat and drink – and sketch, and laze – and shop. Look –
there's the island I told you about!' I drew Liz to the window where
the tiny offshore island seemed to be floating on the lake waters.
'It's so *beautiful*!' I said.

Liz, who was less expressive, just smiled, saying, 'Let's go for a
walk – if you've finished your unpacking?'

'Oh, that can wait. I would like to know when the boats go over
to the island.'

I put the *Guide to Cusio* in my linen bag. I'd bought it in London.
I always needed to know as much as possible about a place before I

visited it.

We walked out into the dazzling sunshine, two young women, Liz tall and fair, myself short and brown-haired. The hotel forecourt led straight on to the square where a row of benches and half a dozen bollards had been placed under some lime trees by the side of the lake. Some old men were sitting there in the shade.

The rope from one of the *motoscafi* plying between the jetty and my floating island was being fastened to one of the bollards. Its engine had just been turned off and water was giddily slopping around as several passengers disembarked. I tried to decipher the timetable fixed to the wall of a kiosk.

'They seem to leave every ten minutes during the summer,' I said.

'We can go any time – I'd like to look at the shops – you go now if you like,' offered Liz.

We had made a prior agreement that one would not mind if the other did her own thing, for some of the time at least.

'Oh, I'd like a walk as well just now – I'll save the island for tomorrow,' I replied.

I made a beeline for a little shop, outside which there were ranks of picture postcards.

'Why do you buy them before you see the place?' Liz asked curiously when she caught me up.

'Then I can know what to look for – they usually photograph the best parts.'

Liz laughed but consented to buy one card for Adrian.

We walked along together out of the square along the narrow street. Here it was dark and cool. The sun slanted over the tops of the high old houses but did not reach down to street level at this hour of the day. There were not many people around; evidently

Cusio was not yet a mecca for tourism. I was pleased about that, but I was still a bit worried lest Liz might be bored.

We walked along past several boutiques with exquisite clothes laid enticingly in windows – there must be other foreign tourists here then? – before we came to a steep cobbled street that turned off on the right and climbed upwards almost perpendicularly. At the top we could see a large church painted a daffodil colour.

'Onwards and upwards then?' asked Liz. 'It's not far – and it'll be cooler in the church.'

'I'm out of practice,' I whispered. I was already out of breath. 'When did *you* last walk in a park? Commuting is very bad for the health, you know.'

There were flowers in tiny gardens banked along the edge of this street, flowers in tubs, in hanging baskets, in troughs. The air was warm and now we could see the sun.

I arrived puffing at the top and followed Liz into the church, which was obviously an extremely ancient building. I trailed my hand pensively in the font. I would like to have genuflected, to have entered into the spirit of somebody else's religion as I did into the more material aspects of foreigners' food and drink and newspapers. I was not a believer though, and I would have felt a fraud.

We looked round for a few minutes at the statues and frescoes, then thankfully sat down. The pungency of incense from the last Mass was still hanging in the air.

Old ladies kept coming in and dipping their fingers in holy water before sitting down and telling their rosaries in front of the statue of the Virgin in a side chapel. It was very peaceful. I was thinking how I wished the world could always reduce itself to a quiet and beautiful place. It was true I would not have liked a world bereft of churches.

Liz was planning – or rather her mother was doing the planning – to marry in the large parish church belonging to the south-west London suburb where her family lived. I wondered whether Liz believed in Christian marriage.

I'd never discussed such things with her though I frequently had long discussions with Eleanor or with my friend Helena on such matters. Was Liz just doing it to please her mother? I knew that Adrian was not a stranger in my friend's bed. Most people had some sex life before marriage at that time, even if you had to pretend they didn't. On the other hand, scientists were often rather more conventional, sometimes religiously Evangelical. Not that Liz was really conventional but she seemed to like rules – even if she did not always stick by them. Sometimes I had the impression that she was rather a shy person. Not with me – for she liked to tease me; and perhaps not with all men, but with some of our female colleagues at the school. She kept up a rather distant and formal air also with her pupils, stuck to teaching her subject, and did not appear to receive their confidences as I was liable to do. I suppose teaching English gets you to know girls rather better than teaching them maths: to know their personalities anyway, if not their minds. I'd always been a little bit in awe of Liz – she wasn't easy to get to know and I'd sometimes felt I'd better be on my best behaviour with her. I hoped our holiday would bring us a little closer.

We sat there together a little longer. I was wondering what I had in common with Liz. We were colleagues, and got on quite well, but I assumed there were always parts of ourselves that each did not disclose to the other – at least that was true as far as my own private inner life was concerned. I know she found me 'earnest' because she had told a mutual friend.

She got up suddenly. 'I need a long cool drink.'

She marched purposefully out of the church with myself in her wake. Back in the village piazza we saw a café and sat down thankfully. Not many people were drinking there, but the chairs and tables spilled out on to the cobblestones so it must be a popular venue at other times of day – or night.

Set just past the centre of the square, at the end nearest the street where we had just been walking, and marooned on the cobblestones like an asymmetrical Noah's Ark, there was a strange building. It had an outside staircase of wrought iron leading like a primitive fire escape to an upper room over an open arcade.

It looked as old as the church, perhaps even older.

'What do you think that is?' I asked.

'The town jail?' Liz suggested. We giggled.

We had ordered Cinzano and soda and when it came it was with a zest of lemon and a lump of ice.

The air was soft and mild and scented. Not too hot now. Perfect.

I sighed with content and began to scrutinize my postcards.

Liz said, 'I suppose I'd better send Adrian a card to say I've arrived – though probably it'll take days to get to him. I shan't bother writing to anybody else. I need a rest from planning and thinking.'

She scribbled a short message. Then, 'Let me have a dekko at your guide book. You might like to go on a coach ride over to the Matterhorn – you said Switzerland was not far away.'

She was probably missing Adrian, I thought. If *I* had been in love, I would have wanted the object of my desires with me in this lovely little place. Without a lover I could not think of doing anything more pleasant at present than exploring the village and the island, but I agreed I might want to be a little more adventurous later.

'I shall get to bed early tonight for my beauty sleep,' said Liz. 'It's been a tiring day.'

We finished our drinks and crossed over the square to our hotel. I finished my unpacking and put on a sleeveless dress of bright green cotton. Along with a handful of other guests, mostly middle-aged, and a few families, we went down for dinner at tables set under long windows open to the lake. Here we consumed platters of delicious lake fish called *avarello*, washed down with Barengo bianco.

Liz said the fish was bream.

Afterwards we slept like angels.

'Shall we go over to the island this morning or this afternoon?'

I had just finished my breakfast – two cups of coffee and two delicious freshly baked crusty rolls plastered with pale butter and jam. Liz, coffee cup in hand, was staring vaguely out of the window. Most of the other guests had departed. We had been a bit late starting our breakfast. She gave a little start.

'Sorry, I'm still half asleep – I'll go wherever you like.'

I was not sure that Liz had believed me when, back in London, I had said very firmly, that we didn't need to be together all the time. On the other hand I didn't want to make her feel now that I'd prefer to be by myself. I suggested: 'You might like to visit another church this morning – or do you want to window-shop?'

Even as I said these words I realized that it was far more likely that I would be the one wanting to visit a church, whilst Liz would always prefer shopping, but it seemed a little patronizing to put it that way. I added, 'I don't mind going to the island alone if there's something else you'd rather be doing?'

'No, there's nothing else I want to do. Let's go there after lunch. We don't have quite such a heavy meal in the middle of the day, do we?' It might be cooler over there. I absolutely must wash my hair first—'

'Right – whilst you do that I shall go and pick up a few brochures in that little tourist office we saw yesterday. They do Maggiore as well as Switzerland – even a day in Milan if you – we – find nothing much to do here—'

'I haven't seen any English tourists – except here at the hotel. Have you?'

'No – you can always recognize the English. I've heard people talking French – they could be Swiss, I suppose. They mostly seem to be Italian though, don't they?' I was pleased about that. I added that lots of people were said to come here on their way to ramble in the regional park, or to camp in the mountains.

I had already read about this vast park and about the plan for new conservation areas, when I was boning up on the various villages around the lake. It always pleased me to find a place where the ordinary inhabitants of a country came for their holidays. My books said that this particular holiday paradise was popular with both the Italians and the French. There were walkers, nature-lovers, backpackers, flora- and fauna-searchers, and it wasn't yet a popular place for British tourists. What I had said to Liz about its being visited a great deal by English clergymen and intellectuals in the middle of the last century was true. They had been the sort of people who climbed mountains, and liked classifying flowers and birds and insects. Wasn't there an Englishman of that time who climbed the Matterhorn and nearly lost his life on it?

Liz was following another line of thought, saying meditatively, 'I shall wash my hair now and dry it on the balcony before the maid comes to clean the room.' Really, she was very undemanding company. I had actually made her laugh at supper the night before when I imitated the unfortunate girls I had taken the previous year to Germany. They had spent most of their time looking for fish and chips and ogling American servicemen.

I went off alone in search of a better map, and a chat in the tourist office in my best, if inadequate, Italian. I was not to be disappointed. The little office on the main street was crammed with enquirers. Two harassed young Italians were trying to explain in French to a married couple in heavy walking boots which train to take to link with a bus that went up to the edge of a commune in the mountains on the other side of the lake.

I eavesdropped with interest. There was always such a lot to see, to do, to hear, to learn. A few weeks ago I'd never heard of this place and now I was full of information about it and about the little island, and had even more queries. When it came to my turn, and after my halting enquiry, a little book was pushed towards me: *The History of the Basilica*. I bought it, and a map, and decided to sit and study them at a café table in the piazza. I chose the café we had not patronized the previous day. There were only two.

What would it feel like to live here? For how long did you have to inhabit a place to understand it? If you lived here as a child you'd have explored the nearby villages, the shores of the lake, the mountains in all weathers. It would not be difficult either for anyone who grew up in Italy to become an expert on churches. There was also a vast number of public monuments that the locals probably took for granted and ignored. It would take a long time for a visitor to get to know and understand the place. Yet first impressions were often said to be the best; a stranger might notice things that no longer impressed the local inhabitants.

This island now, it seemed small and manageable, I thought, so I would begin with that, and would start that very afternoon.

Planning such things made me feel content.

Again I was sitting opposite the strange frescoed building in the centre of the square that we had pondered the day before. It was beautiful, supported by colonnades with a sort of loggia underneath. The guide book, when consulted, said it was the *Palazzo della Communità*, the sixteenth century town hall, built in 1582.

I looked up, blinking in the sun that had now reached the square. So many buildings here clearly belonged to that semi-sacred time for Italian painting and sculpture, the cinquecento. The guide – written in English – called it high renaissance. Other things here however were even older; the same guide book said that all the region had once been settled by the Romans. Liz teased me about my love for and dependence on guide books. 'You are such a culture vulture!' she said.

I paid for my drink, got up and walked past the palazzo (or town hall, as I supposed), and over to the lake. The island was so near it looked as if it had just been chipped off the promontory on which the village stood. Today it resembled a white mirage rising from the waters, already shimmering in the heat. A cluster of buildings appeared to cover almost all of it: a church, a large building I later discovered was the convent, and small villas built all round its edge, with gardens that sloped down to the water.

The heat was beginning to affect me so I sat down on a bench under the lime trees next to a gently snoring old man with a handkerchief over his somnolent face. With an effort I opened the guide book again. Ah, here it was: *The island basilica has many frescoes, as well as a famous pulpit.* It was apparently older than the sacred cinquecento, not quite ancient Roman, but of the twelfth century.

I shut my eyes and breathed in the warm air, with the sound of lapping water in the background. It was rarely that I could relax and rest. Even though I had plenty of energy I found London to be a tiring place, so escape was very precious. I walked back to the hotel dining-room in a happy daze. Liz was already there, her newly washed hair shining in the sunlight from the lakeside window. I admired the way she looked, at the same time as thinking how pleasant it would be to go on holiday with a person who was as keen as I was to read up a place, pore over maps, to drink in local colour – a man, probably a husband . . . .

Not having a husband, I was used to going off alone, and sometimes I felt a trifle guilty over my own capacity for solitude. Ought I to distrust it? I must not bore Liz though, with my attachment to the guide book. Cusio had not been her own choice. Even if she had agreed to come along with me for a last fortnight of spinsterly freedom, I knew that for her it would be only the first of many wonderful future holidays.

It *would* be pleasant to be here with a husband, I thought.

A little boat with an outboard engine went over to the island at three o'clock with both of us on board. I had put my sunglasses on to shade my eyes from the dazzle of the light on the water, and I looked at the island drawing near. I didn't need to consult the book. I remembered what it had said: The Abbot of Cluny had been born here on this tiny island.

I debated whether to say anything to Liz about that, then decided against it. She would raise her eyebrows in mock boredom. He *must* be the same abbot who had founded all those Cluniac monasteries, one of whose ruins was to be found near my uncle's

farm in Essex. How strange it was that people born here long ago –
and so far away from England – even if in the twentieth century
you came on a plane – should travel all the way to cold damp East
Anglia! Must have taken months. Here in Italy I found East Anglia
difficult to believe in. I supposed the Abbot would have wanted to
spread the Word of God to the benighted English. Everything here
had happened *earlier* than at home – and had probably been in the
long run more important for the history of civilization.

We disembarked, along with a noisy band of young Italians on
holiday. The crossing had taken only a few minutes. The island
church stood back a little, not far from the landing-stage. A shallow
flight of steps led up a gentle slope to its great door. We toiled up,
and pushed open the padded door.

Inside, it was not quite so warm, dark at the end where we came
in, and certainly full of delightful odours. A few other visitors from
a previous boat-load were walking round quietly, looking as if they
might not be very conversant with the ritual of such places.
Candles were haloed in gloomy corners, but the nave was well lit.
The church was larger than I had imagined. Larger – and even
older. But it was a basilica after all.

Liz grabbed my *Guide to Cusio* before I could read aloud
anything from it. She intoned in a fake Italian accent: 'The island
is named after the saint who cleared it of serpents and has a basilica in his honour, built between the eleventh and thirteenth
centuries.'

She sighed. 'I shall do my duty and go to look for the remains of
the fifteenth- and sixteenth-century faded frescos.' They were on
the walls further way down the nave so I did not follow her straight
away but walked down to look at the famous beautifully carved,
black marble twelfth century pulpit, about which the guide was

also eloquent.

The other tourists had gone now. I looked up at the gilded dome over the nave and almost tripped over the feet of a man who was on his back underneath the great pulpit, which was supported by four Norman-looking columns of black marble.

'Oh! I'm so sorry – I didn't see you,' I said in English, before I could gather my wits. Had I interrupted a Mecca-like devotion? It did not seem so, for the young man had spread a large sketch-pad on the floor, and I discerned some of the pulpit motifs he'd already copied. He'd been looking at the underside of the pulpit and behind it. It looked a little squashed on its far side against a wall as though something else had been built near it long afterwards, but they hadn't been able to move it from its original site. I thought, all these churches are the same, with accretions of centuries. We can't really imagine what they were like at their very beginning.

The man came half out of his hiding place, looked at me for a moment and smiled, and then bent down to his sketches.

I tiptoed round to look at the pulpit from the other side. It was indeed made of marble but I thought the black might once have had a greenish tinge. A quick further consultation of the guidebook revealed that the columns were 'porphyry'.

The carvings – when I finally made them out – were wonderful. On one side there was an eagle, a lion – I thought at first it was a unicorn – an angel and an ox, all looking splendidly primitive.

Liz was coming back up the nave and I also realized there was another young man leaning against a nearby column. He stared at Liz as she came up to me.

The young man who had been sketching got to his feet and said in English, pointing to the black pulpit: 'It comes from twelfth century.' He was very attractive, with wavy brown hair, looked like a man happy to inhabit his own skin. I felt immediately that he was interesting. He had a mellifluous light voice.

'Is all the church as old as *that*?' I asked.

'From the beginning there was a church, but then we are always making additions,' he said.

Liz came up to us and chipped in. 'It says the oldest fresco is 1421—'

'Yes, yes, but the best thing is this,' said the man, pointing to the pulpit.

The other young man came up to us then. He had a slightly pasty complexion and what my Aunt Muriel would have called 'bedroom eyes'.

'These are almost like pre-Norman carvings,' I ventured.

'Yes, true – but we say Romanesque,' said the young man who had been under the pulpit. 'These carvers come in eleven hundred and are influenced by art from a long way away I am sure . . . .'

I smiled and then I said, 'We mustn't disturb your work,' and moved away, not wishing to be a nuisance standing in the way of Art.

I went to look in my turn at all the frescos. Liz came with me. Some were faded and scribbled over but there were others whose style reminded me of the Wilson diptych familiar from museum visits at home.

'There's the saint arriving on the island,' Liz pointed out, and we both stared at a brown-robed man holding what looked like a shepherd's crook. Fish were swimming vigorously around him but several nasty looking snakes with forked tongues were hissing at him.

'What they call serpents might have been dragons,' she said.

'Dragons are mythical – some people think that they might have been the memory of dinosaurs,' I replied.

There were many other frescos, the most interesting from the fifteenth century, some faded, some as if they had been painted last year – a Nativity, a Queen of Heaven with a little earthly crown, men with bobbed hair and, the best in my opinion, a large portrait of the Trinity: God with a large white beard sitting, knees wide apart, feet in sandals, arms outstretched, holding a wooden cross on which the Christ figure was hanging. It was almost as if the son was a marionette, the arms of the cross being held by the old man and yet he was partly sitting on the skirt of his father.

'Where do you think the Holy Ghost is?' I asked Liz, but she shrugged and I guessed she was a little bored.

'Apparently the crypt is closed today for repairs,' she said. 'It's where they keep the bones of the saint.'

'I know – I saw a picture of his coffin – it looked like Cinderella's coach without the wheels – a pity we can't see it today.'

After a time we went back into the nave and studied the little box-like gallery that bulged out over marble pillars, looking as though it was indeed part of a theatre. The young men seemed to have disappeared.

'Do you think they were professional artists?' said Liz, as we came out into the bright sunshine.

A little further along the lake front we saw the backs of the two young men as they leaned against a wall that overhung the sloping landing. The small motoscafi were still arriving and others looked to be permanently moored on the island shore.

'I don't see why not – lots of painters come here. Let's walk round the island,' I suggested.

A winding lane followed the contours of the island shore and took us around the few acres of the place. In walls on the side next to the lake were mysterious garden doors that must have led to the little villas set by the water's edge that I'd seen from the other side.

Everywhere, as in Cusio, were the balconies and urns heavy with bright flowers, some of whose names I did not know.

'It's just heavenly!' I exclaimed.

Liz laughed. 'Though I don't suppose there's much to do for the young people who live here.'

'Mm – I suppose they have to travel a long way to a secondary school—'

'Oh don't let's think about *education*,' said Liz with a shudder.

'Think what it must be like here in the winter,' I pursued. 'No flowers? Do you think the lake freezes over?'

Liz did not answer but strode on ahead and arrived a few minutes before me round the corner of the landing stage from which small boats were still arriving and departing. We took the next one together.

I noticed one of the two young men now talking to one of the sailors. He did not look up.

'Let's go back for a shower?' suggested Liz. 'I feel so disgustingly hot and sticky.'

After cooling down we drank lemon-scented tea in the hotel lounge. I felt restless:

'I'll go window-shopping with you if you like?' I offered.

Liz took me up on my offer and before dinner we ventured out once more along the cobbled street. There were the beginnings of the evening bustle in the air. Several shops appeared to open at six o'clock and then they were full of Italian holiday-makers. Other shops were quiet, almost empty of custom. I stopped before one that seemed more like a gallery than a shop. The landscapes in its window were vivid but not garish. Liz stopped with me, resigning herself to my enthusiasm for pictures.

One painting struck me immediately. It was longer than it was broad, a picture of tiny houses at the bottom of a steep valley, a few houses even perched half-way up the mountain side, all in shades of biscuit and green, except for a tiny splash of the scarlet of some alpine bloom in one corner.

When we went in we discovered that the shop did indeed double as a sort of gallery. I wondered if there was a studio at the back. The walls were completely covered in paintings of all shapes and sizes, mostly already framed, but there were a few prints too, and cradles of paintings and drawings in every available space on the floor.

A picture on the far wall of a tall woman standing by a grey lake caught my eye. I tried to decipher the signature – wasn't it the same as the one on the picture of the mountain outside?

'You like?' asked the assistant, a round-faced woman in a long yellow and black robe like a peignoir.

'Oh yes, very much – but we only came to look,' I replied nervously in French. My Italian sometimes deserted me and left me tongue-tied, which I hated.

'That is OK – please look around.'

'I think it's the same artist as the one who painted that mountain landscape in the window,' I murmured to Liz. 'I do wish I could afford this one!'

'Save up – buy nothing else and you might,' replied Liz, looking swiftly through a cradle of drawings in the corner. I saw her interest was not really being aroused. I pointed to the still lives that adorned another wall: luscious groups of lemons and oranges and grapes, or of spring blossoms – magnolias, camellias; there was a painting of a breakfast table with the sun making white cloth shine with unnatural radiance.

On the other side there were more landscapes, some chocolate boxy, some austere, all unmistakably of Cusio or its environs.

I went outside again to look more closely at the landscape I'd liked in the window. I thought the little Alpine village in its fold of valley was painted almost as if the artist had been in a helicopter looking down on it. He must have climbed high with his sketch book. In the distance the tiny houses were like dolls' furniture. Did anyone still live there? It looked hidden, but there was an ochre-coloured church standing out behind the huddle of roofs.

'Valstrona,' I read. 'Campello Monte. Thirteen hundred and five metres.' I went back into the shop and plucked up courage to ask its price.

It was far too dear, even if I starved for the rest of the holiday – which was not likely.

'It's in the countryside of our great *Monte Rosa*,' said the woman. 'Have you been to our mountain?'

'I've only seen it in the distance behind the lake,' I replied.

I had seen the irregular jagged edge of the great mountain looking like a primitive comb that very morning from our window. The greatest mountain of the area – even, after Mont Blanc, the second highest in Europe. I waited for the lady to talk about skiing in winter and chairlifts but she did not, so I looked through some of the smaller pictures. It must be lovely to paint in a country where you could know the sun would be there day after day.

'I'll be back,' I said when I left with Liz to walk back to the piazza.

'I wonder if those two painters we saw in the church live in Cusio,' I remarked.

'I expect they just come for the season.'

'I was just wondering if any of the paintings we've been looking at were theirs.'

'Too much of a coincidence, surely?'

We had walked back once more to the square along the narrow cobbled street and were sitting down in 'our' café. It was seven o'clock and already people had drifted to the pavement tables of the only two cafés the place appeared to possess.

'I feel like another drink,' said Liz. 'Art leaves me thirsty.' She yawned.

I said, 'They all stroll up and down half the night here, don't they? *Passagietura* or *passeggiata* – a word like that.'

'Spotting local talent, I expect,' said Liz.

There were couples, along with occasional small groups of men or of young girls, walking slowly along. They did not look at all like tourists.

The sun was still warm, lower in the sky now. It would set over the island. A cheerful elderly waiter served us with our chilled glasses of *Prosecco*.

Liz nudged me. 'On the other side of the square – isn't one of them our church artist?' she asked. I shaded my eyes with my hands. *Three* young men were walking across the square from the waterside in the direction of the café. One of them had a roll of canvas under his arm.

'I'm not sure – I didn't really have time to look at them very closely,' I half fibbed.

'Oh, I think one of them is the pulpit man,' said Liz. We tried not to stare as the three men came across and sat down at a table nearer the pavement but not far away from us.

More young men and women were now strolling along the pavement or in the square. A group of two men, two women and a little boy came across to greet the men at the table. They lingered there, laughing and joking. Dusk would not fall for some time; we could return later. Sitting there in the square was so pleasant; the warmth, the ease, so seductive.

'We'd better go in for our supper,' Liz said eventually.

I could not help thinking what a lot of organization it had taken to have, once a year, a few hours of this pleasant holiday leisure. If only I could organize my life to live in such a place instead of cold London. I supposed, looking at the people around, both villagers and Italian holiday-makers, that their lives were just as busy, just as fraught as was my own teaching and commuting existence. Maybe everything just *seemed* easier here because of the climate?

We finally got up and moved away, passing the young men as we did so. The group with the child had now gone. As we passed their table one of the men, not the one who had been sketching the pulpit, but his friend, he of the pasty complexion and bedroom eyes, smiled and raised his hand. I allowed myself a small smile, but Liz swept by ignoring him.

The men had gone away when we came out of the hotel at about half past nine and crossed the square. I suggested we might take a short walk and then sit down for a coffee.

We walked in the same direction as the day before. The shops were still open. 'I'd like to have another look at that painting of the woman,' I said.

'You do that – I want to buy a canvas bag – I saw some yesterday. See you in the piazza in about twenty minutes – OK?'

I found the little gallery-cum-shop again without difficulty and stared at the pictures in the window. The painting of the tiny mountain village had gone! In its place was the woman by the grey lake. No sign of the lady assistant. Inside the shop a young man was arranging several drawings on a large table. I thought he was one of the young men who had been sitting in the café an hour or two ago. Not the pulpit man, nor his friend, the lascivious-looking man, who had smiled at us, but the other. I went into the shop.

'Could you tell me please how much the painting costs of the lady by the lake – in the window?' I asked, this time in reasonably correct Italian, since I had rehearsed the words in my mind. If it was anything like the other one it would be far beyond my means.

The man looked surprised, scratched his head and said: 'Ah – I am not sure.' Then, in English: 'I can ask – I am just here whilst the others have their dinner.'

'I expect it is very expensive but I like it so much. Who painted it?'

'That is a painting by a friend of mine, Sandro Montani.'

Daringly, I asked, 'Is your friend a person who sketches in churches? I believe we saw him today over on the island.'

In Italian, the young man replied: 'He takes commissions for guidebooks and so needs many drawings of churches.'

'I will call later,' I said after a pause. 'Tell him I like his painting.' I was being rash, for I wouldn't be able to afford that painting either, but I reasoned that artists like to know if people admire their work. The picture, which I lingered over once more before going back to meet Liz, was not large and was in what they were beginning to call mixed media. I saw that the grey lake was really a mixture of dark green and brown and blue and white. The woman in the centre, painted sideways on, was wearing a long dress of a pale eau-de-Nil colour that looked like an antique robe. The sky under which she stood was a whitish grey. I bent to decipher the artist's' name. 'Sandro', the young man had said. Here it looked like a squiggle then an M then a double squiggle. I gave up trying to work it out; I'd better walk back to the square.

I strolled along the piazza along the cobbled street, and imagined I was Italian and on my holidays and really belonged to the company of men and women and children – it was not exactly a crowd – who were continuing their *passeggiata*. There was no sign of my friend on the café terrace. Should I go back to the hotel in case she had gone back there first? I couldn't be bothered. Liz would come along to the café if she didn't find me in our room.

I sat down alone at a table at the back of the terrace. They were in no hurry to serve clients. Everyone was still enjoying the warmth given off by the cobblestones, and the lingering scents of the day. My feeling of ease returned. I opened my bag and took out the newspaper I'd bought that morning. Italian was not as easy to read as it looked. I was puzzling over a strange verb-ending when, looking up and into the distance, I was surprised by:

'Are these chairs taken?' At the same time as I heard this, my eyes dazzled by the sun now setting over the island, I saw Liz in a patch of darkness making her way towards the café.

The man who had asked about the chairs was the bedroom-eyed man who had waved to us, he who had accompanied the artist in the church. Behind him, hanging back a little was the man from the shop.

'Oh – my friend is coming over,' I replied, a little startled. 'The other two chairs aren't taken.'

Both the men sat down as Liz came up to the table with an interrogative lift of her eyebrows. They stood up as she sat down.

'I am Marco Ronchetti,' said the flirtatious-looking young man.

'Mario Sartoris. You were in the shop – I believe you are

English?' said the other more hesitantly.

I had time to think that Mario and Marco sounded a bit like a music hall turn, before recovering myself and saying: 'I am Vivien Butterfield and this is Elizabeth Grove.' Liz looked slightly frosty but I saw no harm in talking to two young men. I said to her: 'The artist whom we saw sketching in the church this afternoon painted that picture I liked in the shop! You know, the one of the woman on the lake shore.'

'Really?' Liz sounded a little cross.

The erstwhile shop assistant, Mario, who I had decided was a sober, quiet, sort of young man, not as extrovert as his friend, said in English: 'Sandro will be here soon and you can ask him how much he wants for his painting.'

Marco said in Italian, with a grin: 'I do not speak much English. Mario here is an intellectual so he can talk to you in your own language.' The men were both polite but I noticed that the flirtatious one kept ogling Liz.

'It's about time I learned some Italian,' she said, surprising me.

'What about your painter friend – Sandro? We heard him speak English this afternoon,' I asked.

'You will be able to talk to him, for here he comes!' replied Marco.

We looked across the square and saw the man who had been sketching the pulpit that afternoon strolling along in our direction from the other side of the square. He had a parcel under his arm that looked as if it might be another painting. He did not seem at all surprised when he reached the café to find his two friends sitting with some unknown ladies.

'Sandro Montani,' he said as he shook hands with us, before sitting down and placing his parcel under the table. I realized that he was taller than the average Italian and a trifle slimmer, and awfully handsome – which I had not had time to notice in the church. I tried not to stare at him. His hair was a lightish brown, almost the same colour as his hazel eyes. His nose was probably a little too long for perfection, but he had a generous mouth, and I could not help imagining what it would feel like to be kissed by it. His eyes carried a message of a slightly amused reserve, giving nothing away. In short he had the face and demeanour that attract women because they make it appear that their possessor has hidden depths, and you would like him to take notice of you. I knew I ought to stop this mental flirtatiousness. Everyone said that Italian men just wanted to seduce you. Italian girls were so strictly brought up they didn't get the chance with them. I felt however that I would not be averse to a little future seduction by such a handsome and talented man. As it would probably not be against my will, it would not be seduction, would it? I was wary of such feelings, even as I registered their onset, for I had often experienced them before.

Next to him, Marco of the enticing eyes was cast in a darker, almost swarthy, mould. He had permanently raised eyebrows as though expressing surprise at the foolishness of others, an aquiline nose, and a smile always lingering on his full lips, about to break up his features. You could tell he wanted to give a certain impression, I thought, but might be no respecter of persons, something in the curl of the lip giving away a certain indifference. I would not wish to be seduced by *him* . . . . I might be quite wrong – I ought not to go so much by first impressions; I knew that was a weakness of mine.

As the men talked quite unselfconsciously to each other, yet not ignoring us, I learned amongst other things that Mario, the gallery man, lived with his mother. I immediately imagined a tiny middle-aged widow who adored her only son and fussed over him. Mario was shorter than the other two, wore steel-rimmed glasses over dark deep-set eyes and never raised his voice. He was not unattractive but Liz was later to call him dull.

'You didn't introduce yourselves properly to me,' said Sandro, addressing us both in a pause in the conversation.

'Oh – this is Elizabeth, and I am Vivien,' I replied quickly. 'I was looking at a painting of yours in the shop – it's more like a gallery—'

Sandro smiled and turned to Mario. 'Made a sale old man?'

Mario said: 'No, Sandro, you are too expensive for young ladies—'

Sandro then asked us if we'd like another drink.

'I don't think so,' replied Liz. 'Do you, Vivien?'

'I might have a tiny coffee.'

'It will stop you sleeping,' stated Marco with a slight leer.

'Not a thimbleful, surely?'

'It is very strong,' said Mario seriously.

'Well, if you all think I should abstain, I will have a glass of mineral water.'

'So will I,' Liz changed her mind.

Sandro got hold of the waiter and ordered himself a beer and San Pellegrino for the women.

Then he said in English: 'My friend Mario helps out in the gallery. Which painting did you like? I have several there.'

I was a little disconcerted. As I would probably never have the money to buy any of his pictures, I didn't want to give the wrong impression of somebody whose mind might be changed – as it had been over the coffee. I said: 'Well it was a very different sort of picture from what I imagined would come out of your sketching in

the church this afternoon. It's the picture of a woman by the lake –
in shades of grey-green and white, and she's wearing a very pale
green dress.' I'd begun my sentence in Italian but had to end it in
English.

'Does la Signora Elisabetta speak our language too?' asked
Sandro looking at them over the rim of his beer glass.

'No,' said Liz shortly.

'Then he will have to speak yours and that will stop me from
understanding you, alas!' said the roué, Marco.

Just then a group of Italians shouted over to us from the front of
the café which they were passing on their own *passeggiata*. Four
young men came up, leaving a group of women and children for a
moment.

'*Ciao* – Alberto –' Hand-shaking all round.

'Enrico – Raffaelo – Luciano—'

The men smiled at us but after a few words returned to their
families to continue their slow promenade. Sandro turned to me.

'It is a good picture of the lake – the lady who posed for me is my
friend Raffaelo's wife. Somebody already wants to buy it.'

'I also liked a picture that was no longer there this evening – a
little village in the mountains with tiny houses—'

'That one is going to an exhibition we are having soon here in
Cusio.'

They were all so friendly, so open, I felt I had known them for
ages.

Marco said in Italian: 'Sandro must paint the English ladies –
they would be good subjects.'

He seemed to be teasing but Sandro looked first at me, then at
Liz. After a pause he said: 'One day I wouldn't mind doing a few
drawings of you both.' Liz did not react, but I probably looked

enthusiastic, and Sandro went on: 'Just now I'm busy with commissions for guide books – you saw me sketching the pulpit. They want me to do some pen-and-wash sketches of some of the chapels on our Sacro Monte as well. For this kind of work I often take photographs first and then work up the drawings and paintings later. We must show them our little "holy mountain",' he said, turning to his friends.

'We might take a picnic there,' said Marco.

'Oh, that would be lovely,' I said. I had read up their Sacro Monte in the guidebook. A mile away up above Cusio, in a sort of park on the hill overlooking the lake, there were twenty seventeenth-century chapels dedicated to St Francis. It was a place I'd hoped to tempt Liz to visit with me. 'I know a little about it,' I added.

Liz said: 'Viv will be sure to have read it up. She is a searcher-out of monuments and beauty spots. Even religious ones.'

Mario said, turning towards me in a kindly way: 'Then you will know that this place of pilgrimage was begun in 1591 but not completed till the eighteenth century, and there is even one chapel left incomplete. It is very interesting.'

Sandro returned to the subject of his painting. 'Later this week I may have more time for you to sit for me,' he said to Liz.

'We cannot pay for portraits!' exclaimed Liz hurriedly.

'I didn't mean I wanted you to *buy* anything! Just that you might both sit for me?' He lit a cigarette. 'Perhaps you are soon leaving Cusio?'

'They've only just arrived,' said Mario.

'I hope you're not turning into an artist who earns his living doing lightning sketches of tourists, old man?' said Marco in a slightly jeering way. I saw he was jealous of Sandro.

Sandro laughed. 'It would most likely be very lucrative with some of them – the middle aged ladies for example.' Turning to Liz again, he said: 'Whilst you are here you will want to visit the environs – go over to Maggiore – even to the Simplon?'

'I think the lake and your Sacro Monte are enough to be going on with,' she replied.

I added: 'You might advise us of other places that are worth visiting?'

'Certainly we shall,' said Marco, 'but unfortunately I have to leave you now – I dine with my mother and have not yet eaten. Shall I hope to see you in the shop tomorrow?'

When he had gone Sandro and Marco drained their glasses.

'We are always in the square in the evening at about nine,' said Marco. 'You are staying nearby?'

I pointed to our hotel across the square.

'It's true there's not much choice in Cusio – but I hope you will enjoy your stay,' said Sandro formally. 'And I am serious when I say that I should like that you both sit for me.'

'We shall see,' said Liz. The men shook hands with us, and were off.

I was excited. A genuine artist – and such an attractive man! I decided he was a very interesting person.

'Do you think anything will come of it?' I asked Liz over a final cigarette in the hotel lounge that night. My friend had not said much since we left the café and I feared lest she might consider me at best imprudent, at worst silly. I thought they had been friendly young men, and Sandro was certainly talented.

'Of what? Oh, you mean the Italians? Mario and Marco – I didn't find much to say to them.'

'Sandro is certainly a handsome man,' I ventured.

'Now, now Vivien! At least he doesn't look like an ice cream merchant – the Marco one does, doesn't he? I find the Mario one a bit solemn though.'

I thought that unfair. He probably had a nicer nature than his friends, and would make somebody a good husband. 'We don't need to see them again if you don't want,' I said.

I had certainly received the impression that the men would not thrust themselves upon us. They were not uncivilized. I trusted my own judgement as to their being reasonably well-brought-up, even if Italian men had that reputation of pinching women's bottoms and following them. It was *I* who had wanted to talk to *them*, had even encouraged them. I wasn't specially interested in sitting for Sandro, though he was certainly the one who attracted me the most, but it made such a difference on holiday to know people who lived in the place, who were not tourists, were intelligent. The men were about our own age too, and anyway, I thought, artists and intellectuals were the sort of men I had always liked best.

Since Liz said nothing more, but looked enigmatic, I added: 'I'm sorry if you thought we were being picked up – but the man in the shop was really interested in talking to me – and they are all a friendly lot.'

Liz lay back against the leather sofa with her eyes shut, but finally pronounced: 'Don't apologize Viv – I know you like talking to foreigners, and – well, there's not a great deal to do here, is there? I mean in the actual place. I don't mind sitting for him if that's what he wants.'

I felt a little crushed. I said: 'He mentioned Maggiore – and Simplon, and – the Sacro Monte nearby – there's heaps of places to visit.'

'I suppose so. Perhaps they'd like to accompany us daily?' said Liz dryly as we took the lift to our room. I did not know whether she was being ironic or sincere.

My enjoyment of Mario's conversation did not stop me from daydreaming over the handsome Sandro. Not over Marco, though. His attractions were too blatant, nor over Mario who was possibly more intelligent.

We did not see any of the young men the next day, but I more or less made up my mind to book a coach trip to Switzerland during our second week. Liz favoured a trip to Maggiore, specifically to Stresa, maybe at the week-end but had made no definite plans. In the meantime the weather was gorgeous.

The next evening, when it was cooler, we walked in both directions round the peninsula on which stood Cusio. There were large and imposing villas perched above the road, with gardens of palms, and red and white oleander, magnolias, pink roses, enormous white lilies, geraniums, camellias, and a mauve-tinted flower, another plant whose name I did not know. I felt an urge to explore the hill behind the little town. Surely that was what the men had called the Holy Mountain – the 'Sacro Monte', but Liz suggested we waited for a cooler day.

We discovered there was water-skiing on the lake, even if neither of us wished at present to indulge in it. Intrepid swimmers, however – among whose number I was not to be found – could breast the waves in a secluded area beyond the little harbour. Liz was keen to go there and I encouraged her. The two of us were used by now to spending an hour or two apart, so on the Friday morning Liz went off to swim with a young Englishman called Graham who was staying in our hotel.

Feeling relieved, as though I had invited a friend to a party, watched her standing round looking – and feeling – bored, and then seen her talking to someone at last, I went off to sit by the lake. I watched a motor launch chugging up and down and across the water to villages opposite and to the town at the head of the lake. Smaller boats were still going off to the island every ten minutes or so.

All was peaceful. I got out my sketch pad and tried to draw the scene with its nearer green hills and its higher white mountains beyond, but soon gave up and took some photographs instead. I could use them later if I wanted to try to paint the scene in oils. Water colours would be a much more stringent test of competence. I wondered if Sandro would agree – I'd never dare tell him about my own daubs.

I got up eventually and walked back into the square, past the strange old *palazzo della comunità*. I'd like to climb to the top of its wrought-iron staircase. Shields were painted blue and scarlet on its pink stucco; the little bell tower rang out the hour. I took another photograph. The building was closed. It never seemed to be open. Perhaps it was a winter thing, only for the inhabitants, not for the tourists. Then I saw, posted up on the arcade underneath, the notice of an exhibition of paintings that was to start here the very next day. There was to be a *vernissage* to which all were invited. Of the artists whose work was to be shown, one was an Alessandro Montani.

I said nothing at lunch to Liz who might, I feared, still be bored by my enthusiasms – especially for paintings and for talking to young men, but I determined to go and have a look when it opened on the Saturday evening. Liz went off to sunbathe on the hotel roof.

I decided to explore the town further – there were two other churches I hadn't yet visited. Also, I wanted to poke around in a second hand book shop I had discovered. I was happy.

Thoughts of the handsome and gifted Sandro did, it is true, occasionally disturb the even tenor of my Saturday morning – but then I was used to living a good deal in my imagination.

It was Saturday evening and I was getting ready to go to the *palazzo* to look at the pictures.

'Do come with me, Liz,' I kept saying. 'There'll be lots of paintings and we might even see Sandro's—'

'Well, if you really insist,' said Liz, surprising me rather. 'I don't suppose we have to *buy* any of them, do we?'

'No, of course not – I mean, you can if you want. It said "entrance free" – I suppose it's just one of their tourist attractions.'

After we had finally arrived before a tall open door at the top of the outside staircase, we entered a vast room. Groups of Italians, and a few hotel habitués, were milling round. The *palazzo* had only this one first floor room, divided into two by moveable screens.

'I suppose they used to have meetings of the townsfolk in the Middle Ages in here?' I said to Liz. Liz shrugged her shoulders.

The walls were empty at the end we entered, but at the far end some stands had been set up for paintings and there were more behind the screens.

The two of us wandered round a little vaguely, inspecting etchings, water-colours, self-portraits, still lifes – and countless impressions of the lake in different seasons and many moods. Quite a few women were circulating, but not many men, except for what appeared to be the mayor, or whatever he was called, and his friends. I finally found a picture I liked and was so absorbed in it that I lost Liz.

A voice in my ear said: 'That *is* a good painting isn't it?'

I turned, hoping it was Sandro, but it was his friend Mario,

71

dressed immaculately in a grey silk suit with a purple flower in his lapel.

'Sandro is being fêted,' he said. 'He has sold his picture of the mountain village – the one you liked.' He crooked a thumb behind him and I saw Sandro, glass in hand, surrounded by some middle-aged women who were also holding glasses of wine. I fancied he was looking quizzically at this fan club. 'Let me get you a drink – come this way,' said Mario.

I looked round, but Liz had melted away. Now Marco had seen Mario and was weaving his way in our direction. Oh dear, Sandro was the one with whom I wanted to talk. Why was it always other men who were more interested in me? The story of my life, I thought, and took a large gulp of the extremely cold white wine. It was a local vintage, and quite delicious.

'Lovely!' I exclaimed involuntarily.

Mario looked amused. 'Wine is not so common in England?' he asked.

'Not cold and dry – not at parties anyway.' I remembered the warmish sweetish beverage proffered by the Head Mistress at colleagues' leaving parties.

'You must look at the pictures,' he said. 'Sandro is always saying he would like to paint Cusio and the island in winter in the snow.'

'I love Impressionist snow paintings. What kind of pictures do *you* like best?' I asked him.

My own favourite painting at that period of my life was by a Scotsman. I had discovered it when I was sixteen. I might tell Mario about it. The wine might help my words to flow.

'I enjoy some of the Expressionists,' said Mario, 'though I suppose painting has become something different since the Romantic Movement. One is safer with the old masters. What about you?'

I considered. In the 1890s, Hamish Murray had been a painter fond of the roomy interiors of tall-windowed houses. In my favourite painting there was a parquet floor, two lit lamps standing on a spindle-legged table in front of uncurtained unshuttered windows and a moonlit sky outside. At the back of the room, a woman was seated at a piano in a long pale grey gown but in the front of the picture a woman in a pale green dress, her hair in a 'Cadogan', gold slippers on her feet, was dancing with a small baby in her arms. The baby had a fat blue bow round his little night-dress. At the door a white-frocked nursery maid, looking almost bridal, was waiting for the baby to be handed over to her and taken to his cot. The lamps cast great shadows on the floor and walls, yet the whole picture was airy, spacious, springlike, the women all happy, obviously rich – except for the maid.

This picture had remained in my mind as an icon, representing a kind of yearning for the 'beautiful life' I'd thought I might lead one day ... with a baby, with leisure, with money .... The people in the picture looked as if they belonged seventy years back, but I knew I had placed them privately in the old manor-house of my village childhood. I also knew that it was not a great or even a good painting.

How could I convey to this young man my feelings for such a picture when I knew my appreciation was inextricably mixed with a more personal feeling? The people in the painting were far from Italy, and far from my present life, but still there in my imagination, a dream, not a fantasy, for they had once truly existed, belonged to the world I wanted, needed, to inhabit .... I did try to convey the sort of painting this was, and my feelings about it, omitting the baby, but I felt my explanation was lame.

Mario listened carefully, and then said: 'We have such paintings

– we call them *genre*. It is a nineteenth century English taste but no worse for that.'

I was surprised; he was more knowledgeable than I had supposed. I was about to say I had better take a good look now at the paintings on these walls when Marco finally came up to us and I saw that Liz was following in his wake.

Sandro had vanished again. He was probably in no hurry to renew acquaintance with two strange foreign women. Maybe his mentioning of our one day sitting for him had been mere politeness. Mario greeted his friend and Liz with the usual *'Ciao'* and handshake. I had sensed in the last few moments that Mario might be attracted to me – to my *mind* anyway – but perhaps I regretted having said too much about my artistic opinions. It was a failing of mine. He would not want to listen to an ignorant Englishwoman stutter out in bad Italian a description of a painting he had never seen. Yet he had seemed to grasp what I was saying.

I excused myself eventually and went to look at what we had come to see, the paintings that adorned the back wall. It was difficult to see them properly since I was not tall and there were people blocking the view who were not really looking at them either. Liz joined me.

'Marco has a wife,' she said. 'The other two don't.'

'How do you know?'

'He said so.'

'I think Sandro looks more married than Marco,' I said.

'I expect he has a girlfriend. Look – here he comes!'

Thinking about Sandro's putative girlfriend made me feel a little depressed. When he came up to us, for once without his circle of admirers, I stood back to observe him.

The company was thinning a little; it was time to go. If only I were rich and could buy one of his pictures, even if the best, the mountain village, had been sold and the other, of the lake-shore lady, said to be modelled on Raffaelo's wife, was most likely also about to be snatched up.

Marco was saying: 'We shall all celebrate now in the café. Yes?'

Sandro looked at his watch and then seemed to decide he could spare us all another twenty minutes. Other artists were greeting him and shouting to each other as we all filed down the outside staircase.

Mario took my elbow. 'Would you like to go over to Lago Maggiore tomorrow?' he asked me as we walked across the square.

Oh dear, I must not encourage him. Yet Sandro might be going too?

It seemed however that Sandro might be otherwise occupied, for he intimated in the café – where he did not stay long – that his plans for Sunday were not yet finalized. I temporized, said I might go on a solitary walk: 'I like walking by myself.'

When we arrived back in our room I kicked off my sandals and stretched my arms high above my head, feeling the need for a release of tension.

'I think I shall go to look at that cemetery on the hill tomorrow,' I said to Liz. 'I don't fancy spending a day with Mario – he's nice but I don't want to encourage him.'

'Suit yourself,' replied Liz yawning. 'I must say that I don't feel like visiting a cemetery, but I might go for a swim.'

We left it at that.

I had always enjoyed visiting graveyards and cemeteries. When I was a child I had accompanied my grandmother to a churchyard near her tiny Dorset hamlet. There, the heart of the great Thomas

Hardy was buried. It was Nan who had told me he was a great man, and the peaceful afternoons we had spent at different seasons of the year, tidying up Nan's own family grave, remained in my memory as times of great happiness.

Now I stood in a cemetery in a foreign village, reached after the long climb up the hill behind the lake. It was a much larger grave-yard than the one in Dorset, was probably used for many villages round the lake.

Looking at the neat graves, each with its photograph of the deceased, some of whom had died young, I felt it was a bit like a picture gallery. There had been no picture of Hardy – even as a child I knew he had been cremated.

Here, flowers were everywhere: in urns, in vases, growing on graves or massed behind them. I walked round the outer perimeter and then on the paths between tombstones. At the far end I came upon a handsome headstone and discovered it marked the grave of an Englishman from the last century.

CARLO WALKER, said the inscription, with the photograph of a 1890s-looking man in a floppy velvet hat.

Tears pricked my eyes when I read the story of his life engraved there. An artist, apparently. One who had never gone home. What had the local inhabitants thought of him? I knew that some of the clerical Englishmen had stayed long in Cusio, middle-aged students who ate and drank and lazed and walked – and often made a few sketches, before climbing the mountains behind the lake, or further away over in Switzerland.

I wished I knew what it was like to live here all the year round, and what it had been like to live here in the past. Or to live *anywhere* in the past. It had been my interest in past lives that had impelled me to go to university when I was eighteen to study

English literature. I was well aware that this passion for the past was regarded by many people as peculiar or, if not strange, unsuitable for a young woman who had her life before her. I had spent much of my childhood and youth being told things were 'unsuitable' – which had only succeeded in making me determined to do them or feel them.

An old man raised his cap to me as he passed on the way to another grave, and I lingered in the cemetery for a moment.

You were born nostalgic, a friend had once told me. Yet here I was in Italy, longing not only for an understanding of the past but also longing for a future that was different from the present, so that I too might carry on life . . . .

With a husband and children ... with a man like Sandro Montani? I knew nothing of his real character; he appeared to be an easy-going man in some respects, but I had glimpsed times when he seemed to go into himself, and abstract his thoughts from whatever was happening around him. It was because he was an artist – and I had a great respect for artists, for painters, poets, composers. As I stood looking unseeingly at some other grave, on which grew many bright flowers, I wondered whether Sandro's physical presence and his demeanour belied his real self. He was so terribly attractive to me: not all that tall, but well-muscled and with a regularly handsome face and eyes that looked a little cynically out at people. Yet I had always been as interested in men's minds as in their bodies. There was a challenge in men that I did not find in most women and I don't think it was purely a sexual one.

I did not think that he would have been born in Cusio, but his grandparents might have been, and might therefore be buried here. What had his childhood been like?

I was even embarrassing myself with this sudden strong sentimental interest in Sandro's family and background. After all, I didn't know him, was just infatuated with a face, a talent, a gesture, a voice. I ought to be ashamed of my daydreaming.

Liz had always judged me backward in the courtship stakes, for I had never even been engaged, even if – often – in love. I'd had several men friends and one or two short affairs, as well as the long one with Peter, but nothing had come of any of them. I feared that in spite of my impetuosity, or probably because of it, because of a certain willingness to lay myself on the line, I was not a man's woman. I understood that most men prefer the chase; they don't like being its object. Here, stimulated by the foreignness of a place, a place where I could be peculiar – because all foreigners were peculiar – I felt liberated, ready to confront an adventure. I walked out of the cemetery in a slight daze that had not been caused only by the hot sun.

As I turned to descend to the lake once more, I noticed a path under trees that led further up the hill. There was a brown signpost announcing 'Sacro Monte' in curly white letters.

'Sacro Monte', I repeated to myself. The words were almost the same as 'Sandro Montani'.

The Italian language was so magical.

When I got back to the hotel Liz was still out and I was drying my hair on the balcony when she returned.

'You missed a trip to Stresa,' she exclaimed, throwing her handbag on her bed.

'You said you were going swimming with Graham.'

'I did – and then Marco came to swim and invited me to go with him to Maggiore. We couldn't find you. Then Sandro came up and we three went over the peninsula on a little mountain road – you'd have loved it—'

'Sandro was there too?'

Oh, how I wished I'd known!

'I enjoyed my walk,' I said, and described the cemetery to Liz as we changed for the evening.

'Sandro says he would like both of us to sit for him,' said Liz. 'We passed his studio – it's in one of those old houses before you get to the turning up to the church.'

I thought she seemed more cheerful.

'They were sorry not to see you. Mario wasn't there. They think he's a bit of a goody-goody, always with his mother—'

'Well, she's a widow – I suppose he's just dutiful.'

We did not see any of our new friends in the café that evening and went to bed early.

The next day, a Monday, almost a week since our arrival, I was passing the gallery shop when Mario hailed me from the other side of the street. He crossed over.

'We've decided that tomorrow will be the day we picnic up on the Sacro Monte,' he said after solemnly shaking hands. 'Please do come – and your friend. It is a beautiful spot.'

'I saw the lane that leads there yesterday when I was at the cemetery,' I said. 'We'd been thinking of going over to the island again tomorrow – but I'd love to go to the Sacro Monte.' If Sandro is going, I thought . . . .

'Did you enjoy the graves?' Mario asked me with a slightly amused glint in his eye.

'Yes – I like cemeteries, you know.'

'We'll see you tomorrow morning then?'

'Shall we bring food – I mean if we are to picnic?'

'Some fruit and bread perhaps? Sandro will be taking

photographs for his next assignment – all those baroque edifices – he'll be painting them all winter!'

Liz agreed it would be nice to go with the men though she didn't think baroque chapels were her sort of thing.

I went to the tourist office to enquire about going over to Zermatt to see the Matterhorn at the end of the week, but I was a bit reluctant to arrange anything ahead in case I missed seeing Sandro again! My holiday was to last for only two weeks. I was already dreading its end, so much did I look forward to the sight of handsome Sandro. I'd seize the opportunity to talk to him tomorrow on the planned picnic, and I revolved possible topics of conversation in my head.

The climb up the hill behind the village was steep. We passed the now familiar cemetery gates and turned up opposite under the trees. Beeches and larches gave a variegated green shade; underfoot the ground was covered in pine needles from their last season.

I had discovered more about the three men. Only Mario was apparently from Cusio itself; Marco was from the town at the head of the lake, and Sandro usually spent his winters at home in Novara. The three always came to the lake for a few weeks in the summer since all their grandparents had been born in the place, and if they were strapped for cash, there was always work of some sort in the tourist season. Sandro had his painting; Marco was some sort of sales rep for Fiat and Mario was training to be an antique and fine art dealer.

Sandro walked between Liz and me and I stole a look at his profile. The touch of his hand on my elbow when for a moment I seemed to be about to slip gave me a delicious sensation, quite different from the one I'd had when Mario took my arm after the exhibition.

Mario was carrying the picnic basket and we women had brought peaches and a long loaf. Sandro had his camera and sketch book in a knapsack on his back. 'They've reopened the café – we shall be able to get a drink up there,' he said.

I was unprepared for the strangeness of the site when we finally arrived on a lane that led to a large baroque church with peeling stucco, on the edge of the park. The church seemed stuck there as if it had once belonged to a village. We walked further along the sandy lane and paused for a moment to look at the view of the lake spread beneath them.

'Shall we go into the church?' I asked.

It looked deserted, neglected.

'It's not too interesting,' said Sandro, so we did not linger there, though Liz poked her nose in for a moment.

We all walked on to a clearing from which several paths branched out to the twenty or so chapels we had been told were hidden away, each one said to be unique. A first little chapel could be seen not far away on the right.

'You can view them in any order you like,' said Sandro. 'I'll meet you all at the well in the middle – you can't miss it. I have to prospect around a bit to see which sites I'm going to paint.' He got his camera out of his bag. 'You can't get lost – just keep on going round and round if you lose your way.'

I wanted to explore for myself. As usual, I had been reading it all up in the guidebook, had pored over descriptions of the contents of these strange buildings with their cupolas and domes and pillars, and I wanted to absorb the atmosphere alone. Liz joined me for a time, and Mario was not far behind us. Marco said he was going straight to the café in the hollow for a drink.

'Let's look in that big chapel you can see behind the trees over there,' I suggested. It had a number – all the chapels were numbered in roman numerals.

'I think I'll just go back over there near the church to take some snaps of the view of the lake – and perhaps look in a nearer chapel,' said Liz. 'I find baroque rather creepy.'

I walked on to the next chapel and looked through its open door. Just inside the door was a grille preventing any visitor from going in any further. Behind the grille, in the half dark, were groups of coloured, life-size terracotta figures, some looking as if they had been freshly repainted.

'They're from the life of Saint Francis,' said Mario, appearing suddenly behind my shoulder.

'Liz would say they were "creepy",' I said. 'She's not easily impressed .... Was it a sort of fashion? Building chapels to fill with terracotta statues – they do look real, don't they? Much more real than the statues in Catholic churches – graven images, some Protestants call them ....'

'The figures are not really here to be worshipped – this is just an ordinary village scene. It was just an excuse to use their skills, I think, even though it was all supposed to be in honour of the Counter-Reformation,' said Mario. 'On the other hand people still fulfil their religious obligations here.'

'I guessed they must have been built because of the anti-Calvin – or was it Luther? – movements – my guidebook doesn't go into what was happening at the time in Europe.'

'Let's walk over in that direction and find another chapel,' suggested Mario. We did.

The various chapels were planted here and there in no particular pattern that I could discern, and without a plan one was soon lost. The others were nowhere to be seen as my companion and I inspected a beautiful little well under its stone canopy and brown tiled roof.

'I wonder if you can still draw water from it?'

'Possibly. It's handsome isn't it?'

By the time I had begun to feel hungry we had inspected a further ten chapels and an infinite variety of scenery.

'We ought to look for Sandro,' said Mario.

He might still be busy taking his photographs, though we hadn't come across him so far. We walked over to what looked like the largest chapel, behind the next slight rise, and then back to the well again, against which Liz was already leaning.

Mario, who was a polite young man, decided to talk to Liz, so it was I who, wandering not far away, came upon Sandro sitting on a tree stump in front of a chapel, a book on his knee.

'Are you still busy?' I asked.

'I'm getting hungry. How do you like the place?'

'I'm in two minds, I suppose. I like it because it's beautiful, and because of the art of the buildings and the scenes with the people – they look quite real. Some people might think them a bit spooky.'

'Spooky – what is that?' he asked.

'Well – ghost-like. A sort of ancient museum. I mean, did people come specially to see it right from the beginning?'

'They came – come – not just to see the chapels but to *pray* in them,' said Sandro solemnly. Then, with a short laugh: 'I too find religious monuments strange – even churches. And you can't be an Italian without spending half your time living near to churches and a lot of your childhood leisure *in* them.'

'Yes – if we didn't know they were churches I've often thought how frightening some of the big ones would be – all deserted and shut up. In Catholic churches you always get candles, so it's more cheerful. Not here though.'

Sandro rose.

'Have you decided which ones you are going to paint?' I asked him.

'It is all in here.' Sandro patted his camera, slung in an elegant box round his neck: 'Avanti!'

I had felt quite nervous having him to myself at last, if only for a few minutes. Nervousness was the reason I often talked too much. I stole a glance at his profile as he walked by my side: long straight nose, well-defined lips, an arc of dark eyebrow.

He turned, and I looked away hastily as if I had been caught in some misdemeanour. It was true that Marco was more sexy-looking with his inviting eyes, but it would not be much of a triumph to get *him* interested in you. Sandro was a challenge, I felt. Then I rebuked myself for being so silly. Perhaps the sun had addled my brain.

For our picnic we all found each other eventually and went to sit in a clearing on some sliced-down tree boles. The men had brought hunks of spicy sausage, some hard cheese and cold hard-boiled eggs. Mineral water was in two tall glass-stoppered bottles that came accompanied by a set of metal tumblers.

'Gracious me, how domesticated you are,' said Marco to Mario, whose contribution this was.

The fruit we had brought had been devoured and we had all decided to find the café in the dell for coffee or another drink – and a lavatory, I hoped. We trooped along a shady ride, passing a set-apart chapel on a rise. Its door was shut.

'The toiletta is down there.' Mario pointed the way. He really was most thoughtful.

Liz and I followed a path to what looked like another miniature chapel in the trees but turned out to be an ancient Ladies, and managed to negotiate the primitive arrangements there. Then I ran down a slope to the café which was set in a little garden with sets of rustic tables and chairs. I waited for Liz to catch me up. She looked pale.

'Are you tired?' I asked. 'We should have brought sun-hats.'

'No I'm OK. I always find looking at statues and stuff tiring. I'm just thirsty.'

For the time being our group appeared to be the only customers. Sandro already had his sketching pad out.

'Well, what do you think of our Sacro Monte?' asked Marco. 'Bit boring isn't it?'

'Oh, no, I find it really fascinating,' I said, since Liz said nothing. I *did* find it interesting; the place grew on one. The park alone would have been beautiful even if it had possessed no ancient chapels.

'Let's see,' said Liz, and Sandro held up a page on which he had sketched two women sitting at a table, their chins cupped in their hands.

'You will come and sit for me, won't you? My present studio is just a room I rent from a friend – 37 Ilona Street – as you walk away from the piazza it's next to the hairdresser's.' Liz looked doubtful.

I said, 'I could come one morning before lunch when Liz is swimming – you don't want to paint us together, do you?'

'No – all I need are some lightning sketches to think about and then develop in the winter. I already have a large portfolio.'

I wondered how many foreign women he had invited to sit for him.

'I've to do more drawings on the island this week as well,' he added.

'Have you ever painted the cemetery?' I asked him.

'No.'

'Viv *adores* cemeteries!' said Liz.

'There was the grave of an artist,' I said, 'yesterday when I walked there. He was English.'

'Oh yes, lots of your compatriots came to our country in the last century – the English love Italy, don't they.'

'English artists do, naturally, I suppose—'

Marco put his oar in complacently. 'Of course we are the best country in the world for art.'

'And tourism,' said Mario. 'They say it's the sun that brings them all.'

'Yes, Stresa will soon be like Blackpool – but more English people go to Spain than Italy,' said Liz.

'The food is better here,' I said.

'Really to get around and understand a place and appreciate it, you need a car,' Liz went on.

'And more time and money. Spend a whole winter here. Go to the opera and to all the great cities and towns—' I expect I sounded childishly enthusiastic.

'You'd like?' asked Mario.

'Oh yes, I'd like – but I have to earn my living.'

'And Miss Elizabeth, she must also earn her living?' Sandro asked.

'Liz is to be married next month!' I said. It was Liz's turn to look complacent.

'And the *marito* – he does not mind that you come here without him?' asked Marco.

'I should think not,' replied Liz coldly. 'I am not a slave, you know. He is busy finishing some work.'

'Englishwomen like to go around with each other. I have noticed this before,' said Marco.

'It's a long walk back – I think we should go soon,' said Liz.

Eventually, after long cold draughts of Swiss beer, chosen rather than coffee, we wended our way back to Cusio, all a little weary, a little sunburnt, not talking much.

Later I said: 'I hope you didn't mind I told them you were about to be married?'

'No – why should I?'

'We've got to know them a lot better haven't we? They are all so nice – especially Sandro.'

'Yes, I saw you making sheep's eyes at him!'

'Oh Liz, I wasn't – at least not intentionally. I'm sure you're the one he'd like to paint. Italians always like blonde women. Will you sit for him?'

'I might give him an hour or two,' said Liz.

'I always feel you pooh-pooh Italian men,' I replied. 'Don't you like them?'

'They'd pass in a crowd with a push, I suppose,' said Liz airily.

'Which one do you think the most handsome? Don't you find Sandro attractive?'

'You ought to be careful with that one! Hidden depths.'

'It's all right for you – you've *got* a man,' I said, adding: '*I* wouldn't mind being seduced by him, you know. Though I expect it's not very likely. He's got a girlfriend, Mario says.'

'Well then, you don't have to feel romantic about him. Men like to think they're doing the chasing.'

'I know that. I expect you're missing Adrian,' I said sympathetically.

'Oh, I'm fine – don't worry about me, Viv.'

'I'd like to go to San Rocco island again tomorrow,' I added dreamily after a pause.

Liz laughed. 'Nothing to stop you, is there?'

The next afternoon, a Wednesday, I took one of the boats over to the island, wanting to walk round the place alone and to have another look at the church. I was not an unsociable person but I always did need plenty of time to myself, so I had suggested that Liz might like to go swimming again.

Liz said OK, she might come over later, she might even persuade young Graham the Swimmer to accompany her. He had turned out to be a twenty-seven-year-old accountant on holiday with his parents and regretting it. 'You go off for your walk,' said Liz.

This time the boat was a motor launch and the air a little petrol-laden but once I'm embarked I sniffed something hot and flowery. I felt a mixture of melancholy and happiness, not unusual for me, I suppose. I wanted to think over yesterday's conversation with Sandro and I could not do this in the presence of another person.

He might even be over on the island? Though I did not intend to dog his footsteps I'd go to the church first, where he had been copying, light a candle, sit and think . . . .

There were a few other tourists in the building, and several old women telling their rosaries, the dry sound of their lips a faint whisper on the air, air that was now heavy with flowers and incense. Tall white lilies with golden calyxes stood in the half dark before the altar. Perhaps there had been a funeral. The sanctuary lamp was glowing.

I sat down and tried to assemble my thoughts but they refused to arrange themselves into anything but a sort of aching wish that I might be accompanied by Sandro Montani, that he might take my hand, put his arm round me, kiss me, ask me to stay for ever with him . . . . I shook myself. I knew only too well the snares of the imagination. Since I was fourteen I had entertained daydreams of a fantasy life with a perfect lover. Even when I was with Peter I would still find myself occasionally having them.

I got up and went over to a corner where a Madonna stood above a pool of candlelight, each candle a halo wavering in the gloom, the smell of wax mingling with more lilies nearby. I put a few lire into the box in the wall, chose a small candle and lit it from one burning steadily on the front row. *'Old Nanny Netticoat in her white petticoat,'* came into my head irreverently. I remembered the candles we'd had at home during my wartime childhood when they had bombed Southampton. The blackout had been total, and the candlelight had fascinated me.

Then I muttered a *Pater Noster* because I liked the sound of Latin words, and because Catholicism belonged here, as it did on the Sacro Monte. It *would* be lovely to belong to something ... if you could believe it . . . .

'Please make me less of an adolescent,' I believe I murmured to the statue. It did not reply.

As I came out of the church into the glaring sun I wondered if Sandro Montani was a believer. Marco probably was; Mario not. With artists you could never tell. They were intuitive people.

I decided to walk round the island in the opposite direction to the one Liz and I had previously taken. There was only one lane, so you ended up back at the landing stage whichever way you went. The massive convent that had once been a monastery, then a seminary, loomed above everything on the island, rising behind the heavy foliage of ancient trees.

'Grüss Gott,' a Swiss-German female tourist with a small dog

walked past me.

I craned my neck to look at the bell tower of the seminary. Would you know you were on an island if you never went out of the convent? How had they taken over all the stone and bricks to build all this hundreds of years ago? On rowing boats? There was so much I did not know about. Sandro and Mario would know about things like that.

The saint was supposed to have walked across the snake-infested, or dragon-infested, water to come here. Before that, had it been uninhabited, with nobody to convert? A hermit could have been happy here.

The entrances to the many villas' gardens, which we had seen before, were all along the lane on the side next to the water but I walked on further this time, and peered into one or two of them. How wonderful it would be to own a house like one of these, with the sound of lake water lapping at the bottom of your garden. There was something about islands that I liked. Bounded, separate, nothing you could do about them . . . . Suddenly I felt quite sleepy.

There was a rustic seat under a chestnut tree at the side of one of the gates on the lane so I sat down to rest for a moment, lulled by the sound of the lapping water. A bird was singing. I felt sure it was a nightingale.

The next thing I knew I was jerking up my head and rubbing my eyes. I must have fallen asleep – how shameful at my age! It was drinking wine at lunch that did it, I supposed. I looked at my watch. I'd dozed for half an hour.

I got up, inspected my face in my handbag mirror and then continued my circular walk, ending up again in front of the steps that led to the church. Sandro might be in there now, sketching . . . .

I pushed open the inner padded door, sat down at the front near the pulpit. The church now appeared deserted. I'd better check on a boat for my return to the mainland.

Just as I got up to go out again I heard someone coming up the staircase from the entrance to the crypt behind the chancel.

It was Sandro.

Then, coming in through a side door from outside, Liz appeared. What a shame, I thought. I might have had Sandro to myself for a few minutes.

'There you are! I've been exploring the island – didn't find you anywhere,' said Liz. She appeared slightly out of breath, but added, 'There's nothing much else to see, is there?'

'I'm afraid I fell asleep,' I said.

Sandro came up to us: 'Well, hello there. When are you both coming to my studio to be my models?'

'I'll come tomorrow morning, if that is convenient,' I replied boldly. 'Then Liz can sit for you after her swim.'

'Very well. And now you must excuse me – I have to finish my pulpit.'

Dismissed, I thought, but Liz said: 'Let's get the next boat back and go and eat ice-creams.'

'OK. I feel like a long cool *limonata*. There's no café on the island, is there?'

We left Sandro to his sketches and found a boat waiting at the landing stage.

'Which way did you walk round just now?' I asked her. 'You ought to have seen me and woken me up.'

'Oh I only got as far as behind the church the other way round before I gave up – too hot. I'm not surprised you fell asleep.'

'How was your swim?'

'Graham was with his parents in Zermatt so I didn't bother.'

'Sandro might have invited us to stay on a bit – I was meaning to go down to the crypt,' I said as the boat, only half full, set off for the shore. Actually, when I'd seen him in the church a few moments before I had suddenly felt the urge to embrace him there and then. He was quite unbearably attractive.

'You know, Viv, you should be careful with Sandro. If you let it show you think he's the cat's whiskers, he'll get vain, and that's not good for a man. I think you ought to talk more to the studious one – Mario.'

'Yes, he's nice but—'

'More your type,' she said. Then she sighed and changed the subject. 'Do you really want to go over to Switzerland? I heard the hotel was taking a party on Thursday to the Matterhorn in their little bus.'

'I wouldn't mind – but you've been before, haven't you?'

Liz had been on several holidays with her cousins to Lucerne and Interlaken and had even skied one year in Zermatt.

'I don't think I'll bother going again myself,' she said.

'I might go – but I'd like to walk to the "Holy Mountain" again – and we might go over to Maggiore,' I said.

'I believe that Raffles friend or whatever he's called has a car and would take us over there. Marco was saying something about it yesterday.'

We left it at that.

The next morning I put on my nicest linen shift and went to sit for Sandro. His studio was a large room over a shop next to the *parrucchiere*, which I had learned meant the hairdresser's. Stone stairs twisted up from a flagged ground-floor entrance with overflowing pots of flowers and greenery that extended even up the staircase. I felt I hardly even needed to knock, so loudly was my heart thumping. After a pause I did knock though, quite softly. Immediately the door was opened by Sandro, a paint brush in one hand and a rag in the other.

'Oh, hello. Come in.'

'You said to come and sit for you this morning.'

'Yes, well – sit here.' He gestured to a decrepit sofa, put down the brush and the rag and took up a stick of charcoal.

'Just sketches, that's all. Is Elisabetta to come too?'

'Yes, but she's swimming at present. Where do you want me to look?' I sat down.

'Just look through the window – that's right – elbow on the arm – nice profile. It's kind of you to come – I'm trying to finish this painting of a storm on the lake.' He gestured to his easel. 'Things done quickly are often the best,' he said as he kept tearing off papers from his sketch pad and dropping them on the floor.

After about ten minutes, he said: 'There we are,' bent down, retrieved the sketches, and put the charcoal back on the table, which was piled up with paints and more sketches.

Was that all? I had better have a look at his painting of the lake before I left.

The paint swirled blue and green and grey and black, with a tiny white boat lost in the middle.

'I'll probably use the poses you've done – one can never have enough of the human form,' he said. He held up one of the sketches and I saw the fluid outline of a sitting woman, almost as if I had been reduced to a gesture.

'I must go,' I said. 'You sketched us at the Sacro Monte, so you've done quite a lot.'

He smiled then. 'You must both come to Stresa next Saturday. Marco's uncle has a restaurant there and Raffaelo can take us by car over the Mottarone – that's a mountain between here and Maggiore – with marvellous views of our lake and the big lake. You can see the Alps as well from there.'

'Oh, I'd love to—'

He took my hand and held it for a moment. Then he turned away, saying: 'Mario or Marco will let you know. And Elisabetta can come round here tomorrow – for me to sketch her.'

He dropped my hand, seemed to have made all the effort of which he was capable. How abstracted, far away in thought he was most of the time. I was just a 'figure' for him. The whole sitting had taken only half an hour.

As I was going down the stairs he called out after me: 'Tell your friend—' Then the door was shut.

'Oh I don't think he's really keen on sketching me,' said Liz at lunch when all this was reported to her. 'I wouldn't mind taking him up on the restaurant invitation though.'

'I'm sure he'd be pleased if you sat for him. It would only take about half an hour – he's very quick.' My friend shrugged her shoulders.

'What about your going to Zermatt tomorrow then?' she asked me after lunch when we were sitting in the hotel garden writing postcards. At least, I was. Liz was idling in a hammock.

'Oh, I might not bother – if you've already been there—'

'No, really, go by yourself – the old mountain is worth a look. Graham thought we might swim from the beach at the other end of town. It's said to be quieter. You'd be back for dinner – or we could meet in the café. I just don't think I'll bother dragging myself round to Signor Sandro's as an artist's model.'

In the event I made up my mind quickly. I *would* go on the Swiss trip. It would be a change from the lake – and away from my Sandro-directed yearnings. The hotel said the list was already in the tourist office – it would open again at four and there might still be time to book.

I walked along the cobbled street to the office at four. Just as I was about to go in I heard my name called.

'Viviana!' It was Mario.

'I'm just going to book for Zermatt,' I explained.

'I shall accompany you – would you like that? I've never been on one of these trips.'

What could I say? Mario was nice, but his presence would only keep on reminding me who he was *not*.

'Lovely,' I said, trying to sound pleased. 'Liz will go swimming instead with Graham – she's been to the Matterhorn already.'

'*Ebbène*! I will accompany you.'

As the girl in the office wrote out our tickets in a laborious hand, I remarked: 'Sandro said something about going to the Mottarone at the weekend. He said your friend Raffaelo has a car and would take us all – to a restaurant in Stresa.'

'Oh, did he? Yes, it would be possible; but he has not asked me. He will have mentioned it to Raffaelo, I suppose. You were at his studio?'

'Yes, he was sketching me – he wants to draw Liz as well.'

'He likes English women,' said Mario dryly.

'I am not very English looking. I do think he's very gifted.'

'Cusio attracts artists,' he said as we walked away from the tourist office, each with a ticket for the next day's trip to Zermatt.

'Not just painters. Musicians – and even philosophers.' We stopped in front of a book shop. Mario went on: 'Over eighty years ago the great Nietzsche visited the place with a woman poet. Can you guess where he was walking when he fell in love with his companion? She was, by the way, a Russian lady.'

I tried to think. Suddenly inspired, I hazarded: 'Up on your "Holy Mountain"?'

'You are correct. He wrote about when they heard the nightingales. We did not hear them when we were up there, did we? Or we were making too much noise.'

'I believe I heard them on the island,' I said.

'Ah!'

'What happened then?' I asked him. 'I mean, to Nietzsche?'

'Oh, she rejected him – it was too sudden.' Mario looked at me sadly. 'He never had any success with the women, I'm afraid. He suffered a lot from it. Later he said that Sacro Monte was the most beautiful dream of his life.'

'How melancholy.'

I was wishing it was Sandro telling me all this! If Mario were to continue in this vein tomorrow my trip might be a bit of a strain.

'Never mind,' said Mario. 'It was not the end of his life. He wrote a famous book and said the idea came to him in Cusio. Later, of course, he went mad.' Then he laughed, and said: 'I have to serve in the shop today. I shall be waiting in the "parking" where the coach leaves tomorrow. Six o'clock. Don't forget – you must get up early.'

Vivien, I groaned when I was by myself, why did you let yourself in for this? One of those early starts they were so fond of when all you wanted was to turn over and go back to sleep . . . .

★

Later, I was to have confused memories of the day spent with Mario. Most of the time we seemed to have been sitting in a coach looking at mountains coming closer and closer. When we crossed the silly little frontier, next to a sweet shop, I had that catch in the throat that frontiers and all the history of a place always gave me. Then there was the Simplon Pass just before Berg and then the turn-off to reach the Matterhorn from the back door, so to speak. In Switzerland I was pleased that for once I should be able to make myself understood, German having been one of the languages I had learned at school. Mario, without a word of German, thought this admirable, but added complacently: 'The Swiss always speak *my* language.'

When, after leaving our coach and travelling on a local train, and then a rack and pinion railway, we finally arrived at the platform from which the Matterhorn, just across the way, could be viewed, the sun was bright on the snow, the air cold. Mario pointed out the Monte Rosa which he thought more beautiful than the strangely shaped Matterhorn.

'All their mountains are called Horn,' he complained. Perhaps something about mountains did purify you, I was thinking. Everything seemed a long way away – Cusio, and the lake; even Sandro.

Back in Zermatt, Mario and I ate apple pie and cream and drank Swiss coffee at a pavement café. I was surprised to find him undemanding company. By now Liz would have probably have been moaning about something and I could imagine Sandro might be a trifle morose away from his home ground. Mario though took a lively interest in everything and even followed me into a bookshop after lunch.

I bought Katherine Mansfield in German, having already

bought the same writer in Italian in Cusio.

'Why do you want to read her in translation?' exclaimed Mario, mystified.

'I just like the fact that she is everywhere now – and to see what her stories are like in other languages.'

'Here is another of your English writers,' he said, pouncing on a German copy of *Tessa der Durbervilles*. 'Should I read it?'

'Yes, you might – it will be translated into Italian.'

'Is my English not good enough?'

He sounded hurt.

'I'm sure it is. Thomas Hardy lived very near where I was brought up. He is still very popular with the English.'

'And here too, I believe. I shall buy it in English.'

The return to Cusio was the morning's journey in reverse, but the mountain air had made me a little sleepy. I knew that Mario would like it if I allowed my head to fall on his shoulder as he sat by my side in the coach, but I did not want to encourage him. If only it were Sandro sitting next to me, Sandro talking to me about the scenery or the books he had recently read.

He is never there, the man you want, I thought, clear-sighted enough to recognize the old truth: the man who opens his mind to yours, who is friendly and approachable, and who may even want *you*, is never the one your senses yearn for. Not that Mario had actually done anything to show me he might want me in any way other than that of friend and companion, but the way he focused on me, his eagerness to converse, the interest he appeared to take in my own opinions, all made it abundantly clear that he liked me.

Why was liking not enough? If Mario had been more assertive and at the same time more mysterious I might even have fallen for him. Perhaps.

The only difference between him and his friend was that in Sandro's company I felt something you might even call a chemical affinity. It was strange that Sandro did not feel the same affinity with me. Was I forever condemned to fall unrequitedly in love? Lots of people would call it lust, I supposed, but truly I felt it was more than that.

When I arrived back at seven o'clock that evening Liz was making up her face in the bathroom mirror.

'Did you sit for him then?' I enquired, throwing my handbag on the bed and myself after it. I must wash and change, but felt disinclined. On the other hand I felt quite hungry.

'No. I went to his studio, but he was busy doing something else. He didn't do any sketches of me, but he mentioned again about going to Stresa on Sunday in his friend's car. I went swimming this evening just before you got back. Did you enjoy the Matterhorn?'

'Oh what a shame! I was sure he'd be delighted you'd taken him at his word—'

'Sandro Montani had other things to occupy himself with today,' said Liz severely. 'He did say he would do some drawings of me in my big sunhat tomorrow by the lake. What about Mario?'

'We had a good day – he is very nice. I enjoyed Switzerland,' I answered primly.

The next morning, our last Friday, I decided I would walk alone again to the Sacro Monte. Liz was to go swimming with Graham, and apparently his father too, and would later meet Sandro down by the lake to see if he wanted to do a few outdoor sketches.

'He said we could eat ice-cream if he didn't feel like sketching,' she said, idly swinging her sun-hat on its two ribbons.

It was a very hot day, making me wonder if I was foolish to want to walk over a good mile up a hill. There was such a strenuous climb out of the village, as there was in all directions, except by boat, if you wanted to get out of the place. Still, it wasn't noon yet, when mad dogs and Englishmen walked abroad, and I could find the woodland café again, have a long cold drink, and a sandwich.

I toiled up the narrow path behind Cusio, reached the entrance to the cemetery hot and out of breath, turned left and began to walk under the cool dark beeches. The other day we had not had time to see all the chapels, so I would go to those further from the entrance, and take some photographs on the way.

It all seemed strangely darker and quieter under the trees than it had on my first visit. Then the church hove into view, and the sandy lane. I decided not to follow the outer path but to cross the grass to the chapels in the middle. One or two of the larger ones were said to contain the best scenes and figures but there was no telling where they were to be found. I had seen a picture of one of them we had not seen, the carnival one, in which monks and children and horses and fine ladies were strolling along a street with the brown-robed figure of the saint in their midst. I thought it might be number thirteen. Now, as I walked across the park, away from the splendid vantage point with its views of the lake and the peninsula, I was thinking how very strange it was to leave life-sized terracotta people stranded in such buildings for three hundred years, like abandoned dolls or idols. I had always thought statues resembled dolls, and remembered what I had said to Sandro the other day about the strangeness of religious buildings. These were neither idols nor dolls, though both dolls and idols had a symbolic significance not possessed by 376 lifelike figures, dressed for the most part in clothes belonging to the ordinary people of the century in which they had been carved.

I shivered a little, in spite of the heat that was now beating down on the wandering path. The thought came to me that in fact these figures were just *people* from the real past, folk who had worshipped in a certain way but whose memorials were more to do with human beings, not part of a divine story.

I supposed there must be guardians here: someone must look after the twenty chapels. A whole crowd of people must always have been employed to keep the buildings and their occupants clean and tidy, open as they often were behind their grilles to the elements. Preserving the park and all its inhabitants must need a lot of work.

Suddenly, and as if to answer my own question, I heard the unmistakable whine of a vacuum cleaner. I followed the noise and came up to one of the larger chapels I didn't remember seeing before. I looked through the grille, saw the real people mingling with the older figures. A woman was manoeuvring a snaky cleaner and a man was testing electric light bulbs.

It reminded me of a stage set: the whole of the place was a theatre. Perhaps here religion had always had something of the theatrical? To be truthful, I preferred the little village churches of Dorset to the monuments of the Counter-Reformation. I must be an irredeemably Protestant sort of agnostic.

I gazed a little longer at the cleaners who were taking no notice of the life-sized statues and figures and did not look up at me either. In this chapel – I could not see its number – the saint appeared to be ascending to heaven – or was perhaps on his way down – with a few onlookers cheering him on. I could make no sense of this particular scene so turned and walked back to the path. As for the figures, if somebody came and mixed them up, so that episodes from St Francis's youth were put down in another chapel purporting to represent him at the end of his life, how long would it take for anyone to realize? It must be a temptation for the cleaners. They might sometimes take a terracotta figure home with them? I'd be tempted myself!

Another chapel eventually hove into sight. Now I had lost my bearings. Many of the chapels resembled each other – I had seen rectangular ones, round ones, and polygonal ones, but had not been able to distinguish the earlier from the later. So many of them had been restored as well, at different times. How ignorant I was. I supposed a person like Sandro or Mario would know whether something had been built in the sixteenth century or late in the eighteenth.

One of the chapels had not even been finished, and it must be a little further on from where I was walking. Going from one to the other of all these similar but not quite the same buildings was like owning many dolls' houses but not being able to see them all together. Like the Queen living in different places with a tooth-brush in each bathroom . . . . I shook my head – it must be the sun, making me have such strange fancies . . . . Then there were the paintings and the frescoes. How much zeal and effort over all the years – or had the painters, like the sculptors, just seen it all as a job of work they would be paid for?

After a further few minutes' walk I glimpsed another chapel I calculated I had not seen before. There seemed no rhyme or reason to the order of their numbers and I was too weary to try to work it all out. This one however *was* number thirteen – I saw it in roman numerals on the front. It looked a bit like chapel number eight, if I remembered right. Sandro had said, I seemed to remember, that the architecture of number fifteen was the most beautiful. Oh well, I'd walk over to it after looking at thirteen.

I made my way across the sward, tall, thin-trunked trees a little way away. I supposed if I had been a serious researcher I would have insisted on bringing a map. I stood for a moment, opened my shoulder bag and fished out the crumpled guidebook. It was in Italian but seemed to say that this chapel had been built at the end of the sixteenth century by a native of Cusio, and in it the saint was being led half-naked in the streets of Assisi 'protesting against carnival excesses'.

I put the book back in my bag and plodded on. I saw a chapel built like one mushroom sitting on another, even looking pleasantly homely but here now first was number thirteen.

The door was open. I went right up to the grille, and looked into the darkness. Yes, here was a lively carnival scene. The figures looked as if they had been 'improved', I thought.

I blinked, looked again. One of the male figures had moved! No, something *behind* him had moved. My heart began to pound. Nobody else had been in front of me, I was sure. Should I take to my heels? There might be a rapist or a murderer hidden here. Then I thought, how absurd. Nobody would wait here for hours for a tourist to approach.

I shut my eyes for a moment, then opened them cautiously. One of the men in the crowd behind the saint, dressed in brown as far as I could see in the faint light from the window – for the chapel was in shade – was actually tapping St Francis on the shoulder.

I was not the sort of woman to scream, but my mouth was dry, my tongue almost stuck to the roof of my mouth. My hands tightened on the grille. If a figure had come to life I only had myself to blame – the hot sun, my silly fancies. Then, as I turned to escape whatever or whoever it was, I heard a voice.

'Vivien?'

From behind the saint's outstretched hands there emerged – a man. A man with a sketch book.

Sandro Montani.

I was going mad, thinking Sandro was everywhere.

'Sandro!' I half gasped, half squeaked.

He came up to the grille. 'What are *you* doing here?'

'I might ask the same of you. Liz said you were going to meet her by the lakeside—'

'Oh dear, I forgot I'd said that,' he said. 'I wanted to sketch the backs of the figures – the bits you don't see.'

Liz would be disappointed, but I myself must make the most of this chance encounter. I took my camera out from my canvas bag.

'Stop there a moment – I shall take a photograph of you next to St Francis,' I said, a slight wobble in my voice the only remnant of my fear. I'd need a flash.

Sandro waited patiently for a few seconds as I fiddled around before snapping him. Then he opened a door hidden in the grille and came through. (That photograph never came out – the flash wasn't working!)

'Shall I take one of you – I didn't think you'd like the place enough to return?'

'No, don't bother. I wanted to walk by myself,' I said. How very good-looking he was.

He put his sketch-pad back in the bag round his neck and took my hand.

'What about a drink? It's bloody hot – good thing their statues are not made of wax.'

I abandoned any idea of looking for number fifteen. All I could think of, as we walked back across the sward and turned by the central well and then down to where the café was, I might be frightened of a rapist but I'd still be very happy to be seduced by Signor Sandro Montani.

In the café I drank a whole glass of light Italian beer and repaired my face. He laughed. 'You look fine—'

'No – I'm boiling!'

We began to talk about Mario, then about Cusio. I asked him about the terracotta figures, told him some of my fancies and asked whether it was possible to get hold of a map of the chapels.

'I don't think one exists – at least I've never seen it. Did you see that one of the fresco painters was from here – he had the same name as myself?' Sandro asked me.

'Montani?'

'Yes. I should like to draw Sacro Monte in the winter. Pen and wash would be the best medium – all the whitenesses – the white sky and snow over the ochre of the buildings and the trees dark green – but white in all the colours.'

I wished I could cover his hand with mine. How I wished we might never have to get up and leave the café, longed for him to kiss me, make love to me there and then, under the trees. Even if I never saw him again.

He was saying something about the day after tomorrow when he hoped we would all go to Stresa in Raffaelo's car.

'I might have asked my girlfriend,' he said, 'but she has to go to her sister's wedding.'

'Is she in Cusio then?' I was able to ask him quite coolly.

'No, in Novara, where I live most of the time. She's a medical student – *una donna simpatica e intelligente*.'

I asked huskily: 'Will you marry her?'

'Perhaps, when she has finished her studies. At present she is delivering bambini.'

What would a man like Sandro want from a wife? Bambini, I supposed.

If I spoke aloud the thought that had just come into my head, what would he think of me? It was shameful. I was wishing he might seduce me and make me pregnant! I didn't even want him to *love* me – or even imagine he could ever love me – but I longed for him to find me physically attractive. It was quite elemental how I wanted him to want me. I scarcely knew him . . . . But I was used to dissimulating my desires.

'What is she called, your girlfriend?'

'Luciana.'

'What a pretty name! She must be clever to want to be a doctor.'

'Oh, here in Italy you get your university degree through knowing the right people. Luciana works hard but her father is rich.'

'Even if she is rich she may need to work? I think that's a good thing,' I said boldly.

'*E vero.*' He got up. 'I think we must go – I must do some more work in the studio.'

'Liz will have been waiting for you by the lake.'

'It was not a definite promise – tell her I am sorry but I was behindhand with other work.'

I thought, he had not really forgotten but had just changed his mind. All artists are selfish. As we began the long walk back to Cusio, he said: 'Promise me you will both come on Sunday – we shall be in the piazza at eleven o'clock with the car to drive over the mountain. There will be splendid views worthy of your attention.' He paused, and then added: 'You know, Vivien, you are a *donna simpatica.*'

Immensely touched, I stared at him, my heart thumping away. I came to a halt, stood stock still. Then he turned, took my hand and then very slowly kissed me on the brow. He then continued his walk, and I must perforce follow him.

'You are returning to *Londra* on Monday?' he asked in quite an ordinary voice.

'I'm afraid so. Sunday will be our last full day.'

We walked on in single file now as the path was narrow. There was nothing more I could say to detain him. What a bonus it had been, this meeting on the Sacro Monte – and his chaste kiss. Now I must try to forget him.

He said *'Arrivederci'*, turned on his heels, and went off, I presumed back to his studio.

I went over his remark: *Una donna simpatica* … I wouldn't tell Liz about that. Or about the kiss. I supposed it was meant to be a sort of compliment, that sort of kiss?

Wishing Sandro loved me brought back all the years I was with Peter Richardson.

When I arrived back in the piazza I went and sat down by the lake. I didn't feel like going into the hotel straight away. Anyway, Liz would probably come down to the lake herself, and if not I'd go and look for her in our hotel.

I sat on a bench, partly shaded from the sun, and allowed myself to think for a few moments about Sandro Montani, so near and yet so far. I knew perfectly well why I wished he would find me sexually attractive – even seduce me! It was Nature's time clock inside me, always reminding me that in eight years I'd be forty. I couldn't believe it – it seemed so old. If I were seduced I might become pregnant and this time I'd have the baby. Sandro – or whoever the father was – need never know.

One of the reasons Peter and I had split up was because just when I had made up my mind to end the affair, I had become pregnant. Then, after desperately hoping there might be some way of having the child I had to set about dashing my hopes, for Peter left it to me to decide, and I just could not take him away from his other children. He said he was still in love with me after five years together, and I believed him. I had tried to think clearly. On account of the very situation we were in, I wasn't sure that we would stay together.

In a way, I suppose getting pregnant should have been the sign that I should take the risk. It didn't work out that way. Instead, it made me realize quite clearly that it was impossible. We didn't live in a polygamous country. I was young, and I discovered I already nursed the vague hope of finding a real husband one day. You couldn't expect to start a marriage already burdened with someone else's baby, could you? I knew Peter would hate his child to be brought up by another man. He just wanted me to stay with him whilst he had his cake and ate it. His wife was not so young. I had discovered in myself an unsuspected sort of morality, a strong feeling that live children were more important than putative ones. Peter must not leave *them*.

I suppose I could have used a different kind of morality that sees the unborn as something sacred, but I did not feel that. Time however was passing for me if I was ever to find a man to be the father of the children I was quite sure I wanted.

I had acted quickly in that cold grey February of 1959, and arranged for an – illegal – abortion. In those days you either had the baby or ran the risk of putting yourself outside the law. As everyone knew, if you had enough money if was not a difficult thing to arrange. As usual, the poor paid with their lives or their happiness and the slightly better off escaped. What I thought of as a 'tadpole' had to go down the sluice during my half term weekend. I had acted so swiftly – though my agonizing seemed to have gone on for months – that only seven weeks elapsed between the discovery and its solution. I knew that what I must do would eventually end our affair but I didn't now believe that was why I did it. If I had been born to a different sort of family, living in the village manor house rather than a Dorchester suburb, in a family as enlightened in these matters as I thought I was, things might have been different. If I were to keep the baby, my parents, Hilda and Edgar, would have to be told and I just could not upset their lives in that way. My father and mother would never be able to cope with an illegitimate grandchild. I could have unburdened myself to Father, I suppose, but he would have been shocked or distressed, and I had been used for many years not to ask for support from either of my parents in a crisis, whether financial or moral. I had panicked at the sheer *impossibility* of their knowing what had happened. I could not imagine what they would say or do, and I felt responsible for their happiness. In the past, they had made sacrifices for me as well as for my brother Roger, and I didn't want to hurt either of them. My grandmother would have understood better, but by 1959 Nan had died.

I looked up through the lime tree branch, remembering these oft repeated thoughts, and coming to the conclusion that if anyone were to have told my parents it should have been Peter, not me.

I wished the world was different. I always thought of the unborn baby as She, though at the time it never occurred to me that I was robbing my parents of a granddaughter. In 1958 my brother had just married and was soon to become a father – in the end he was to have a large family – so that had eventually salved my conscience as far as their grandchildren were concerned.

Maybe also when I got over all the trauma I realized that I would not be forced into a lifelong bond with Peter. Shortly afterwards we parted, for what would we do if the same thing happened again? You can never go through all that again, had been my reasoning. I had to make a new life for myself. My lover had wanted me eternally committed to him but he had too many obligations already. If my decision was just shorthand for not loving him enough I had to accept that.

I should have thought of all that before I began the affair with Peter, I suppose, but you don't always think ahead in your twenties. Now, some years later, I felt more hard-bitten and more ready to blame Peter – which I hadn't felt like doing before.

As I sat on by the lake I wished I did not have to remember all this. It was still painful. Not the abortion so much as my failure of nerve. I had been a coward. Even so, I had never really thought I could have done anything else, even if a part of me regretted my decision. At this present moment, as I sat on in the shade, that long-ago decision was making me realize how much I now wanted a child. Other things being equal, which in my experience they never are, there were compensations in my present freedom. Freedom for what? I asked myself as I watched the little boat disgorge its passengers on the jetty. I'd never told Liz any of my story, thinking she might be shocked, I suppose.

Peter had looked heartily relieved when I'd told him my decision. Did he realize that if my parents had been dead I would certainly have had his child, and insisted upon managing alone? Not because it was his baby, so much as that it was an affirmation of life, and on the whole I was in favour of life. The abortion had effectively signed the death warrant of our long love affair, and I was no longer pretending that loving a man didn't above all still mean the possibility of a family rather than a husband.

I found Liz on the balcony of our room reading a magazine.

'I met Sandro on my walk,' I said. 'He apologizes for not meeting you – said he had some important work to do.'

'I expect he just forgot,' said Liz carelessly but not crossly.

'Well, I did say we would accept their invitation to go over to Maggiore on Sunday – you will come, won't you? He said he might do some sketches of both of us there.'

'What else did you talk about?'

'Oh, just about the chapels – he was actually *in* one of them behind the grille! We went for a drink.'

'Did he try to seduce you then and there?' she asked ironically.

'No, he didn't.'

'Were you disappointed, Vivien?'

I was used to my friend's teasing, laying myself open too often to it on account of wearing my heart on my sleeve, so I just smiled, saying: 'He has a fiancée, I believe.'

'Did he tell you that?'

'Yes – she is called Luciana. Shall we go and look for a cup of tea or do you want to go over to the island again? I haven't had much lunch – I saw some delicious cakes at that little *pasticceria*.'

'Always thinking of your tummy – love ought to make you lose your appetite.'

I was not sure that Liz would accept the Sunday drive; was prepared for her to cry off at the last moment to get her own back on Sandro for making her wait in vain by the lake on the Friday. On the Saturday we shopped as the men were all busy.

On Sunday, Liz, wearing a large sun-hat, was ready in good time and we strolled into the piazza looking for the men.

'Raffaelo's car is at the end of the street where it meets the road,' said the voice of Mario. Marco was not with him.

We all walked along the narrow street to its furthest end where it met the sloping gardens of the hillside villas. Beneath them the lake waters were glittering silver in the sparkling sunshine.

Sandro was next to the driver in the front seat of his friend's large old-fashioned car. Raffaelo, who was to do the driving, was a dark, rather soft-spoken young man. Sandro raised a languid hand to us in greeting.

'There is room for three people in the back,' said Raffaelo. 'We shall pass at the foot of the Mottarone mountain but not ascend it – you must look at the view out of the windows.'

'Oh, why not go over the top? You can see miles and miles – all the peaks of the Monte Rosa, scores of other mountains – many small lakes as well as ours and the Maggiore. On a very clear day even Milano and Torino,' exclaimed Sandro, waking up.

'No time – have to meet my family at noon,' said Raffaelo shortly.

Sandro relapsed into a rather sulky silence. After all it was his friend's car and his friend's time, and beggars can't be choosers. He looked a little tired.

Liz was keeping quiet but had taken off her hat. She had said nothing to Sandro about his forgetting to meet her on the Friday, or deliberately not going to the lake after telling her he would.

Mario, the peacemaker, said: 'It is not clear enough today to see the furthest distance – there is a heat mist. It will be for another time. English people come in winter when there is skiing here.'

'You have never skied in your life, Mario, have you?' murmured Raffaelo at the wheel.

'There are botanical gardens too,' I said. 'I read about them. How long will it take to Stresa this way?'

'About half an hour – it is high country,' answered Mario. 'Very impressive even without going to the top.'

I was thinking I would rather have made the excursion over the Mottarone and seen the fantastic view than spend my time guzzling in a smart lakeside resort. Liz would probably not have agreed.

The road out of Cusio had turned at the bottom of the little hill at whose top was the cemetery, to join a main road that climbed higher and higher. The higher we went, the more mountains came into view from across the lake. The countryside was green and fertile, a stream running along the bottom of a valley. I kept turning to look at the view. Sandro was silent, ignoring everybody, but Mario obliged with the names of the villages we could see and of the mountains on our left.

After about half an hour the road joined another better tarmacked one, and we began to descend. I saw a long shining lake beneath us.

'Maggiore,' said Mario with a proprietorial air.

Liz roused herself. 'We came a different way before?'

Sandro turned, and actually smiled at *me*. 'Yes. Now we shall all have a cool drink by the side of the lake.'

Raffaelo parked his car and departed to meet his family. He was to meet us again at seven o'clock for the return journey. The lake lay shimmering for miles and miles with wooded islands visible from where we stood. There were a few gulls blown inland circling around, and we could hear the hum of traffic along the tree-lined avenues, and the plashing of paddle steamers.

'What about the cool drink?' I suggested.

'If you can walk a little further?' Sandro led our small party along the lakeside to a gleaming white hotel built on the very edge of the water. 'The food here is good.'

Good, but very expensive. We must both pay our share. It was not as if Sandro and Mario were our boyfriends, and even if Marco's uncle owned it, he would be expecting us to pay for a good meal.

The dining room was immense, already half full with Italian families: babies in high chairs, grandparents, waiters gliding like ballet dancers. It had long windows opening on to the lake, fortunately in the shade.

'It is not so much for tourists here,' said Mario. 'We must eat the lake fish.'

The wine list arrived. I asked to have a look. There were names I didn't know. '*Gavi* or *Barengo bianco* with the fish? and *Barolo* and *Barbera* if we eat meat – they're red aren't they? I don't see *Sizzano* though—'

Mario laughed. 'It is unusual to find a girl who interests herself in wine – but some of the ones you have named are from Piedmont, and here we are in Lombardy, you see, so there will be different wines.'

'Oh – really? Gracious me! Local pride, I suppose? So we have crossed a frontier?'

'Indeed.'

Sandro had taken out his drawing-pad and all the way through the long Italian Sunday lunch that followed he was making little sketches of us all.

'Can we look?' Liz asked when we got to the dessert stage, a frothy chocolate cream confection that I wished I had more room for. He handed her his cartridge pad and she riffled through it. 'You have got Vivien to a T,' she said. 'Do you never draw men?'

'Oh, sometimes – all my friends have had to be models in the past. I draw you both today because you are soon to leave Cusio. Will you be sorry?'

Liz did not reply, but I said, 'I wish I need never go home – it is so perfect here and you have been so kind.' I sounded a little over the top even to myself and hoped I was not drunk.

'Two weeks is not long,' said Mario.

'And it has gone so quickly.'

'Will you come back?' asked Sandro, taking his pad back.

'I hope so,' I said fervently.

'I am ready for England,' said Liz.

'Well, you are to be married,' I said.

Mario was looking at us under his dark eyelashes. 'Won't *you* come back, Viviana, then?'

'I'd love to, but usually I go to France.'

'There are other parts of our country you might like better than here,' Sandro put in. He was looking at his own sketches in a vaguely appraising sort of way.

'Roma for example and Firenze and Venezia,' said Mario.

'I'd always wanted to come to your lakes,' I said. 'When I was a little girl I had a collection of postcards from an old neighbour and there was one of Gardone by Lake Garda. I vowed I'd go there one day – but I came here instead.'

Liz was looking at me curiously. 'Viv is a nostalgia freak,' she said again.

'What *is* that?' Mario asked. I explained.

'If you come back, I might do proper portraits,' said Sandro.

'May I take one of your sketches home?' I asked.

'Oh, most are not good – this morning's are not too bad, but I can do better.' I did not insist. He thrust another page under Liz's nose and she looked at it idly. She pushed it over to me.

'Let me see.' Mario leaned over to take a look. 'Yes, you have made them look *incantevole.*'

'We *are* enchanting,' I riposted, but Sandro was looking reflective. We had probably not enchanted *him.*

Liz said: 'It is quite a good likeness of Viv but you have made my features too regular.' She got up then, saying she must go to the *toiletta.* Whilst she was away, I offered to pay my share of the bill.

'No! No!' Mario, who was paymaster, waved my offer away.

I had looked up the Italian word for to tip – *dare la mancia* – so said now that we could do that.

'We shall accept that,' said Sandro pontifically. I counted out a few notes and then followed Liz.

'I didn't think much to his sketches,' said Liz, powdering her nose energetically.

'The one of *you* was good – you should give it to Adrian.'

'He doesn't give them away – haven't you noticed?'

When we both returned the bill had been paid and a walk by the shore was suggested. Liz went on ahead by herself. She must be missing Adrian again. Well, they would be back together soon enough. Mario came up, asking me something in Italian. After a pause, I replied: 'I think you mean "A penny for your thoughts." '

'Well then?'

'I was just wishing again that I need never go home. I'd love to stay on here – but duty calls.'

He seemed to hesitate a moment, but said only: 'I think Elisabetta is ready for London – when is the wedding?'

'Very soon: her mother wants a big one but she and her fiancé want a quiet one.'

'In a church?'

'I think so – yes.'

'Yes, it is what mothers like.'

He was so nice. I wished again I had fallen in love with him instead of Sandro, who was now down by the lake skimming pebbles on its waters. We were opposite a small island now with a line of trees and a church spire.

'Life here is not so free as in your country,' said Mario. 'You would not really want to live as a member of our bourgeoisie.'

'I don't know. It's true I like to be independent, and for that I must work.' What a liar I was. I'd be off like a shot if Sandro wanted me.

'You could teach English in Florence.'

'I have already done that – in France. I'm saving up to buy a small apartment in London.'

Sandro was sitting under a tree now and Liz was walking back.

'I think we must go soon to the car,' Mario said.

The sun had sunk a little in the sky but people were still walking up and down, a few waiting for a boat to one of the islands, all the young women in sleeveless dresses and short skirts showing off their long brown legs. It was true that the presence of sun made people different – happier. If you could be certain of sun every day – the occasional storm here soon let the sun back – your whole life would change. For one thing, you might be less ambitious, I thought.

In the car on the way back we were all quiet. Sandro seemed a little less touchy than in the morning. We had to get up early the next day but Mario insisted we all met for a farewell drink at nine o'clock in the piazza café.

Liz went off in search of Graham, to ask him for his address, having promised to send him a few of the snaps she'd taken of him in the lake. I lingered a moment dreamily upstairs before supper, then forced myself to begin to pack. Liz had already done her packing.

Why must all good things always come to an end? I did not want to say 'goodbye' over a drink, but how else could you say it? I wasn't hungry for supper; we had all eaten quite enough for one day.

Later, we went over to the café, just after nine. Mario, and this time Marco too, were already there at a table under the awning. I asked the men if I might take some photos of them. They were agreeable, but: 'Wait for Sandro,' Mario said. About ten minutes later Sandro himself turned up.

If he had cared he might have asked for a snap of Liz and me together, but he was ignoring both of us, in spite of agreeing to come along for the farewell drink. He was a strange man.

I took pictures of the men separately and together, and one of Liz, and Mario took one of me.

'I do hope they come out,' I said. 'I'm not very good at photography.'

'I'm afraid I left my camera behind – my film's finished,' Liz said, rather pointedly I thought.

Raffaelo joined us for a few minutes but Sandro left with him soon afterwards. The 'parting drinks' had fallen a little flat, and there was an atmosphere of slight constraint. I hate thinking about farewells so I really cannot remember all the details of our last meeting, but I do remember feeling rather depressed. I kept saying thank you to Mario for all he had done to make my stay so pleasant. Liz was subdued and looked tired. She seemed to cheer up once we had left Cusio.

As the plane taking us home went over the Alps, I took my final holiday photograph. Mario had asked for the one of myself, and I had promised to send it to him eventually.

We were flying high above the clouds. Liz said suddenly: 'I'm really really glad to be going home.'

'At least we've both had a good rest,' I said. 'I always need at least two weeks to recover from the term.'

'Are you ready for London again now?'

'Not for the new term.' I still felt low in spirits. Returning to England always had that effect upon me.

I had supposed that Liz would be coming back to teach for a term at least after the wedding, but now she said: 'I shall never teach again – you don't know how I loathed it! I shall get married and go off somewhere straight away with Adrian, and I shan't ever go back to school.'

'Will Adrian be able to keep you both?' I asked her. Liz did not usually talk about her private affairs.

'If he gets the commission in the North he was angling for just before I left, yes. I'm waiting to hear – he's a dreadful correspondent and I just daren't ring him up in case he hasn't.'

Adrian Hill *had* received the commission he wanted, and when he was asked to move to Leeds in the September the couple had as quiet a London suburban wedding as they could get away with. They then departed to a rented flat in Headingley for six months. I was amazed to discover that Liz had already given in her provisional notice at the school at the end of the summer term. Now she gleefully followed her husband to the wild north.

She was to announce her first pregnancy not long afterwards. She had a rocky time of it with – twice – a suspected imminent miscarriage. However the baby, Emma, arrived healthy. I remembered Liz telling me she wanted to start a baby straight away. It was a good thing Adrian had been able to secure that lucrative work. But then, Liz was lucky, always had been. If I envied her I did not let it show, and our friendship continued at the two ends of the new diesel line from King's Cross.

When the Hills returned to London at the end of two years, I was surprised to find how fond I was to become of Emma, the first of the three children born to the Hills, and the only daughter.

Liz said I could be Emma's unofficial godmother, the official ones having been chosen by her mother from among several pious relatives. Gradually though, as the family increased, Mrs Grove relaxed her hold upon her daughter.

As my thirties went on, I felt, from time to time, a little lonely. Sometimes I felt weightless, as if I had been left with nothing, was a seedless husk. Sometimes I suddenly found myself in floods of tears, immensely surprised to be weeping them. I realized then how much I regretted what had happened to me years before, whilst knowing I could not have acted otherwise. What was denied me was because of my own decision. I had taken full responsibility for it at the time, even if I wondered more and more whether more of the responsibility should have been ascribed to Peter.

Mario did write to me. Sandro of course did not. I replied once or twice to Mario, and sent him a Christmas card and the snap of myself and one or two I had taken of the men together, but what was the point of continuing our correspondence? I dreamed occasionally of Sandro Montani, and went on attending art exhibitions just in case he should have a picture exhibited or for sale in London.

As time went on, whenever I visited the Hills, who bought a roomy Edwardian house in Wimbledon, I found that I continued to get on very well with little Emma. Much later, I got on well even with the not-so-little Emma of fourteen or fifteen. Better in fact than the child's mother did. Liz, who was now calling herself Lizzie, said that mothers always had to take it in the neck from daughters. 'Boys are so much easier,' Liz would moan.

I did not consider Emma a difficult child; it was just that she was unlike Liz in temperament. The little boys might be less complicated, but in my opinion also less rewarding. Emma's adolescence was much more stormy than that of her brothers. I sympathized with her, although I was fully aware that it was much harder to be a mother than a godmother. I often wished Emma was my own child.

For years, the desire for a child of my own did not leave me. Knowing Emma helped a bit. I knew I ought to develop other interests, fall in love again. By the time I married it was too late for me to produce an Emma of my own.

PART TWO

Return to Cusio
January 1995

It had already been snowing when I arrived in Milan on that January day last year. I found the long-distance taxi I had arranged to meet me in the airport forecourt, next to one or two buses for foreign skiers. I do not myself drive, even if conditions are good. The journey of about seventy-five kilometres took us about two hours because the roads were congested around Milan and further on there had been a fall of snow, though not a big one, the previous night.

We went by Lake Maggiore and then took the road round to Cusio. I'd wanted to cross by the scenic route from Stresa over the little mountain but was told the weather was not good enough for that and the preferred way in winter was across to the head of the little lake and then down to Cusio.

Once we'd arrived on the only road that led down to the old village by the lake the sun came out. My taxi stopped in a parking lot on a slope near tennis courts peppered with snow. There was a path here leading down to my hotel. Once the hotel minion, posted at a first floor entrance, saw me, I had my luggage taken away. I paid off my taxi, and followed the boy, hoping I wouldn't slip and start my holiday by breaking an ankle. There ought to be an easier access – I hadn't realized that the whole of Cusio was now pedestrianized and that cars were not allowed in the centre of the village at all. We went across a courtyard and ascended some steps and I found myself in a handsome first floor lobby. There was another entrance beneath this looking out on to the village street for those who arrived on foot.

The Hotel San Giulio was open all winter. It had a vast modern extension around a very old building. I was told by the proud manager that like most of the biggest of the ancient buildings of Piedmont it too had once been a convent. It had been modernized during the last ten years, and was busy all the year round, host to vast numbers of business men and women who stayed there for conferences. My time there was to be no exception. I had not arrived in some gloomy out-of-season quietude but in a bustling New Year centre. 'The snow will not stay long,' one of the clerks at the desk in the marbled entrance hall assured me. 'Here it lies only for two – three days.'

I didn't remember the original hotel, which was not the one where Lizzie and I had stayed years ago, and I took some time to get my bearings. The hotel we had stayed in thirty years before was not open in the winter season.

When I finally arrived in my large second floor room that overlooked the lake it was already getting dark. I opened the balcony door and let in a rush of cold air. You forget that Italy has shorter days too in winter, and that it can be cold. Even though I had wanted to see the place under snow, I think it had been more of a mythical snow, not real 1995 snow or real 1995 winter.

There across from Cusio, riding on the dark lake was the little island, and there were a few stars already peeping through the black sky.

I might be a little mad, but I was happy as I went down to the first of the delicious dinners that were waiting for me, and was waited upon as if I were indeed a princess.

When I awoke the next morning I saw there had been another light fall of snow. It wasn't the weather for long walks, but the air was bracing, and it was still sunny. There was a dazzling January sun piercing through layers of grey and silver, and from my window I could see that the roofs of the convent buildings on the island were now white. The scene looked just as it had done on those photographs I'd seen in London. I wondered if the person who had taken those photographs lived here.

Would boats go over to the island in this weather? I didn't see why not. The lake looked unruffled at present and unless more snow came back in a blizzard I'd eventually try to find a boat to make the short crossing. People must cross over for provisions all the time.

After eating a croissant, which was sweetened with jam, and drinking two large cups of coffee, I wrapped up well and put on my rubber-soled boots. I'd potter along the main street, see if any of the little galleries I remembered were still there, might even ask a few questions if I could summon up enough Italian. I still don't really speak Italian but I can understand most of it and can usually manage a reply with a mixture of Latin and French and a few set phrases, even if the ends of verbs stump me.

The cobbled main street didn't seem to have changed too much, though the shops that were open looked more prosperous. Many

were closed. I was mad to come here in winter! There would only
be village people and business men left; the artists would have gone
back home, to Novara or Milan, between October and April. And
yet I felt that somebody might remember Sandro, even if he no
longer had his studio here. No more snow had fallen and I wanted
to make the most of the hours of daylight.

I went up some of the tiny alleyways that branched off the piazza
and looked more closely at some of the houses that stood back from
them: round a corner, behind a wall or perched over the alley itself.
What I hadn't realized before was that some of these old houses
were veritable *palazzi*. There were also several beautiful covered
arcades, open along the side, radiating from the square. There must
be churches here too that I had never seen. Eventually I walked
back to the San Giulio, feeling quite hungry.

There were several dining rooms. I imagined the biggest one
would have its windows open over the lake in summer, just as ours
had before. Today the long windows were shut and there were
several tables of business people including a few smart looking
young women who did not have the appearance of secretaries. The
maître d' told me they were there for a sales conference. They were
certainly enjoying themselves and making a good deal of noise.

I was ushered by the middle-aged waiter, who had already told
me at breakfast that he was Swiss, into a smaller room where indi-
vidual guests were served. The few diners looked up at me for a
moment and then politely turned away. I supposed it was still quite
unusual in Italy for a woman not in the first flush of youth to sit
and eat alone, and I felt I ought to have brought a book with me.
The service from three young waiters was punctilious. They had
been well trained, and I was enjoying the novelty of it all as I
ordered a lunch of soup and fish and fruit, and two glasses of ice-

cold *Erbaluce*. I was pleased to have remembered the names of the local wines and to find they still tasted as good. They corked up the bottle for me ready for the evening.

That afternoon I walked further along the main street as far as the village square, which I remembered so well. I knew that our old hotel had been just off it. The pavement café, so well remembered, was now indoors for the winter. I lingered a moment by the newspaper shop where I used to buy my postcards, but withstood the temptation. There'd be time to write postcards later.

I stood and stared at the large old building, bang in the middle of the cobbled square, the painted shields still on its façade looking brighter than they had once done. There was the little tower, and the outside staircase with its wrought-iron balustrade which led to an upstairs door over the arched arcade below. I remembered that it had been the *pallazzo della comunità*, a sort of village hall where Sandro had exhibited some of his paintings. Now it seemed to function as a public library too, but it was closed.

A peeling poster on one side announced an exhibition of paintings in the previous August. This was more like it. My heart beat faster. But I didn't recognize any of the just discernible artists' names.

Perhaps everything here would be closed. Why had I wanted to come in winter?

When I walked over to the water's edge and looked out over the lake and saw the island in its pewter-grey waters I felt suddenly better. Liz and I, and Sandro and his friends, had visited that island more than once. I very well remembered the Romanesque church with its extraordinary pulpit and its frescoes, though I had not thought about it for years.

The convent reared up from the centre of the island, at a slightly different angle from my hotel view. The church was on its left, and you could see a dozen or so villas grouped round them, their gardens still fronting the waterside. The trees were bare that I remembered green and thick, nightingales singing in their branches. Hadn't I fed the swans, or was that somewhere else? Did swans go away in winter? I supposed they must still be there somewhere.

I had a memory of always feeling blissfully happy in Cusio but it could not have been true, since I well remembered pining for Sandro. That was an emotion that was detached from the place.

Well, I'd certainly be going over to the island again. I must see it near at hand in the snow just as it had been on the photographs I'd seen in the London gallery.

As I stood looking over to it, cold air on my face, I thought: ordinary people now explored jungles and went on safaris and flew to the ends of the earth, so it wasn't so odd that I went alone to visit a country that was not too far away, even if I had visited other parts of it over the last thirty years and even if the season was the wrong one.

I stayed for a moment near the tiny harbour; no boats were out that afternoon. Cusio *was* very beautiful, even in winter. It was only in my personal time that it was remote. Other people lived their present lives here.

As I stood in the darkening air I remembered the person I had once been. The past had always seemed present to me, even during my youth. What Liz had once called my 'nostalgia'.

As I walked past the lighted shops back to my solitary room I was thinking that both Cusio and I had changed, even if the place was still familiar to me after thirty years. It recalled to me a self I had probably not been for years. This little holiday would, I felt sure, be good for me. There are things one does in youth that set the whole course of one's life. Cusio had not done that for me, but it *had* been some sort of watershed – I saw that even more clearly now. I thought again that people do not fundamentally change, even as they age. Some bedrock of character always remains, in spite of the superficial adjustments that life forces upon them.

I went back to my hotel and drank a cup of their lukewarm Earl Grey tea in a small room with a grand piano. The room faced the lake, well away from the sales conference members whose chatting and clapping I could hear in the distance. On my way back I had not been able to resist buying a few picture postcards of the island. I decided to write my first card now, to Emma Hill. Tomorrow I might write to her mother when I had more to report from the place whose delights we had once shared.

That evening I decided to keep the *Erbaluce* for tomorrow's lunch and ordered a bottle of *Sizzano*, a red wine whose name I also recalled. Wine always keeps me awake, unlike most of my friends who now, I am told, often fall asleep after a glass or two. I was careful not to drink more than two glasses, but even so it was a long time before I fell asleep, more noise from the sales conference revellers in my ears.

No more snow fell in the night but I managed to locate a weather forecast on the little radio I'd brought with me. I translated the woman announcer's rapid Italian into 'more snow will probably fall in the Piedmont area during the next twenty-four hours.'

I went out again soon after breakfast, this time to walk further along the main street, past the square, to where the same street continued with a few more shops and a church. Then it snaked along the edge of the lake before widening and joining the road from above that I half remembered. The hanging gardens of high villas tumbled right down to the road. The trees had branches still covered by evergreen foliage, heavy now with old snow that had frozen there. It was definitely colder here.

I decided to walk back to try to locate the old gallery shop where I had met Sandro's friend and where they had sold Sandro's paintings. I had not yet come across any shop selling paintings. Maybe such shops would only be there in the summer. The winter inhabitants of Cusio wouldn't be the sort to buy pictures of their native lake.

Just before the church I saw the sign *Parrucchiere*: a hairdressing salon. It could not be the same one I remembered from years ago. That one had been next to Sandro's studio, if I remembered rightly. but nowhere here could I recognize the old entrance to the house whose first floor he had rented. Many of the owners and the shops must have changed, and there would have been rebuilding even if a façade was preserved.

At the entrance to this salon there was a little cobbled entry that I guessed would lead to one of those winding stone staircases going up the innards of one of the old houses that were, even thirty years before, divided into flats.

On the left hand wall of the entry there was a little showcase, in it the reproduction of a painting, a child standing in the foreground looking at the lake. It was not a painting I'd ever seen before and the style was not quite Sandro's, but ... I plucked up my courage to investigate.

I walked up the first flight of irregular stairs and found myself in a little passage with a window let into the wall. In the window there wasn't a painting, but a photograph, a landscape: breeze-blown poppies in a field, poplars, grey sky – not a bit chocolate-boxy. Was there a studio up here, with a shop attached? I didn't suppose it would be open for sales, but whoever lived here *might* have known Sandro.

There was a bellpush. What would I say to whoever opened the door? That I was looking for paintings by a certain artist I'd known many years ago so that I could buy one to take back to England. What if Sandro Montani were now a famous artist, his paintings costing more than I could – even now – afford?

I pressed the bell. There was a jangling noise and then silence. Nothing doing. Then I heard a disembodied voice that seemed to proceed from the wall. It said *'Entrate'*, 'Come in'. I pushed the door. It opened easily and I found myself in another dark hallway.

A grilled window flew up next to a door. The face of a youngish woman was framed in it like a ticket seller. She had long messy dark hair that provided a further frame to a pale beautiful face. She reminded me of someone.

'Yes?'

'Is this a shop, and is it open?' I asked in my stumbling Italian, feeling stupid.

'No, *Signora*, my shop is not here but in summer on the via Ilona.'

'Has it been there for long?' I asked. 'I knew a little shop that sold pictures years ago.'

'I think it will have changed owners, *Signora*.' She obviously thought I was ancient.

'Where exactly is it?' I asked.

'Next to the antiquarian bookshop but it is closed, as I already said.'

'In case I come back in the summer or can write to the owner,' I extemporized, 'I'd like the exact address. Would it be possible for you to give me it?'

'Open in summer on Thursdays and Saturdays between ten and noon and two and seven o'clock. Number 12. Ask at the bookshop,' she replied impatiently.

'Thank you.' I would remember the address, and the via Olina was the main street. As she was about to pull down the grille I said in a rush: 'I am looking for paintings by an artist I used to know here many years ago – Sandro Montani – do you know if he still paints and if any of his paintings are in Cusio?'

She stared at me and paused a moment before replying. Then she said: 'I have heard of him. Go to the bookshop, *Signora*, and ask there. The owner may know.'

'That is very kind of you,' I replied. 'Do you know if he still comes here to paint?'

'I believe he is dead, *Signora – è morto*,' she replied and the grille shot down.

I was shocked, but was I really surprised? Since I now knew that his was a name not unknown to people here, I might find out more about what had happened to him in the last thirty years. He was bound to have gone on with his painting.

A mocking little voice in me said: Didn't one of the reasons you came here arise from your curiosity about what had happened to that man? Didn't you hope he might still be living here? I replied to my *alter ego*: No – I could have found out about him without coming here, especially if he were famous. My private reasons are difficult to explain, even to myself. I just have the feeling that no journey here would be a wasted one.

I knew I had not come to Cusio just to see if Sandro was still around, nor to look for that real self of mine who might – or might not – be more available here than at home; I suppose I had come from a mixture of curiosity, and nostalgia for the place.

I would call in the bookshop next morning – I had passed it on my way to the piazza from the San Giulio and seen it was closed on Fridays. I might have another look at that village hall place too, whenever it was open.

As I walked back I tried once more to locate the house where Sandro had lived, but it seemed to have vanished into thin air. I realized if I were ever to come across it again I'd have to penetrate behind some new shop front. There were layers and layers of things here, buildings hiding buildings, with a network of tiny alleyways behind the village, creeping up the hill in the direction of the cemetery.

The cemetery. I supposed I might visit that too, if the weather held?

The next day dawned in grey darkness; snow flakes whirled through the narrow street when I finally got out of my hotel. Nothing too terrible, but certainly not a day for climbing the path that led from the village to the *cimitero*.

After breakfast I put on my stout boots again, having decided, in spite of the weather, to walk to the second-hand bookshop half way along the street. I knew it would be open on a Saturday morning, for I guessed that all the browsers of the Cusio region would make it their week-end Mecca.

Hadn't that gallery shop thirty years ago been near this one? There was no hairdresser nearby any more, even if the new gallery shop was next door to the bookshop in summer. The *parrucchiere* had moved. I looked at the shops each side but both were closed. One looked like a jeweller's. There was no number on the bookshop. It ought to be 11 or 13, unless Italians were superstitious. I supposed other shops had mushroomed here in thirty years for the sale of pictures.

Light was streaming out from inside the bookshop premises. As I pushed open the door I had the strong feeling that it would be here that I would eventually discover what had happened to Sandro Montani.

Books climbed up the walls of a cosy-looking room: old books, not so old books, yellow books, brown books, bound books, unbound books . . . . As I walked inside I had a strong sensation of *déja vu.*

The old man at the desk in the front of the shop looked up. I had some Italian words ready assembled in case he asked me what I wanted but he quickly looked down again and left me to my own devices.

I looked methodically up and down the shelves. I love bookshops, wherever they are. I think if I were in Japan or China without one word of the language I'd be able in some curious way to find my way around a bookshop in Beijing or Tokyo. It wasn't as difficult as that here, for there were English and French as well as Italian books – and anyway today I was mainly on the look-out for books of paintings and photographs.

I found an anthology of English literature for Italian school students published in Naples. It looked as if it had come out in the 1950s or even earlier. Certainly a lot then seemed to be expected of sixteen-year-olds. The extracts were far too hard for most of the students I had recently taught, even though English was their first language! There were many of my favourite poems between its covers so I decided to buy it to read in bed in the hotel, though ten thousand lire seemed a lot for a second-hand paperback. I put it under my arm as I looked around further.

The art books were round a corner on taller shelves. Had I ever been here when it was not a bookshop? It could not be the ground floor of Sandro's old studio. I felt there might be something of him here but I was not sure. In the morning I'd felt like a child playing Blind Man's Buff when the others shout 'Warmer! Warmer!' or 'Colder! Colder!' In here it was definitely 'warmer'. I remembered Sandro saying 'I'd like to paint all the whitenesses'.

I turned round and went up to the proprietor at his desk. 'Do you have any books with pictures of Cusio in the winter? Books of paintings, I mean?'

'Photographs – not paintings,' he replied.

'I saw some photographs of Cusio in London,' I said, 'I hoped that a picture book – of paintings – might have been published too?'

'Paintings by anyone in particular?' he asked.

I chattered on: 'Well, there was a painter I once knew here – many years ago. I've already asked people about him. Someone told me he was dead. I always assumed he would have gone to live in Milan. I don't know how long he went on painting – he's probably no longer in fashion.' I was actually speaking Italian.

'His name?'

'Sandro Montani.'

'Eventually *he* did a bit of photography too,' said the man, and then, softly: 'Viviana?'

I had not recognized this 'old man', but he had recognized me. I felt a prickle go down my spine the split second he spoke my name.

'Mario?' I said hesitantly.

He stood up, a sunburst of a smile on his face. 'I was sure it was you when you came in.'

I dared not say that I had thought of him just as an old man. What was I but an old woman?

'Wait,' he said, and turned to a shelf behind his desk from which he extracted a book. 'Here – I think this is what you want.'

The jacket of the book had that painting of the woman by the grey lake I had seen and loved all those years ago. I took the book, opened it. Facing the title page was a photograph of the island. I looked up. I wanted to ask him if Sandro was still alive, but I must wait.

'It is an anthology of writing about Cusio with one or two reproductions of paintings,' he said. 'I recognized you yesterday in the street. I hoped you would visit my little shop.'

'That was very clever of you,' I said. 'Goodness knows I have changed.' I was not fishing, just speaking the truth. 'Why didn't you tell me straight away when I came in?'

'It was difficult ... to tell you who I was ... you hadn't realized, and I felt foolish.'

I looked at him carefully.

'Take a seat,' he said. Now we were speaking English. He went on: 'It must be tiring – tramping round the place in the snow. Is that why you came back? To find Sandro – and his paintings?'

I felt silly. He would think I was mad, yet his question had been asked quite soberly so I answered in kind. 'No, I wanted to see Cusio again. I'm retired now and I realized I'd never been back since 1964. Then I saw some large black and white art photos in a London exhibition. They weren't taken by Sandro, but I took it as a sort of sign to come back – I'd always wanted to see the lake and island in winter—'

'You were indulging in nostalgia – how unforgivable!'

I sat down on an old-fashioned-looking kitchen chair next to his and he sat down again himself. I wanted to look at him more closely but it would be rude. Perched on his nose was a pair of moon-shaped gold-rimmed spectacles. Taking them off, he said:

'I suppose some people might think thirty years was a long time.'

'You don't?'

'I deal in hundreds of years.' He smiled.

'Sometimes it seems like yesterday when I was young – I feel the same age as I was when we came here for that holiday. I've always wanted to come back. Not really to see people – more as if I'd left something here I still needed. I can't explain ... but I'm *amazed* you recognized me.'

'I don't get many English tourists in asking about books – mostly they're German, or dealers—'

'I'm only an amateur,' I said. 'I always go to bookshops – wherever I happen to be. How long have you been an antiquarian bookseller?'

'Oh, about fifteen years. I got bored with pictures – the art market changed out of recognition. Fashion rules, and I don't happen to like the prevailing one.'

'Sandro was a good painter,' I said. Even out of the depths of my besottedness I saw that, I thought. I still wanted to ask him straight away if it were true that Sandro was dead, but it would seem a bit uncouth when I'd only just met again the man who had taken far more notice of me than Sandro ever had. I remembered how Mario had always talked to me more than to the others – in the café, and at the exhibition in the village hall. The other two men had never taken any special notice of me – except for that hot afternoon with Sandro in the Sacro Monte .... Mario had been a good friend of his, and Mario had written to me for a year or so after the holiday. In the end I had let the correspondence lapse. He had apparently never wanted anything from me, or he had been too diffident.

'I will tell you all I know about what happened to him – I see Marco from time to time. Marco kept up with him when Sandro married and went to live in Milano – his wife's family had a factory there.'

I wondered if that had been Luciana, the medical student, the girlfriend Sandro used to talk about. I *still* dared not say: Is Sandro really dead? dared not tell him what the young woman had said.

'Come and have a drink with me in the San Giulio,' I said impulsively. 'Or is your shop open before dinner in the evening?'

'Not in winter. I could come over to your hotel at about six o'clock,' he replied.

'And would you be my guest for dinner too?' I asked him.

'Oh, yes – for the sake of old times,' he replied. He smiled. His smile had not changed, was still as sweet. There are not many people who can smile really sweetly.

Of course when you looked at him closely you could see he was not all that old – not much older than myself, I supposed, but his hair that had been black was now a pure white and the different spectacles changed his face.

'Not just for that,' I replied. 'I am *so* pleased to see you again. You make the past seem ... well ... real ....'

'I have a few things to take to the post but shall I meet you in the hotel bar about six o'clock and afterwards we can have some supper. I'm afraid our old haunt – the café – is no longer so comfortable in winter – but we could go there if you preferred it?'

'No, come to my hotel and we can have a long talk –' I stopped. Would he really want to talk to me?

He said simply: 'That would be lovely, Viviana. I would also be pleased to take you over to the island whilst you are here.'

I remembered how I had always found it so easy to talk to Mario but that afternoon I realized that *he* found *me* easy to talk to. We had a lot in common. What had we talked about in the past?

'I must not take up your time now – you tell me all your news later,' I said. 'May I please buy this other book before I go?'

'What have you there? Oh, I remember using that – it was in the late Forties—'

'No wonder your English is so good,' I said as he wrapped it for me and I handed over the 10,000 lire. 'I would like to buy that book on Cusio too,' I added. 'I remember so well that painting on the jacket.'

'You must have a look at some of my other books in the back – I shall make you a present of the one you like best,' he said. 'Not of this anthology though, it is of no account.'

I said I'd love to browse further and would come back another day, and then I said *arrivederci* and went out of the shop, strangely moved. I was no longer a stranger here in Cusio. Somebody knew me.

We were both seated at a low table near the window in the spacious hotel lounge. The window looked out at the lake and the island. The island buildings were all white now in the snow, and there was a goose-feather-grey sky over the lake.

I was remembering what we used to talk about. When he had taken a sip of his aperitif he put down his glass and said: 'Do you still like genre paintings?'

'Did I? Yes, I suppose I still do.'

'They became very fashionable a few years ago here, with *Patrimonia* and all that.'

I translated that to myself silently as 'Heritage'. 'Fancy you remembering!' I exclaimed.

'It was a memorable summer for me,' he said. 'Tell me, how is your friend, Elisabetta? Do you still see her?'

'Oh, she married as soon as we returned. She has three grown up children.'

'And *you* married too?'

'When I was very young,' I said, 'there was never the right man at the right time. I didn't meet my husband till I was nearly forty. That was late for those days. He died twelve years ago.' I thought, I was thirty-two when I came here. This man could not have been much older.

Mario looked solemn. 'I'm so sorry.'

'We didn't have any children,' I added. 'It was a great sorrow for us both.'

I thought, what I had wanted more than anything, I had never had, even if I had not missed the experience of love. I wondered if Mario had loved many women.

'I worked all my life except for the eleven years Roland and I had together,' I went on. 'Of course in England now, and I suppose in your country too, marriage and motherhood don't stop a woman working out of the house as well? Not so many women worked in the past as do now. And you – did you marry?'

'No, I never married – in many ways I regret that.'

'Your friend Marco was already married that summer,' I said. 'Though that didn't stop him flirting.'

'He was a flirt but not a bad man.' Mario took another sip of his wine. Then he said: 'Sandro stopped painting not long after he married.'

'Oh?'

'We never really understood why – but he once said he had realized he would never be great and if he could not be a great painter what was the point of just being a fairly good one?'

'I should have thought he'd paint for his own pleasure.'

'Sandro Montani did many things for pleasure, but painting was his religion.'

'It was like a monk renouncing his vows?'

'Yes – exactly. As you may have guessed, he was very popular with women, even if the one woman he wanted – you didn't meet her – Elena – jilted him in the end because he just couldn't keep his hands off other girls.'

'I was told his fiancée was called Luciana.'

'He told you that?'

'Yes. He said she was a medical student.'

'Oh, he had a mistress who was a doctor. He might have meant her.'

I was dumbfounded. How much had Mario ever known about my feelings for his friend? Had he ever guessed how I had longed for Sandro? Would he ever have believed how much I had wanted Sandro to seduce me in that musty chapel, that time he was copying a statue in the heat of a high summer?

'I wasn't one of those "other girls",' I said.

'I know,' he said, and took another sip of his wine.

I had a sudden sharp remembrance of how I'd wished with all my heart that Sandro might make me pregnant. It had seemed such an imperative need then. I must have been a little mad, if no more crazy than many young women? They talk of a woman giving a man a child, but I had, even then – and especially then – seen it the other way round. I must have been before my time?

Ironic that Sandro had dallied with many girls – and yet not wanted *me*. I had realized years ago that if a man like Sandro ever made love to me, it would be – for him – just a lustful episode. Like the many others Sandro himself had probably indulged himself with, I now realized.

I had been prepared for that though: *I* had been lusty too! If young men wanted – needed – sex, Nature needed women to be impregnated. Two, often irreconcilable, desires when a young man and a young woman were together – and both running against the ethos of the years when I was young.

'Sandro was a very attractive man,' I said to Mario now, and I didn't find it difficult to say such a thing to him. 'I don't expect I was the only woman to find him so.'

'No, indeed,' he said, and laughed.

But I had known when I wasn't wanted, I thought.

Mario's face grew pensive. 'Sandro always had plenty of fish to fry,' he said.

My feelings could have grown into love with Sandro, I thought. I could not help remembering the mixture of romantic and physical passion I had once had for him. The memory was quite fresh even if it had merged with others. Sandro had after all only been one of those men for whom in my youth I had felt such a passion. Each time I had been quite sincere. I suppose I must have been susceptible. After Sandro, I'd imagined I had resigned myself – just a little – to disappointment.

'I had little really to say to him – I was too romantic, and a bit silly, I suppose,' I said now to his old friend. I was remembering too, how much I had always liked Mario, the very same man now sitting next to me at the low table in the dimly lit cocktail bar. I found I still liked him. I had always enjoyed our conversations, just as I was doing now.

Had he once found me attractive? Liz had thought so. Mario's replies and counter-questions were in a less accented English than previously; he must have practised the language somewhere. His use of grammar and idioms was impeccable.

As we talked, and as the ever mild-mannered, but far from stupid, Mario looked at me over the rim of his wine-glass, I realized what a blessing it was to be able to be honest with somebody, to talk openly and know you would not be misunderstood. Especially, to talk to a person of the opposite sex. Whatever some feminists say – and I am a great admirer of women and have many women friends – there is always that little *différence* between us and men that lends piquancy to encounters. Even with respectable old gentlemen. I could still talk to him, for here was a person with whom I would always be able to talk. If Sandro had ever understood my unde-clared feelings for himself, would he have told Mario about 'romantic young Vivien?' Yes, most likely he would. Men discuss women as much as we discuss them.

'We all make mistakes when we are young,' said Mario now. I wondered to what he was referring. He went on: 'I made many myself, though not of the same sort as dear Sandro's.'

The very opposite sort, I thought. Then the idea came into my head that Mario might be gay, and that was why we had always got on so well . . . . No, I felt sure he was not . . . .

He was looking searchingly at me. Now was the time to ask if Sandro were still alive. I felt my heart jump behind my ribs as I tried to prepare myself to ask him, and I took my glass and drank from it to cover my nervousness.

Mario was saying something in a low voice. 'At our age,' he said, 'one often regrets the things one has done – or not done. It is a pointless exercise.'

I thought, he could still marry a young woman – even have children. Nature was most unfair in this respect, even if experiments were now taking place for babies to be born to elderly women.

I decided to plunge. 'Is he still alive, Sandro?' I asked him and I sounded breathless. 'The woman I spoke to yesterday in a sort of shop inside a house near the piazza – the one who told me to ask at your bookshop – she said she believed he was dead.'

'Yes, he died a few years ago. You saw his daughter, Chiara.'

I hadn't really believed her, I thought. She had sounded so uncertain.

'His *daughter*!' I remembered she had looked both a little exotic and yet familiar; her face framed in the little window had reminded me of someone. It must have been her father.

'I don't expect she wanted to shock you. There might have been other foreign ladies coming looking for him over the years, you see . . . .'

'I see.' I cleared my throat. 'Was that where he used to live then – that flat at the top of the stairs next to a hairdresser's?'

'At one time. After he went to Milan the first time and came back married to a woman called Anna – Chiara's mother. The marriage didn't last long so the daughter stayed with her grandparents. They owned that house – they're dead too now. Later, Chiara stayed on there alone and she makes her living as a photographer – she has a little shop too in the summer months. She used to make and sell jewellery – she's very artistic. An excellent photographer too.'

'How did Sandro – what did Sandro die of?' I asked.

I feared he might say that he'd committed suicide or caught syphilis or something, but Mario said simply: 'He died of leukaemia – it was such a waste. He'd remarried very happily, although there were no other children.'

I was silent for some moments, trying to take it all in. I was glad I hadn't asked him in the shop.

'How very sad,' I said. 'He was so full of life and talent. Do you often see Chiara?'

'Chiara. Yes, from time to time. I sold her father's book – the one of his paintings in the early seventies, but it's out of print now or I would have offered it to you. I have a copy at home that I can show you if you are interested. He illustrated the old guides to Piedmont as well.'

'I remember,' I said. 'He was drawing pulpits and terracotta statues and things when we were here all those years ago. Did he do many portraits? He sketched both me and Lizzie—'

'That is Elisabetta – Liz?'

'Yes, it was after she married that she began to call herself Lizzie.'

'I remember very well that he sketched you both. Your friend was very English-looking and Sandro always liked English women. He stopped trying to sell that sort of thing when figurative painting went out of fashion though he may have continued to draw from life at home. I believe his wife sat for him – his first wife that is. Later, he tried abstract paintings. His colours were lovely but it didn't really suit his talents. It was when he went back to Milan for the second time that he stopped painting.'

'It was his second wife then who was the industrialist's daughter?'

'Yes, Silvia. He only married Anna because she was pregnant and his parents insisted. Our generation of Italians used to do as we were told.'

'I wonder who has those wonderful pictures now of the mountain and the woman by the lake. I saw them first in the old gallery shop, and then he exhibited them in the palazzo – do you remember?'

'Yes, of course. They are reproduced in the book, but I think the originals went abroad. If only he had continued in that vein – but it was out of fashion – and he too began to despise too much *naturalismo*.'

'Had you known him long when we first met? You were very close friends?'

'Sandro was a very good friend of mine at school and college but we drifted apart after his second marriage, and when he stopped painting. The owner of the gallery shop sold up to another owner, so when I bought the bookshop next door I wanted Sandro to exhibit there instead, but he refused. He said he'd had enough of selling to tourists. He did take some interesting photographs though, just for his own pleasure.'

'Yes, I remember he used to take photos before he painted things, to aid his memory. That London exhibition of photographs I told you about – of Cusio and all around the region – was what really decided me to revisit the place,' I said. 'I believe they were by a Swiss from Zurich.'

'Chiara has taken some excellent art photos,' he said. 'There is a book I can show you – and they are going to reprint them as postcards.'

'It's good that she has inherited some of her father's artistic talent.'

'Shall we go up for a meal?' suggested Mario, seeing I had drained my glass of cold *Barengo bianco*.

'You know this place then?'

'Oh yes, it's where we bring clients we want to impress!'

We went up the wide stairs to one of the dining-rooms on the first floor where the windows all overlooked the lake. Several tables were already full of the conference guests. Mario seemed to be known here. The waiters all hurried to take our order – with less *badinage*, I noticed, than they usually had for me as an ancient lone female.

I told Mario I had remembered the names of the wines we had drunk all those years ago and now Mario added a few more for me. He ordered some red wine called *Bonarda*, another local vintage. Over a delicious dinner I told him more about my London life: my memories of teaching, my busy life until I retired. Then I spoke a little of Roland and our marriage. Even as I went on to tell him of friends, the theatre, how London had changed, the beggars, the homeless, it all seemed remote, little to do with me.

Mario said they had beggars in Italy too, if not in Cusio, and there was a drug problem, and the problem of people released from the old mental hospitals. Problems just like ours at home.

'We shall have our government elections next year,' said Mario. I learned that in spite of being a sort of business man – he *did* sell books and pictures – Mario was in fact hoping that for the first time for fifty years the Left would be returned to power.

'I was never a Communist,' he said, 'but it is a pity that all politicians are tarred with the brush of corruption.'

We talked about politics then, and even about Christianity. Had I realized before that Mario really was what the Italians called an *intellecttuale*? He told me now that he was a feminist but I wasn't sure what this might mean here, even if the Mamma still held the reins of domestic power, as she always had. I remembered how assiduously Mario had looked after his own widowed mother.

When we had finished our supper, he said: 'Now you are here you must let me take you to all those places you want to revisit – the island and the Sacro Monte.'

'Oh, but I must not take up your time,' I said, thinking he might be doing it out of politeness and that my conversation probably bored him. Women of my age are used to being ignored and often suspect the motives of the friendly. He didn't bore me, and I liked being with him, but he had always been a polite person.

'I understand there will be things you will want to do alone,' he said solemnly, 'but getting out and around in this weather would be easier with a companion. You might slip on a path—'

'Or fall overboard?' I added, laughing, and he relaxed and laughed too. 'I had thought of visiting the cemetery,' I added. I wanted to ask him where Sandro was buried, but it seemed none of my business. Mario knew though that the thought was in my head for he said: 'Sandro is buried in Milano. Even if he did come here sometimes in the winter when no other artist did . . . .'

'I remember he said he wanted to do that!'

We arranged to meet the next day, if it was not snowing, and to go over in a motor boat to the island.

'There are not so many boats operating in winter,' he said. 'Only for the inhabitants, not for *turisti*.'

I agreed to his idea and thanked him for inviting me. When we parted I had plenty to think about.

I was not sure whether Mario actually lived above the shop or had a flat somewhere else when I walked to the shop to meet him the next morning. The weather had turned out cold and bright with – thank goodness – no more snow for the moment. Snow is all very well on photographs but when you are no longer young it slows you down. The shop door was shut, but Mario was standing outside with a green paper bag under his arm.

'You will unwrap this in a moment – a little present,' he said.

We walked first of all in the direction of our old café. I had never been inside before; the outdoor tables had always seemed to be part of summer. Naturally at this season everyone was served indoors. A large new plate-glass window looked out on to the piazza, and beyond the trees over by the lakeside we could just glimpse the island under its white mantle.

'Here you are,' said Mario, putting the paper bag down by my coffee cup. Inside was a parcel wrapped neatly in green tissue paper. 'You will guess it is a book,' he said.

I opened it. It was the book of photographs by Sandro's daughter.

'The young woman you saw the other day,' said Mario. As if I didn't remember.

When I had unwrapped it completely I saw the author's name, Chiara Montani, in curly white letters on dark green. The jacket had that view, seen as if from an aeroplane, of a tiny Alpine village in the fold of the hill, looking like a match-box model, I always thought.

'It's exactly the view her father painted all those years ago,' I exclaimed. 'And like the photograph I saw in London.'

'Oh, it's a famous view now,' he said. 'She wanted a different one on the jacket, but this one sells.'

'You know,' I said impulsively as I opened the book, 'I had the impression his daughter could have been English when I saw her the other day.'

'English?'

'It was only a fleeting impression – I suppose I know "arty" girls only in England – and she looked like them, with long tangly hair. Is she a bit aloof? I only saw her head and shoulders. Is she tall?'

'Medium height. Brown hair. A bit like both her parents I

suppose,' he said, after slowly savouring his first mouthful of coffee. 'I can show you Sandro's book later in the shop,' he added. 'Paintings don't sell as well as photographs. I agree that photographs *can* be an art form.'

I was looking at Chiara's pages. Some photographs had been taken in winter, just like the ones I'd seen in the London gallery, and there were those evocative footmarks in snow, and more illustrations of the delicate wrought-iron tracery of gates and banisters.

'That wrought-iron is another speciality of the district,' said Mario.

There were colour photos too, some of autumnal trees with leaf-strewn paths under them; others taken at night from a distance, looking down from a height over motorways, long necklaces of the shining ruby beads of back lights of cars mixed with the diamonds of front lights from traffic coming from the other direction. Strange, almost surreal.

'These are interesting. I wonder if she knows the man whose work I saw. There are similarities.'

'You could ask her. If you still want to go over to the island this morning, I believe there will be a small motor boat waiting about now.'

'Oh yes, I do.'

It was very cold on the jetty but the little boat was snug. Even so I was glad I had wrapped up. There were only two other people being taken across, an old lady and a young man who might be her grandson. The boatman reiterated the time of his return in case we might be stranded. We would have four hours to explore.

'There's a restaurant here now,' said Mario. 'Italians spend a lot of time eating and as it's Sunday it will be full of islanders after Mass.'

The paths were snowy, but I had my boots, and the wind that whipped us as we came round from the makeshift jetty did not worry me. I had my fake-fur hat on. Mario too was wearing a squashy brown hat.

The tall convent building loomed above everything else on the island but we decided to visit the church first. I wanted to see the interior again. The steps up to its big front entrance were swept clear of snow.

Strange how you remember little bits of things from the past, and yet they are never quite the same as you had imagined. When we entered the church I did recognize the wonderful pulpit, opposite the door by which we had come in, and I remembered Sandro on his stomach underneath it. The nave however was smaller than I recalled, and the frescoes more beautiful. The perfume of incense was no longer so pervasive: Vatican Two, I supposed. Also, there were notices asking people to 'behave themselves in the house of God' that I did not remember seeing in this place before.

'You were always reading a guidebook on your holiday,' said my companion as we walked around looking at frescoes and holy remains.

What I was remembering just then was the excitement of being young and the effect other people had upon me then. Even now, I was just as interested in the Mario of sixty-plus and his reactions as I was in the basilica. Would I never change?

I thought, here am I, in a church, in a foreign country, on a winter Sunday, an ordinary Sunday for the people who live here. Worshippers have just left, and others will return in the evening. I don't belong here but neither do I belong any longer in a little village church in Dorset ... I am a dislocated person.

'Did you ever visit the crypt before?' asked Mario, breaking into my introspection.

'I can't remember – I don't think so. Let's go there now.'

As I followed Mario down the stairs to the entrance to the seventeenth-century crypt behind the chancel, I suddenly felt that I still belonged in a way to the past. I ought to shake off this mood of nostalgia. It was a sort of enjoyable grief, had nothing to do with the kind man who was accompanying me.

Mario was now pointing out that much of the basilica had been restored at different times, some of it quite recently. It seemed the past never stayed the same. 'A mixture of Romanesque and baroque,' he said. 'Strange, but it seems to work.'

In the crypt I suddenly had an odd feeling, as though I had been there before, though I didn't think I ever had. I seemed to remember that Sandro had been in the basilica and had been down in the crypt that day I had fallen asleep and missed Liz on her walk round the island, and I remembered him standing in the church, looking so handsome.

There in the centre of the crypt was the famous gold casket looking still for all the world like a fairy carriage and with the mummified remains of what I was sure was not the saint lying inside, skull on pillow. Mario did not even look at it. I bought a few postcards, half wishing I might light a little candle as well – but what could I now pray for?

There was another little door in the wall of the crypt. It suddenly opened, and a young man came in. I saw stairs behind the door leading up to the outside. The young man gave a slightly old-fashioned bow, said 'Buon giorno,' took a pencil out of his pocket and then busied himself copying some legend in Latin at the bottom of a faded fresco.

'We haven't seen all the frescos upstairs,' said Mario, so we finally plodded back up the stone stairs again. He led me to a further wall where I saw a beautiful painting of the Holy Family in the stable, beneath it several male saints standing to each side of the Queen of Heaven.

'When was that painted?' I asked Mario, whom I trusted as a fount of knowledge.

'End of the fifteenth century,' he replied.

'They could sell reproductions for Christmas cards,' I said flippantly. 'The colours are lovely. Make your fortune.'

'Copyright,' he said shortly.

We looked at some other not quite so ancient paintings. I said, 'I suppose our churches at home were once full of frescos and colour before the Reformation.'

'Sandro wanted to paint modern church frescos,' said Mario quietly.

'I didn't know he was a believer?'

'I don't know what he believed, but he was interested in the spirit of a place, and often said that modern churches needed the work of modern artists. In Italy on the whole people prefer the traditional.'

Somehow I found the idea of Sandro Montani painting frescos incongruous. I had seen him copying or sketching in this very church for the guidebook he had illustrated, but the idea of a religious Sandro did not accord with my memory of him. I'd have been less surprised if it were Mario who turned out to be a practising Catholic.

'Was he a practising Catholic then?' I enquired now.

'Who knew what Sandro believed?' replied Mario. 'We never discussed religion.'

As we talked we came up to the nave again just as an old woman came into the church. She crossed herself twice, sat down and bowed her head. There were snowflakes on her coat.

'The snow's come back,' Mario whispered. 'Do you still want to walk round the island?'

'We can go for lunch first,' I replied. 'And then when we have eaten it may have stopped.'

'True – it never stays long, you know, in this part of the world.'

Now I was feeling reluctant to go out again into the cold, confessed to myself that I would honestly prefer at that moment my own physical comfort to the retracing of those steps I had once taken thirty years before. But I was determined to see all I could of what had, for whatever reason, brought me back to Cusio, even if the spirit was willing but the flesh not quite so keen.

Outside, the snow was not falling heavily, was more like a light dusting of icing sugar on a sponge cake. But even snow like that can accumulate and so I was glad to be led into a pleasant and surprisingly large restaurant which, as Mario had predicted, was full of Italian families dancing their reasonably informal dance of Sunday lunch.

As we waited for the *pasta alla funghi* which we had both ordered, feeling hungry after our peregrinations, and drank some red *Sizzano* – Mario said: 'I have something to confess.'

'Oh?'

'I told you I saw you in the street the day after you arrived in Cusio – I was sure it was you. I even imagined you might want to visit picture galleries – so I told Chiara that if an English lady came up her stairs, attracted by the painting at the bottom, she would please tell you to call in the bookshop for more information.'

'Well, Mario, I'd have visited your bookshop in any case!' I replied, a little amazed and a little flattered. 'As a matter of fact I'm really more interested in books than in paintings,' I went on. 'Fancy you thinking I'd call in that place of hers.'

'I knew you were the sort of person who does not forget – the sort of person who likes sometimes to revisit a place. I was away from Cusio myself for many years but once I returned the idea did occur to me that you or your friend might come back one day. And I was right, wasn't I? At least, about you.'

'Oh, Lizzie would not want to return here,' I said. 'She's not a sentimentalist. And she wasn't as keen on the place as I was.'

I nearly said 'as keen on Sandro', but stopped before I said too much. After all, I did not really know Mario well. I felt I did but that might be just a delusion. What man wants to be told a girl was in love with his handsome friend and spared hardly a thought for himself? Not that I had possessed much common sense in those days. I reflected that even then I should have realized that Mario was a much better companion than Sandro. I supposed I'd in fact spent far more time with Mario than with Sandro. It had been the *idea* of sex with Sandro – with the wrong man – that had got in the way. I felt sure that if Sandro could be resurrected he would not remember me!

I changed the subject slightly as we drank our coffee. 'I seem to remember that on this island in summer there were nightingales – that I did hear them singing. Was that a false memory?'

'There *were* a few nightingales – *usignoli* – on San Rocco,' he replied. 'You don't hear them so often here now. There are some on the Sacro Monte also.'

'One sometimes remembers the right things in the wrong place or the wrong things in the right place, but I was sure I heard one singing here. They're not so common at home now.'

'You must tell me one day about *your* countryside – I mean where you lived as a child. I promise I will read more of your Thomas Hardy! I have already read quite a lot.'

Then we talked of other things. Mario was very well informed. He spoke of the mysteries of physics and astronomy, and I talked a bit about my reading and how baffling I found scientific discoveries. To pass from the universe to the intricacies of human genes seemed an easy step with someone who was both interested and knowledgeable. All the incredible micro-world existing in an unimaginably large universe ... Mario spoke then of the frame of astronomical time and I asked him about the dinosaurs who were said to have perished over sixty million years ago when a meteorite hit the earth.

'Our planet will come to an end one day,' he said, and my earthly preoccupations seemed for a moment very paltry.

'I shall never grasp it all,' I said. 'How can we begin to understand?' I thought of Mother dying and life going on .... 'Time is everything,' I remember saying, the wine having improved my Italian no end.

When we came out of the restaurant, the snow had stopped but a wind had sprung up. We decided to walk just as far as the convent walls, not to go right round the island.

'I always wondered where birds went in winter,' I said. 'I used to think as a child that they made their nests to live in, not just to rear young, and that they were tucked up cosily in the cold weather.'

'You have a tender heart,' he said.

'No, but as I prefer warm weather I like to think of everything and everybody cosy and warm.'

'Strange to want to come here in the winter then?'

'That's because English people are romantic and espouse lost causes and unseasonable pastimes – as a sort of test, I suppose. It wouldn't be the same to return to a place at the same season. Since things would have changed it would be better not to expect to see them exactly as they were.'

'You are a puritan, Vivien,' he said.

'Climate makes us what we are,' I replied.

I thought, at this moment I am *here*. Nowhere else. Just here. Again, at last. Without nightingales. Who would miss me if I never went back home? I could die here? Or become a nun in this very convent that we are staring at on its little island hill? It did not look very welcoming.

'Do you think they have central heating?' I asked him.

'I doubt it – it is possible that the Reverent Mother does – not the poor little novices.'

'So novices come here still?'

'No, now *I* am being romantic. I doubt many have the vocation nowadays. In spite of the modern world, the island is still however the centre of religious life for the whole district.'

'The convent doesn't look very old,' I remarked.

'No, it's only about a hundred and fifty years old – rebuilt, as so often happens.'

'Yes, there is something I think we would call neo-Gothic about it – that's come into fashion again in England.'

And here were the doors in the wall I remembered from years ago. I wondered how many people had died on the island since I was last here, how many been born.

We walked on as far as a beautiful intricately patterned wrought-iron gate, a snow-covered garden path beyond.

'There used to be a bench here,' I said to Mario. 'I remember sitting on it – and I fell asleep.'

'Perhaps that's where you thought you heard the nightingales?'

he said. 'In the gardens. Shall we turn back?'

'Just a minute. Let me take a picture.' I dug down into my shabby old bag where I had thought to place my camera.

'May I have you on one picture? I want to take the convent and the tops of the trees as well – I like unusual angles.'

'You may take a photograph of me so long as I may also take one of you.'

'OK,' I said. 'I kept an old photograph, you know, of you and Sandro at the café table.' I didn't say that it was the picture of Sandro I'd wanted to keep.

My own photographs, unlike the ones I imagined Chiara took, were quickly done. I don't believe in fiddling about with complicated technicalities. 'Snap' describes the sort of photograph I take. I'm not technically proficient.

We walked back and round to the church. The gift shop was closed. The wind was colder now and I did not imagine that dusk was beginning to fall. We heard a boat give a preliminary hoot by the landing stage.

'It will go back in ten minutes,' said Mario, looking at his watch. 'Have you seen all you wanted?'

'I think so – you know it's funny, I remember silly things like sitting on that garden seat, but I can't remember very clearly now what we all talked about at the café. I always had the impression Sandro was an easy prey to boredom when he was not sketching. Your other friend – Marco – was a bit of a Jack the Lad.'

'Explain please.'

I explained as we walked down to the landing stage.

Mario said: 'True, Marco had an eye for the women but he was a faithful husband.'

'I'm surprised. I used to think I was a good judge of character –

I don't think I'm usually wrong about people but we didn't know each other very well, did we?'

'Oh, one can have one's perceptions clouded,' said Mario with a smile. 'On the other hand if you have long conversations with people you usually discover quite a lot about them. I would say that you for instance were a serious minded person *al fundo* as we say.'

'Like you, Mario. Some people don't like long conversations, do they, so you never really get to know them.'

'There are other ways of knowing, especially when you are young.'

'Yes, of course, but one can be wrong about them too.'

Mario persisted: 'Your friend Elisabetta for instance – she never said much – certainly not to me. She did not seem at all like you. And yet you are still friends.'

'Well, if we chose people just like ourselves we might not end up with many friends. Anyway, I do have other friends,' I said, thinking of Eleanor and Oliver, 'with whom I probably have more in common.'

'So where did you meet Elisabetta?'

'We taught in the same school. She was a mathematician.'

'Really? Well I would not have guessed that. So I too can be just as mistaken, I suppose. Yet there are things about which I am sure I am not mistaken.'

I looked at him interrogatively but he changed the subject. By now we were huddled in the boat which soon cast off.

As the boat chugged us along in the choppy grey waters of the winter lake, I looked back at the little snow-covered island. It was now a fairy-tale isle riding on the waters, sentinel pine trees at one end, pollarded limes at the other, with an iced wedding cake church, white roofs crowding round the edges and, rising self-importantly in the centre, the convent, almost as high as the church campanile.

I was not looking forward to going back alone to my hotel but I knew once I was there I'd enjoy thinking over the day. I would leave it to Mario to suggest another outing.

Snow fell again in Cusio that evening, and I knew it would not be possible to go to Sacro Monte the next day. There would only be two more full days of my holiday left after that, for I was to leave on the Thursday morning. I prayed that the snow would stop and we might go up on the Tuesday.

The next day, in answer to my prayer, Mario telephoned me in the afternoon with a suggestion.

'I could take the car up tomorrow by the main road on the other side – it would be hopeless trying to climb up the healthy way.'

'I mustn't take you away from your shop,' I said.

'Oh, I do most of my business by direct mail,' he explained. 'The shop is a luxury and I can shut it whenever I like – so provided you have stout boots and can walk around when we arrive—'

'Of course I can, but I'm still a bit worried that my trips down Memory Lane are taking you away from your work – even if it's only telephoning and answering letters.'

'It's good for me to get out – I'm too close to becoming a hermit,' he said. 'Anyway they will have cleared the paths, I'm sure, by tomorrow. The whole place has to be looked after and is always visited whatever the weather. The administrators' cars and the monks from the church have to be able to get up there.'

When I put the telephone down I wondered why I still felt the urge to go up to the Sacro Monte, which would most likely be a spooky place in winter.

I'd decided not to go to look at the cemetery, but something was impelling me to revisit the Sacro Monte, the same something that had made me decide to come back to Cusio in the first place. Yet nothing had really happened to me there, and now I'd met Mario again, there was nobody else to find . . . . I thought, Sandro is dead. Sandro who talked to me one day up there among the little chapels.

That night I dreamed of a baby, like a little doll or a little wax angel, with wavy golden hair. Still with the shreds of the dream clinging to me, I took my guidebook down to breakfast. What did I really need to know about all those chapels up on their holy hill? Was I looking for God up there?

The waiter saw my book open on the table and cried, pointing to a reproduction of a fresco from one of the chapels, '*Bellissima!*' They always said that.

I didn't suppose I'd ever learn enough about the buildings to really understand them and appreciate their detail. It was the all-over feel of the place that attracted me, and also because it was now also fixed in time, in my own past.

Well, on Tuesday morning we did manage to get the car up the winding road. We left it in a car park the other side from the cemetery and walked back along the snowy lane that led to the hill of chapels. Someone had been there before us, for there were footprints in the snow. Fortunately it had not drifted and although it was very cold the sun came out as we reached the church that I remembered.

'We needn't walk far,' I said. 'Just to a few of the nearest chapels. It would take hours to get round them all in the snow.' The snow had piled up here in mounds and was heavy on the trees.

'Most of the place needs more money spent on it,' said Mario gloomily as we stood in front of the railings on the lane opposite the church and looked out over the lake. This view of a white country was splendid. There was mist over further mountains but nearer hills across the lake were snow-white, and nearer at hand we could see the white roofs of the little 'palaces' of Cusio beneath us.

'Really,' I said, 'I think I liked the place because of the woods and the feeling you were near to Nature here.'

'Not to heaven then?'

'No, more to natural things even if they were tamed – and then the chapels had been here so long they almost looked natural themselves.'

I had with me a new guidebook to the place. The shop I dimly remembered was shut. At least I now had a little map.

'They could easily spend more on the place with the profits they get from the guidebook,' said Mario, flicking through it now.

'They don't charge to walk round. I suppose they could do that?'

'No, because it's owned by the Commune and the Church – and I suppose the Council of the region – the three Cs. The commune is not rich but business men make quite a lot from tourism. The Church is always grumbling how poor it is but we are a bit far away from the beaten track for the region to spend more on us. I believe there have been many cleanings-up and repaintings – and they cost money.'

'How good your English is!' I said.

'Should I not say "cleaning-ups"?'

I looked at him affectionately.

I was also wondering who paid for it all in 1583, when the book said 'the community' had begun all the building. I guessed the Church had taken the money pilgrims left after visiting the chapels.

'Anyway St Francis is a saint for the Green Party!' I added.

Mario read aloud from the guidebook. I loved hearing his voice speak Italian. 'The foundations of the first two chapels were laid in 1591,' he read. He looked up. 'You know, they never brought their plan to completion, and they altered the numbers on the chapels. Now there is a way of going round if you are religious – and then you can pray in each one!'

'They were mostly completed by the end of the seventeenth century though, weren't they?' I asked.

'No, they originally intended thirty-two chapels. Well, in the first twenty-five years they'd built twelve.'

'It's a lot when you think how long it takes to build anything now – at least in England. Do they still build sanctuaries in Italy?'

'I don't think so!'

We moved away, went over to the Convent Church of St Nicolas and looked through its door. There were Christmas mass survivals, a nativity scene, greenery brought in and a smell of wafted incense.

'They have the Christmas Eve crib here,' said Mario. 'I suppose because it is the easiest and nearest place for pilgrims to visit.'

I peered at the small plan in the guidebook. If you looked carefully, the path went round and round almost like a maze. As we had started at the wrong place we'd better walk to the entrance we'd come up long ago and start looking at the chapels in the right order.

'Let's just walk back to number one,' I suggested. 'It's too cold to stand around with the book.'

'Just get the general feel,' said Mario who always seemed to know what was in my mind.

'OK. I shan't try to work out which is which.'

But as we walked slowly across to a small chapel under trees whose boughs were laden with snow, I could not help remarking: 'I wonder where the one was where Sandro was copying the figures. He gave me such a shock the day I came up here alone – I thought a statue had come to life.'

We came up to the chapel, stopped and peered through the wrought-iron grille. Everything seemed smaller than I remembered it, and there were a few clothed figures looking a bit drab.

'No, it could not have been this one – I seem to remember it was number thirteen – or fifteen.'

'Yes, fifteen is said to be the architectural masterpiece. I don't know about the sculptures in it though – if I remember rightly it's a curious subject – the saint receiving the stigmata—'

'Obviously *you* don't need a guidebook.' We leaned against the grille. It was utterly silent and I shivered. 'I remember him saying – and that could be why I wanted to come here in the winter – he said he'd like to draw it all in the winter. "All the whitenesses," he said.'

I turned round as I spoke. Under a whitish sky – a pale grey when compared with the snowy ground – the ochre buildings, now partially snow-covered too, and the green conifers were like a stage set. The fancy came to me that it had all been waiting for me for thirty years. The island and its church; the mountain and its chapels . . . . The only place I wouldn't see again would be Sandro's old studio.

'Do you remember much about the time we all came here?' Mario asked.

'Yes – I loved it. My recollection of the chapels is a bit hazy though – too much to take in.'

'I've been here dozens of times but I remember that day. *You* were very enthusiastic, but I remember thinking your friend looked rather bored.'

'Well, we can't see them all today – it would take hours.'

'You must see number eight though – the saint is taken up to heaven in a real chariot!' urged Mario.

'It seems quite another place today ... it was just ... different – then.'

'Summer – and youth.'

'They always say – in England – how innocent we all were thirty years ago. Do you remember – nobody cared if you smoked tobacco, and hardly anyone had heard of heroin and there were fewer cars and no heart transplants, and black-and-white television ....'

'And everybody was supposed to behave themselves,' said Mario.

'But they didn't.'

'Let's just walk over there and then we can go back to the church. Are you cold?'

'Not really.'

The snow looked wetter, thicker on the further paths. We trudged over to number eight and it was quite startling.

'It's the one the children like best,' Mario said.

'The saint flying through the sky? Very clever – I suppose it looks more like a miracle. There were no flying chariots in those days.' I thought of the aircraft that had brought me here, and I was still trying to remember which chapel it had been where Sandro had popped up on my second visit. Try as I might I wasn't quite sure.

'I think we shall not drink today at the forest café. It will be shut,' said Mario.

'Right. Let me take some more photographs of all this, and the snow, and then we can walk back.' I took several snaps of Mario in his fur hat and then we walked back down the lane. As we trudged along I felt grateful for his kindness in taking me around like this.

I wished I could reciprocate. The only thing I could think of was to offer him hospitality in London.

Suddenly he said: 'Do you remember my telling you once about Nietzsche's visit here in the 1880s?'

'Yes, I do, as a matter of fact. You told me that he dreamed the most beautiful dream of his life here.' I remembered how I had wished Sandro would talk to me of such things.

'And *you* said it was a melancholy thought,' said Mario.

'Did I? I suppose I was being sorry for him. I need not have been. It wasn't Cusio that sent him mad.'

'No, but he always remembered the place.'

I wanted to tell him that I had suffered from unrequited love myself, and not just here with the elusive Sandro. Now I came to think about it, I supposed I had spent quite a large part of my first forty years enduring such passions. A woman my age couldn't say such things. Not even to Mario, who had probably suffered in much the same way. Now, as we reached the car, still safely under the trees, he was saying something about Sandro.

'Do you remember – you have a good memory, I think – how Sandro always made a pretence of ignoring women?'

'I suppose that is the way of the accomplished seducer?' I replied, not really thinking about what I was saying.

'Yes, sometimes it was for that reason.'

'At other times he could be rude,' I said. 'He always looked a bit bored, except on that morning I found him here in the chapel. We had a nice talk in the café then. Later, I discovered he had been supposed to meet Liz to sketch her but he just forgot.'

'Sandro did not "just forget" anything,' said Mario.

'Well, he did sketch her later in Stresa. I wonder if he kept those sketches. I'd love to see what we both looked like then.'

Mario started the car and very carefully edged it into the lane, keeping in first gear, for the descent was steep.

'Tomorrow I shall do my shopping,' I said. 'I am really grateful for this morning – I'd never have got up here by myself.'

He smiled. 'I too have enjoyed it – and when you have done your shopping tomorrow you will come to my shop and see the book of Sandro's drawings I promised to show you?'

'Thank you – I'd love that.'

Mario had told me he had to see a client at two o'clock so once we arrived back in the village I returned to my hotel where I chose a large bowl of soup for my solitary lunch. It was delicious.

'You went for a snow walk?' asked my waiter.

'Yes – up to the Sacro Monte.'

'Well, you are very brave!' he said.

I finished writing some postcards – I had neglected them in the days since meeting Mario and I didn't want them to arrive too long after my own return. When I cast my thoughts forward to my return to England I could not quite believe in it. I sent my brother a picture of the island, and then found a detail of the famous pulpit that would please Emma Hill. I'd already written to her once, but not yet to Lizzie and Adrian, though I had already sent off postcards to Eleanor and Oliver. I read in my room after that but my thoughts kept returning to Mario Sartoris.

If he had really been attracted to me he would have persisted a little longer thirty years ago. What was all that talk of Nietzsche about? I must have made it clear that I was not interested in Mario 'in that way' but then Mario might not have been in me either. He had written to me, as I have said, two or three times in the months subsequent to my holiday in Piedmont, but for some reason I had let him drop – probably because by then I was chasing some other Sandro-like, but English, will o' the wisp. I had liked Mario years ago, and I still liked him, finding him still such a pleasant and easy companion, and now even more grateful for sensible conversation and, it must be admitted, the attentions of a nice man. Now we were old and grey, liking was more important than the excitements of youth.

I was, however, well aware that men continued to attach great importance to their sex lives. Women varied in this, I was told. As for myself, I was quite resigned to my solitary widowhood. Mario had surprised me by remembering so much of those two weeks long ago; that was unusual.

I went to bed quite early so that I might get up in good time to visit the hairdresser and have some shopping accomplished before I met Mario at the bookshop. I wanted to buy something for my baby great-nephew, my brother's grandson, though what, I could not think. I'd buy Lizzie a scarf in memory of our first visit to Cusio, and Emma might like an art book.

When I woke in the night it was out of a confused dream that had taken place at the Sacro Monte. I knew it had been there, even if the buildings were vaguely like Greek temples and people were wandering round in long white dresses and cream-coloured doublets, costumes that I knew, in the dream, belonged to the English Elizabethan period.

I looked at my watch. Half past four – the worst time to wake. Too early to get up, but difficult to get to sleep again. The dream had left me with the feeling that Sandro Montani had been part of it, though I could no longer recall what he had been doing. I tried to remember: the words 'sacred' and 'Sandro' mixed up in my mind. Monte and Montani were very close in Italian, it was true. If the dream had included the sacred I could no longer remember what it was. Then the word 'wedding cake' came unbidden into my head. I'd seen the snow-covered convent the other afternoon like wedding-cake icing, hadn't I? The 'temples' of my dream represented the churches I'd visited, and the chapel. What *had* been happening there in my head?

I gave up and switched on my radio. There was very faint classical music from one station that might lull me back to sleep.

Everyday reality intervened by the time I had finished my breakfast on Wednesday morning and was walking in the direction of the hairdresser's I'd noticed previously. Life was not a dream; and I needed a haircut, and I wanted to buy a silk blouse for myself as well as some presents. I had the strong feeling though that morning that I did not really belong in Cusio: I was just a tourist like those who came in the spring and summer.

I was in the *parrucchiere* by ten o'clock. It was quite near Chiara's flat and workshop and I had debated whether to ring her bell. Finally I had plucked up my courage and done so, but there was no answer. Either she was away or she preferred not to bother with me.

The hairdresser needed all my capacity for mime since my Italian was so rusty – or had never existed – for the words I needed. I got by with *tagliare* and *shampooing* and *gel*. Although it was only a little shop there was some piped music in the background. I recognized *Volare* which I was sure had been playing when I was in Italy in 1964 and probably long before that. Some things did not change.

A song followed, one that I did not know. 'What is it?' I asked the girl who was drying my hair very vigorously in a big white towel.

'Oh, my mother likes that one,' she answered. 'It's *per un'ora d'amore.*'

I thought, 'for one hour of love'. It was clear what sort of love that would be. The song sounded light-hearted.

Young women did not change much either, I discovered as I went on chatting in my bad Italian to the girl who was now cutting my damp hair. It was much easier to make myself understood in matters more interesting to me than hairdressing. I understood her quite well, and her assistant, who looked about fourteen, when they complained of the quietness of the place and how they much preferred the Big Lake. There was nothing to do here. I had heard exactly the same sentiments expressed not long before in Dorset.

'You must go to the market,' they said, 'in the piazza. They have some English clothes – very cheap.'

I went out into the cold air feeling reasonably fashionable, wishing to enjoy my shopping spree, for I had discovered that I had quite a lot of currency left, even when I'd calculated the tips and extras. I would not buy in the market for once; I would go to the better boutiques. Usually, I avoided shopping in London, finding it tiring and often a waste of time. Here, however, the few shops that were open sold cheerful knitted jumpers that did look a little 'foreign'. Most European countries have their goodies made now in Taiwan or China but I was pleased to see 'Made in Italy' on the red and black silk tunic I bought.

For Lizzie I purchased a blue and silver scarf that would match her silvery fair hair and at the jeweller's I bought a magnificent miniature silver rattle for my great nephew Ralph. I went along to Mario's shop thinking I'd buy Emma a book there as well as look at the now out-of-print book of Sandro's paintings and drawings.

There was an electric fire on in the shop, on the floor by Mario's desk, and already one customer, a man with a military bearing who was looking methodically through some books on flora and fauna.

'Viviana! I suddenly feared when I woke this morning that you might go home tomorrow without saying goodbye,' said Mario.

Why had he thought that? It was a strange thing to say after all our deep conversations of the past few days. I had imagined we were good friends.

'I wouldn't do that when you have been so kind. Taking me all over the place!' I exclaimed.

'It's Sandro's book you really want to see, isn't it?'

Not for the first time I wondered if he had been a little jealous of my long-ago interest in his friend – and even now in that friend's creative work.

'That – and you, of course,' I replied, and then he smiled.

'What time do you leave tomorrow?' I told him and he looked gloomy.

'Here is the book. It is mostly studies from life. The only copy I have left, so I can't sell it in case a rich American takes an interest. One who might be willing to try to discover where all these drawings, and some of his pictures, are now. Then there could be an exhibition in Chicago and Chiara made a rich girl,' he said.

'I rang her bell,' I said. 'But she was out.'

'She telephoned me yesterday at my flat. I told her we had met. Here you are.'

He dived down under the desk and brought out a brown paper parcel. I wondered for a moment where his flat was and why he had never taken me there.

'Go into the other room where there is a table for looking at large picture-books. I have to do some invoices, so you can take your time. You have changed your hairstyle,' he added. 'It is good.'

I took the parcel into the further room where there was a round table and a chair drawn up. I unwrapped the parcel. It contained a book in a shiny white jacket entitled

Sandro Montani
1930–1981

Inside, opposite the title page, was a reproduction of the *Woman by the Lake*. I looked at the table of contents. Besides some landscapes, and some drawings there were apparently many studies from life: still lifes of objects as well as men, women, children ... many of whom were drawn in the nude.

One was a drawing of a child of about eight, with long hair, an oval face, a steady glance. Underneath, there was the title CHIARA, but I knew it was her without that. She had not changed. Her face reminded me of her father. I went back to the beginning of the book and turned the pages carefully. There were life drawings of many young women. One of them caught my eye because she looked familiar. I looked at it again. A woman lying on a sofa in a recumbent pose a bit like a Goya *Maja*. When had he done that? I was seeing likenesses everywhere. There were not so many men in the life section of the book, but early on there was a portrait of a young man who looked like the Marco I remembered sitting at a café with a tall glass of beer.

I looked for anything Sandro might have drawn that lunch time when we had all been in Stresa, but there was nothing. He must have done hundreds of sketches and kept only the best for his book. I had not expected to see any sketches of myself, so I was not disappointed when I found nothing.

I turned back to the drawings he had done just before he stopped painting. They were more abstract but still with the easy fluid line of his. Then I looked again at the nude young woman.

Mario was suddenly by my side. 'Nearly time for lunch,' he said.

'I'd better not bring your book with me – I wouldn't want to get winey or oily splodges on it,' I said, 'but I must buy something for my goddaughter Emma. She might like a book. Can you suggest anything?'

'I have a very pretty anthology of Italian love poetry, illustrated with woodcuts,' he said, turning into a salesman. He brought it over for me and it was simply lovely.

'Dante, Petrarch, Tasso, Leopardi, d'Annunzio. Montale if you want to be a little more up to date, though he is not easy,' he went on. 'Of course your goddaughter may not read poetry – they say the young here don't any more.'

'Poetry is said to be very popular in Britain,' I replied, 'Emma is not an adolescent – she's over thirty and has always read a good deal. I don't think any fewer people read poetry now than when we were young.' I was saying all this as we went out.

'To your hotel? Or shall we take the car and go back to the Sacro Monte? The restaurant there will be open today.'

'You don't mean the café?'

'No, since you were first here they've opened it up into a restaurant – and there's another one for tourists in a seventeenth-century villa, further along from where we were walking on Monday. *Their* speciality is prosciutto and tagliarini al pesto and dishes of truffles. They do some very good wines too – those local ones you like.'

'I can still remember how they tasted then! I think *Gavi* is my favourite – but I like them all really!'

'Well, the restaurant isn't open on Monday, so I didn't mention it before.'

'I think I've seen enough of the Sacro Monte, and I'm not raven-
ously hungry,' I replied, surprising myself. 'I'd like to take my
purchases back and then treat you to a light lunch at the Giulio.'

'OK,' he said.

'Because tonight I want to get to bed early to be ready for my
morning taxi to Milan.'

'Shall I come to see you off?'

'No, Mario – I hate farewells at airports.'

He was different yet again now; no question of my 'not coming
to say goodbye' to him. He was in a more wistful mood.

I rushed up to my room, deposited all I had bought on the bed,
powdered my nose and rushed down again to the lounge. Mario was
talking to the barman. He ordered me a pale icy vermouth – no gin,
I insisted. We sat down on the banquette by the window overlooking the lake and the island.

'I shall always remember this view,' I said. The island still had
snow on its roofs but no more had fallen since the previous day and
the sun was brilliant.

'You really must come again in the summer,' he said.

'Perhaps I will.'

I wanted to broach the subject of the life studies but I felt a
certain reluctance. I felt I was walking on a broken-arched bridge
and that I could easily turn back. Which was the cowardly way – to
go on or to turn back? As usual I equivocated, mentioned air travel
and the weather and the book I'd been reading late the night
before.

Mario knew there was something I wanted to ask him. Over
lunch, as we were eating our delicious lake fish that looked like an
island in a creamy sea, he said: 'You liked his drawings, I think.'

'What can I say? They were brilliant. I can't understand why nobody wants to reprint the book.'

'Fashion, Viviana, fashion.'

'Is it really as bad as that?'

'Worse – and not only here – maybe not quite so bad here in Italy. The old humanist tradition is lost, you see.'

'I was disappointed not to find any sketches of my youthful self,' I said flippantly.

'You recognized Chiara?'

'Yes – a beautiful child. That chalk drawing – such blue eyes – did Sandro have blue eyes? I always thought of them as brown.'

'Grey, I believe,' answered Mario, tidily removing his fish spine. I could see that he wasn't going to help me ask the question that was burning in my head.

'Did he ever draw from memory rather than life? I mean, did he ever just *imagine*?'

'I don't think he ever *drew* from memory. Paintings were different. You remember how he took his sketch-pad wherever he went. Just like Chiara now with her special camera. He always said he could never invent – all his drawings were based on a particular moment, a light that would never return – those were his very words. Naturally his paintings were different and he'd use many different sketches for them before composing a picture.'

It was not a painting but a drawing I wanted to ask him about.

'One of the drawings of a woman looked a bit like Lizzie years ago,' I said.

'Well, he did sketch you both,' replied Mario, picking up his glass of *Gavi* and sipping it with relish.

After a pause I ventured: 'It was a life drawing of a nude.'

'He must have persuaded Elisabetta to take her clothes off then!'

'Perhaps it was not Lizzie – but it did remind me of her.'

'He sketched you both several times.'

'I'm sure she would have told me if she had posed for him in the nude. She was a very controlled sort of person, not the sort of young woman who would do that – it needs courage and she always kept herself to herself.'

'It worries you, Viviana?'

'Yes, I suppose so.'

'Well, why don't you ask her?'

'Oh, I couldn't do that! Not after thirty years.'

Mario waited, and then said: 'I believe she did pose for him in that way.'

'It seems so very unlikely.'

'Not your idea of your friend?'

'Not just that – it's not my business whether she once posed for Sandro in the altogether – it's my own judgement that I wouldn't be able to trust if it were true.'

'You believe that girls who pose in the altogether are shameful hussies?'

'Shameless,' I said. 'No, of course I don't think that. It just seems so out of character. Anyway, it must have been someone who just looked like her because he only ever sketched her outside – in the café and in Stresa – do you remember? He was going to do some drawings of her in his studio the day I went to Zermatt with you but I remember her telling me she went there but he was busy so didn't get round to doing any.' Yet Mario had sounded so sure when he'd said he believed my friend had in fact posed in the nude for Sandro. 'Do you know the drawing I'm talking about?' I asked him.

'Yes.'

'And you say she *did* pose for him?'

'Yes.'

'I suppose you knew him quite well. Did he tell you about it?' I felt I was standing holding a messy ball of wool, drawing out a strand from it. 'Well, I've been very slow,' I said. 'We really do live and learn.'

I was still not convinced, but the sweet trolley came up just then and I could not decide between meringue with Chantilly cream, zabaglione, chocolate mousse or a dish of fresh fruit salad. I knew I *ought* to take the fresh fruit salad but I didn't. I opted for the meringue. As the confection melted on my tongue with a slight sugary-taste, I was thinking I would like to look at that drawing again. It might be wiser not to, and to forget all about it.

Then Mario said: 'Perhaps he *did* sketch her that day we went to Zermatt but she didn't want you – or anyone to know.'

'Yes, it's true Lizzie always kept things to herself.' I felt he was not telling me all he knew and for the first time there was a slight constraint between us.

We walked out after our meal and stood near the lake. The wind was cold but the sun still shone on the distant peaks.

He took my hand. 'It has been a very nice holiday for *me*, you know, these last few days – seeing you again,' he said. 'Now we must not lose touch. Will you write to me? I can be your Italian pen-friend?'

'If you would really like that, Mario.' Men don't usually like writing letters, I thought. I added: 'It's been a lovely time for me too – I'm truly glad I came.'

I knew I'd miss his company and yet I didn't want him there all the time. I had a lot to think about. Soon afterwards we shook hands and I went back in to pack. Mario returned to his work.

That evening I didn't feel like another large meal so I had an omelette and salad brought up to my room. This is the life, I thought, really relishing my independence. Why should I torture myself over the possibility that many years ago Sandro Montani, who had probably sensed nothing whatever of my short infatuation for him, might have preferred my friend to me? Yet he had said I was a nice woman and kissed me on the forehead! Why did it upset me so much? I was crazy! I had in a way 'found myself' back here in Italy, even if I had not found Sandro. And I had made a new 'old friend'. I would think about the other matter at leisure and consider what might have been the case.

In the morning there was all the flurry of departure – paying bills and leaving tips and checking I hadn't forgotten my keys and my passport and my ticket and my English money, all the boring minutiae of travel. I had no time to brood over the mystery of the sketch of Lizzie until I was being winged across the Alps on my way home.

Had Mario perhaps been mistaken about Lizzie sitting for Sandro in the nude? It was a long time ago. He might easily be mixing her up with some other woman they had met some other summer. I ought to have had another look at the book but I had felt curiously reluctant for some reason.

Yet, as the short journey progressed, and we were given our plastic cutlery to eat our plastic chicken, and I sipped at my glass of wine, my mind roved round the subject – and went off at various tangents. No, other suppositions could not be true . . . . By the time we arrived at Gatwick I had reached and then abandoned several unsettling conclusions. I decided to forget them for the time being. There was plenty to do starting up my home life again. I felt as if I'd been away for a year, not less than two weeks.

I realized too that I had not fundamentally changed since my young days. Given the chance, I'd probably make much the same mistakes, though their consequences might no longer be so dire. I had also regretfully come to terms with the bald truth that however kind Mario Sartoris had been, however much I still loved the place and my memories of it, *I did not belong in Cusio.*

A phonecall from Lizzie a day or two after my return was to bring back some of my original unease.

PART THREE

London

1996

Just recently Emma Hill had fallen in love. Her choice turned out to be an Italian, a young man called Guido whom she had met at a Saturday afternoon ethnic festival patronized by her bosses. Why the *Accademia Italiana* should have sent a representative to the festival was unclear, but the two of them had gone for a cup of coffee after several hours of watching interminable Indian dancing, and matters had proceeded from there.

He appeared to reciprocate her affections, though Emma had not mentioned his name to her mother until she had known him for about six months. I learned these essentials from Lizzie who telephoned me shortly after my return to London.

I knew my friend was quick to come to conclusions. Moreover, Emma must have realized by now how keen her mother was to get her safely married. I think Emma had wanted to keep the relationship to herself for a time. I knew that she was the sort of young woman who might have shied away from a formal engagement or too much family formality, even though she had suffered in the past from a succession of extremely informal young men. Now she was about to introduce this new young man to her parents, for he had asked her to marry him.

Lizzie was not a xenophobe, but that Guido was foreign might make her a bit nervous. The Hill family was so English in its way of life. Lizzie had been taken by surprise and complained to me: 'I thought she was still pining after that Mark man she knew last year – but this must have been going on for some time!'

I had the impression that she disapproved but that as she had not yet met the young man could hardly say so.

I was longing to tell her about my holiday but wary of introducing the subject of the drawing, so I said little about it beyond how beautiful the place was and not a disappointment at all. Lizzie did not appear very interested when I said I had met Mario again. I remembered that she had once described him as 'rather wet'.

'Why couldn't Em meet some nice Englishman?' she asked. 'You can never get to know foreigners so well – Emma says she doesn't even know if he's a Catholic! Will you come over on Saturday? You can tell me what you think of him – she's bringing – er – Guido to dinner – just for the family and a few friends,' she went on. I said I'd be delighted.

The next day Emma herself rang me up and filled me in. I told her I was looking forward to meeting Guido.

'Tell me about Cusio – thanks for your card by the way,' said Emma.

'I sent you two – you won't get the second for days.'

'Your pilgrimage will be something to talk about when you meet Guido – and you speak Italian too! Not that he doesn't speak wonderful English but it's always nice when somebody makes the effort to talk to someone in their own language, isn't it?'

'My Italian is very sketchy,' I said. I added: 'I've got a little present for you that your fiancé might also enjoy – a book.'

'Oh thanks. Vivien you do *promise* to come, don't you? Mother will do an interrogation session if you're not there.'

Lizzie's daughter had always called me Vivien ever since she was a lisping toddler whose attempts at my name had then ended up in 'Bibby'.

'Don't you think he ought just to meet the family first? I mean I'm only your godmother.'

'Which makes it all cosy, and family-like,' said Emma. 'He will understand the idea of a godmother,' she added and giggled down the phone.

I promised to attend. I was touched that she really seemed to want me there to meet the young man.

'He is really such a nice man,' she went on. 'I mean I *like* him – and he seems to like me! He has two sisters and they're both quite high-powered – one's a lawyer – so he's used to women having careers, even if they're married, which his sisters are. Mother gives the impression I might be living in purdah in Naples—'

'Whereabouts is he from?'

'His family all live in Bologna.'

'Will you eventually go to live in Italy, do you think?'

'Maybe if he doesn't get promotion after his five-year contract in London runs out. That's not for ages though and I'm sure he *will* get it. Now tell me all about your holiday. Did it live up to your expectations?'

Whatever *they* were, I thought.

'I met a very pleasant Italian – a man your mother and I met years ago,' I said.

'I've never met a nasty one,' she replied. 'I suppose I am biased though. Everyone keeps telling me Latin men are sexist and not to be trusted.'

I wondered if 'everyone' was shorthand for more heavy hints

from her mother, but I was probably being unfair to Lizzie. 'It's silly to generalize,' I said.

I always tried not to sound like the ex-teacher I was, so I added, in case she should think I was directing my remarks at her: 'I didn't mean you shouldn't go by your own experience – that's different.'

'I'm so pleased you're coming – I know you'll like him,' said Emma. 'I don't really want a party at this juncture, but I suspect Mother is going to invite more people than she said at first. If things are sticky you call tell us about your holiday.'

I knew that by 'sticky' she meant her father's notorious inability to converse about anything not directly related to his work. Usually, he spoke of technical mysteries to do with his profession. Liz, however, was good at small talk.

I thought Emma was obviously trying to please her mother by this formal engagement.

Lizzie telephoned me again the next morning to say they had decided to have a little party first on the Saturday evening before the dinner party. 'Just a few neighbours over for a drink first,' she said. She sounded nervous. 'Might as well do it properly.' She suggested six o'clock as the time for my arrival. Lizzie was always very strict about this if she was giving a proper dinner, not just entertaining a friend in her kitchen.

I felt a little awkward, already knowing more about Guido from Emma than Lizzie might imagine I did. I'd often felt like that before over my goddaughter. I certainly did not wish to claim a special relationship with Emma, even if I knew we got on well and that she approved of me. Relations between mothers and daughters are often said to be fraught and it hadn't been myself who had suffered all the bother of bringing a child up. I'd only ever known the best part. In the past, Lizzie had found Emma's way of life too bohemian for her tastes, but I could never see that the bohemianism amounted to much more than a dislike of the suburbs, which was perfectly natural, I thought, especially at her age. There might also have been a little pot-smoking and an expressed sympathy with rebels. Certainly Emma had announced when she was about twenty that she was a feminist – adding that she was not a 'radical' one! Lizzie had got annoyed and said Emma 'had never known a moment's sexist discrimination.'

'I'm not a feminist for my own sake, Mother, but on behalf of all the women who have such terrible lives,' her daughter had replied.

At heart, Emma was not a very political person but one with a strong sense of injustice as well as a dislike of convention. I'd come to the conclusion that she did not care for fashion, was not a person for espousing up-to-the-minute causes. I'd been a bit like that myself, most likely still was.

I arrived at the house near Parkside promptly at six-o'clock. We were to eat at eight. The neighbours and other friends had also been invited for six. I left my little presents for Emma and her mother upstairs and joined the party in the tall drawing room with its bay window looking out on to a lawn and shrubbery. Adrian had done very well for himself. The neighbours and one or two of Adrian's colleagues were already decorously circulating, along with a few of Emma's old friends from the high school who still lived in the district. One I recognized as Lavinia Someone whom I had once taken to the Children's Theatre with Emma years ago. Now here she was with a toddler at her skirts and a husband hovering dutifully behind.

I was surprised to find Polly and Helena there too, the latter looking a little bemused. Helena's partner, Joe, was already in deep conversation with one of the neighbours. Polly was looking healthy and composed. Lizzie had asked me for their addresses after she'd seen them at my own party just before I left for Cusio. How long ago that seemed, and yet it was less than a month! I hadn't thought Lizzie would want to see the women again. True, we had once all taught in the same school, and there were remarks now at the number of years that had elapsed since that time of our lives.

Adrian was dispensing the champagne – the Hills always gave you of the best. I espied Emma's brothers, Andrew and Simon, Andrew broad-shouldered and perfectly groomed for such parental parties, Simon fair and tall and just as pleasantly polite.

Emma came up to me after a few moments, a young man in her wake, whose hand she was holding. He was a dark-haired, medium sized young man with spectacles.

'Vivien, this is Guido Taviani,' she said. 'Guido – my godmother – Vivien Wilson.'

He detached his hand from Emma's, shook hands heartily and beamed. 'I am so pleased to meet Emma's family and friends,' he said.

His accent was slight, a little less Italian than Mario's, and I suddenly felt a little stab of loneliness. I could not think of Mario as 'my' Italian but I did wish for a moment that I was thirty and doing the rounds with an extremely suitable future husband.

Emma, having to talk to all her mother's friends and neighbours, left us together, and he said: 'Emma tells me you have just come back from Italy?'

I told him, Yes, and where I'd been and about the time I'd once visited his home city and what a competent administration it had compared with most Italian cities. Then we talked about films and were on to books by the time the gathering was well under way. Then Guido went off to pay his respects to others, and Lizzie came up. She was wearing a lovely blue silk dress, and her sapphire and diamond earrings. Her high heels gave her a good six inches over me. I used to wear heels, but once aching feet prevented me enjoying a party I'd regretfully abandoned them.

I thought: I hadn't noticed not being tall when I was abroad, but here, among enormous and well-fed Anglo-Saxons I felt I was a pygmy. Lizzie had often made me feel like that. Years ago I had confessed to her that I envied her being tall. I'd never told her for twenty years that I still did!

She was too polite to say anything just then about Guido, merely raised her eyebrows.

I said: 'I so enjoyed meeting Guido—'

'Good, because I'm putting you next to him at dinner,' she said in a low voice. 'Now I must go and sort out the meal – there'll be eight of us – the family, and you and Guido – and Cousin Selma.'

I had not noticed Cousin Selma before but did so now. She was standing talking to Adrian and one of his sons and clutching her handbag as if it might take flight any minute.

'So long, Vivien,' said Helena as she went out with Peter. 'Lovely young man,' Polly whispered to me. 'Ring you up for a gossip soon.'

'Goodbye, Helena. 'Bye, Polly.' I felt privileged to be not leaving, but admitted to the family circle.

I'd been too busy talking to the young Italian to drink too much champagne and was glad about that when we went into the dining-room about ten minutes later and Adrian uncorked the Chablis. We began with some salmon that dissolved in the mouth with a faintly lemon tang. What would we talk about? I hoped that the conversation would not degenerate, as it had done so often in that room, to the problems of au pairs and schools and burglars. Andrew asked Guido about some Italian football team and I saw Emma looking a bit anxious. Perhaps Guido, unlike most Italians, was not football mad. He answered with an anecdote about some player and then Simon talked about skiing. The boys had obviously been primed by Lizzie to make an effort.

I turned to Cousin Selma on my other side and we talked about nursing homes, on which I was an expert, having long experience of my mother's sojourn in one. Selma's mother was still alive and paying an immense amount of money to be kept comfortable.

Then Emma asked me: 'Was Cusio as beautiful as you expected, Vivien?' and they all looked at me.

'Even more beautiful,' I replied. 'Especially in the snow. You remember the Sacro Monte?' I said, turning to Liz in the interval between her serving the next course.

'Oh yes – vaguely. Did you do much shopping?'

'Got you a scarf,' I said. 'It's on your bed.'

'And did you practise your Italian?' asked her husband politely.

'I'm afraid it is beyond redemption. The people I met – Mario Sartoris especially – spoke very good English. As you do,' I added to Guido.

I waited for Lizzie to ask whether I had seen Sandro or Marco but she did not, was now busy serving the pudding which was a tower of puffy chocolate and coffee nuggets to which you added an ice-creamy kind of sauce. The salmon too had been perfect. I could never cook as well as Lizzie if I practised a hundred years.

The conversation languished and picked up between Emma's parents and Guido – languished again, and then just when you thought it had come to a full stop, picked itself up again. Each

time I opened my mouth, having endeavoured to think of something to say to the young man, or even to Adrian himself, Adrian
brought forth some ponderous remark. I decided to leave them to
it.

How artificial civilization was, even in a pleasant London back-
water, and how not one of us was saying anything remotely close to
our real feelings, though we were not telling lies.

Finally Guido turned to me, saying: 'Emma tells me you have
given her a book of Italian verse.' She must have opened the parcel
I'd left in her room when she went upstairs just before dinner to
powder her nose, not that young women Emma's age seemed to do
that any longer.

'Yes, you will have to translate for her – it's too hard for me to
understand. Usually I buy European poetry with English transla-
tions. Do you read poetry?' We hadn't had time to get on to that
subject earlier.

It would be sufficiently unusual, I thought, for a young man to
read poetry whether he was Italian or English, but of course I was
forgetting that, like my goddaughter, Guido worked for a literary
and artistic concern.

'You must recite me your favourite English verse,' he went on.
'Emma has read me MacNeice – but he is Irish.'

'I shall lend you Thomas Hardy then,' I replied. I reflected that
my favourite novelist and poet would have appreciated this gathering, and what I was thinking about the past and its ramifications
for the present might have intrigued him too. I thrust those
thoughts away. This was hardly the smart society that had so fascinated Hardy, and many years had passed since the London dinner
parties Hardy had been so thrilled to attend.

I was an incorrigible tracer of secret meanings – if unfortunately without enough creative spirit to make anything of my surmises. Yet it is still true that we live on surfaces, and never more so than when we are with the people on whom we want to make a good impression, or at least show them we are still reasonably mentally active. Few indeed are those to whom we may reveal part of our inner life and feelings. Mario was one of the few, and I hoped that Guido might be able to fulfil the same function for Emma. It is rarer than we think, this ability to listen to people. Emma was going to be lucky in her marriage. I had known her all her life and, although one may be mistaken about people, I still thought she had a certain freshness and originality which the years of filing folders and attending meetings had not entirely crushed. Maybe Guido would take her away from that world of work. Then I stopped myself, thinking that women were now supposed to go on working just as men did, and not to want a breathing space when they married. It is however immaterial whether certain people are male or female if they want – desperately *need* – breathing spaces. Guido might be one of them? Which would mean that he would not put a large salary as his priority, and so they would both be over-worked. Especially if they had children . . . .

I was recalled to the present by Emma saying: 'How did you find your memories assorted with the reality of Cusio, Vivien? Were you truly not disappointed? You say it was even more beautiful?' She had obviously been thinking this over, seemed genuinely interested.

'Oh,' said Selma, 'Italy is so lovely – though tourists aren't likely to visit slums, are they?'

'I was not disappointed,' I said to Emma. I turned to Lizzie. 'The lake and the village have hardly changed at all.'

'Much *has* changed in my country – at least my father says so,'

Guido put in. 'Also I think *he* will have changed – so he sees different aspects.'

'Yes, that's possible,' I said. 'Paris has certainly changed, and so have we – and if I hadn't lived in London for as long as I hadn't visited Cusio, I expect I'd hardly recognize the place – skyscrapers, motorways, buildings pulled down, offices everywhere—'

'Milan is the same, but the countryside alters less at home. Emma has promised to take me to a small English village. I have never lived anywhere but in London over here,' Guido said.

We moved into the drawing-room then for coffee. Lizzie busied herself serving it and tried to change the subject as she handed me mine: 'You remember Lavinia Parker? Don't you think she has changed more than Em?'

I answered appropriately and sipped my coffee, even though I knew it would probably keep me awake.

'Did you take some pictures on your holiday, dear?' asked Cousin Selma, who had sat down next to me. 'I always think snapshots are the best thing for bringing back happy times—'

'Yes, I took several. I don't know yet how they've turned out.' I was looking forward to seeing the one of Mario in his fur hat.

I wondered whether Lizzie had kept any of the photographs we had taken thirty years before. Now that I'd seen the real place again, and one of the men, I was curious to compare any other old photograph of Mario and of Cusio I could find with later ones.

'Emma and Guido would *love* Cusio,' I said. 'It's the ideal place for a honeymoon.'

I believed I might sound insincere. I meant what I said, but I mustn't gush. Neither could I ask Lizzie just then whether she had ever posed in the nude for Sandro Montani, though the sight of her moving round filling coffee cups, as efficient as ever, made me even more curious. Would I ever be able to ask her? It might be possible to confront her on the telephone, though that seemed a bit of a coward's way out.

After the dinner party I was busy integrating myself again into my ordinary life. I waited until the snaps I'd taken in Cusio were developed and then I did write a long letter to Mario. I thanked him for taking me round and wining and dining me and above all for his friendship, and I sent him copies of the photo of himself, and one of me, and two or three of the island and the Sacro Monte. I mentioned that Lizzie's daughter Emma was to marry an Italian, and that she had liked the book, but I said nothing about the sketches of the old Liz.

I soon received a reply. He asked me again if we could have a writing friendship: would I be his English correspondent? I smiled over that; it sounded a bit adolescent. I'd always liked writing letters, liking even more to receive them. Nor did Mario mention the famous sketch-book in his letter. I had not forgotten that he had once said in that connection: 'Well, why don't you ask her?'

This was easier said than done, even on the telephone. I had never confronted Lizzie before; I'd always been a little intimidated by her. Really, I could not ask her.

Now that I was back from Cusio, the memory of my old infatuation seemed to have become less important, as if I had managed to inoculate myself in preparation for the rest of my life. Any feelings I'd ever had, any nostalgia that had remained for Sandro and for the many other objects of my youthful adoration, had been apparently dissipated – or chemically transformed – in the enjoyable conversations I'd had with Mario. I thought: I have learned my lesson; I shall no longer yearn for the impossible. If nostalgia had gone, love of a place, and the remembrance of being young still remained. The place was still there; maybe it was the *place* I had really longed to see again rather than any one person, and now that I had seen it I was happier. The place had tugged at me until I revisited it; now I thought I had, if not 'found myself', rediscovered certain aspects of myself by drawing a line under the past – just as I had after Roland died. After his death I had lost one grown-up part of myself, perhaps for ever. Now I was, so to speak, losing the youthful parts. Soon I'd be back to childhood – but one can never lose that.

It would be nice to see Mario again. We had got on so well. He wrote that he would continue to write to me if I agreed, and I saw no reason not to agree.

My holiday seemed to have affected me in other ways too. I was full of ideas, for reading, for visiting stately homes, for listening to music, even for frequenting auction houses. Not that I bought anything, but I had always enjoyed going to sales of Victorian jewellery.

One afternoon I had been to Sotheby's and was walking down Bond Street thinking about that little gallery not far away where I'd seen the exhibition of photographs that were so like those Chiara had taken.

For some reason, the jewellery that I'd just seen, the rubies and emeralds and garnets and amethysts, had made me think about my old village home in Dorset and about the old church and the graveyard. It must have been because the jewels were so quintessentially of the nineteenth century – the century that was now nearly the last century but one.

For some months I had been involved in my own private past, but now it began to seem that it all linked up now to a more distant past. I found the feeling difficult to analyse even to myself, but as I walked by the shops, so full of beautiful things, I reflected upon my own far from luxurious childhood. Had I ever expected to be rich, to wear the kind of clothes I had dreamed about as a little girl, the taffetas and organdies and full skirts of imagination? I had never owned such dresses in my youth or afterwards, but had I always been content to admire them only on others?

I had always slightly despised people whose ambitions were limited to such material things but as I paused to look in some of the shop windows, I realized that I had always envied people who lived in this way, who wore such clothes. Ever since my first sight of a real manor house I had secretly dreamed of one day living in it, of having the kind of romantic family life that fitted a great grey Elizabethan pile with armorial bearings on the porch, gardens of yew walks and flights of shallow stone steps. I was the child of austerity, so as well as envying them, I also feared cornucopias.

I paused in front of one window: on display was a porcelain model wearing a full-skirted, mid-calf-length flared black taffeta dress, the frilly ruches emphasizing the slender artificial legs. Emma would look lovely in that, I thought.

A little further on there was a window dressed with clothes for a girl. A nine year old girl, I imagined, in an oyster-and-silver stiff taffeta with large puffed sleeves. The stuff was almost paper-like, might even stand alone.

I had never had a daughter to buy such clothes for. Suddenly all my new found happiness – or resignation – had gone and I was standing alone looking in the window with such longing in my heart. I remembered looking at a dress in a shop window as a child with much the same longing, though I didn't suppose the clothes in 1940s war-time Dorchester would have been as beautiful as this.

Even as a child I had thought: the dress is beautiful, but I have the feeling it might look better in the window on a model than on a real girl . . . .

It must have been the puritanical ways of the social class in which I had been brought up that had given me – and left me – with such feelings of mingled envy and timidity. Spending had been regarded as sinful. If I had been born in that grey Elizabethan manor of my childhood that still stood in the village I'd have had that child of Peter's. My parents would have accepted it. I did not want to think about that. I had resigned myself long ago to what had happened.

I moved along. The sun was low in the sky now, for after all it was still winter, and I had better find a bus and get home.

Then I stopped for the third time. In another window yet another glittering dress. Would you call it scarlet or crimson? Not vermilion, no, nearer scarlet, long and slinky. Not for a child this time or even a child-woman. When I looked closer I saw it was almost completely covered in sequins. It was like a flame in the window.

I remembered a party dress worn by a girl of about eighteen in the village after the war. She always said her family was related to Hardy's. Her dress, though, had not been crimson or scarlet but a dark rose madder . . . . I cast one more look at the red sequinned swirl and hurried on to Piccadilly. On the bus I reflected that these magical clothes symbolized Youth as well as the Eternal Feminine.

I had always been able to imagine beautiful objects and people: jewels, and dresses – and young men like Sandro Montani. People who have little, *imagine*. People who live in manor houses don't need to, since they possess the reality.

I would always possess an imagination. A man who wrote out of a fairly poor and constrained childhood, his imagination touched by what he did not possess, was remembered longer than the society dinners he graced or the rich hostesses he fell in love with, or the opulence of their careless luxury. For people like me, I concluded, as the bus crossed over into the greyness of south London, even if I had owned what I had longed for, even if I had married young, the reality might have been too much. Imagination could be even more precious than reality: the *idea* of a lake, a man, an island, a sacred place, or even the rich confection of a manufactured fashion.

As the bus followed the seemingly endless boredom of the Old Kent Road, I saw flowers and woods, skies and fields. I recalled the real manor houses of my childhood and remembered more than one poem on the subject of a long ago love returning in force, as a ghost . . . .

You can't linger for ever in the seductive meadows of memory, nor remain perched up high in some imaginary realm, yet what I had been feeling that winter afternoon in Bond Street must have seeped into my spirit, for my mood over the next few days was a little strange and introspective. Not unhappy. I had always been subject to rapidly changing moods and states of mind.

A few days later I woke late to a dazzling late winter sun shining through layers of pale gold cloud. I decided to sort through some of my old clothes for the charity shop. Tomorrow was always a new day: the truism happened to be true. I caught myself remembering that going abroad had usually cheered me up. I had always gone to France, to Spain, to Italy, for my holidays because those countries made me lighter of heart, and in my youth I had certainly felt more alive over there. My common-sense self said: well of course you felt free and light hearted abroad because you were on holiday. I was always more relaxed across the Channel too, happy to concentrate on beautiful places and beautiful objects and able to forget the narrow confines of my own childhood. That childhood returned whenever, quite without my volition, a trivial memory shoved itself into my head. Now, I half wanted to visit Eleanor again, to see the fields of childhood once more, and half feared lest they might catch hold of me for ever. In spite of bringing me face to face with the past, Cusio had been an escape from only one of my past selves.

I wrote again to Mario in reply to his letter and told him this time more of what I had been doing since I left Cusio. I knew he might be the one person in the world who would be interested in my inchoate emotions. I also knew now how to make him laugh, and I described how the other morning I had absent-mindedly watered the waste paper basket and thrown some pencil shavings into a plant pot.

Mario and I had discussed poetry and art but as far as I could remember we had never talked about music so I decided to tell him about my recent passion for Beethoven's bagatelles. I was listening to these – my favourite 'last' ones one February evening when Lizzie telephoned me.

I had been plucking up courage to ask Lizzie, casually, about the drawing the next time I saw her. I'd been too preoccupied with my various solitary tasks to get round to inviting her, but it was my turn to entertain her. After we had exchanged a few words about Emma and Guido, and I had enthused over him – for I was determined to let her see how suitable I considered him – I was surprised when Lizzie said:

'You haven't really told me much about Cusio. I'll not be far away from you tomorrow – Adrian wants me to collect his camera. He always has it repaired at Messenger's, it's the only place he trusts, so I thought I might pop in to see you.'

'What a good idea!' I replied. 'I was going to ask you to come and see me soon anyway – I've been feeling guilty about neglecting my friends whilst I've been easing myself back into London.'

We arranged that she should come round for a light lunch and a chat. Lizzie always drives everywhere and likes to visit me because I have no yellow lines outside my house to forbid parking. I wondered what I could give her to eat. Usually, I ate only soup and cheese or salad and some fruit at lunch time, but I went out and bought a quiche from the health food shop – I wasn't up to making one, but I'd prepare a salad to go with it, and I had a bottle of dry white wine waiting to be opened. Lizzie never drank very much.

Then, casually, I would say that one of the drawings I'd seen in a book of Sandro's sketches looked very like her, and that Mario insisted she had once sat for him. Dare I tell her that it was a nude?

I sat looking out of my sitting room window at the clouds. My flat is on the second floor and I get splendid sunsets. Now I felt constrained. It was really no business of mine that Lizzie had sat for Sandro on the day she said he had been too busy to sketch her, and yet in some curious way I felt it *was* my concern. Mario – and I – might both be wrong, and Lizzie entirely innocent of a fib.

Yet Mario had been so sure . . . .

The quiche was a success. The wine too was light and delicious.

I need not have worried about introducing the subject of Cusio for Lizzie appeared really interested and even broached the subject herself. I was surprised. I told her a bit about the place and how I'd met Mario again, which she'd probably heard me say at her dinner party. Then I brought out my recent photographs. 'You remember him?' I asked. 'The serious-minded one.'

I remembered that she had once despised Mario as a softie, a hanger-on. I waited to see if she would mention the names of the other two men.

'Oh yes, I remember him. He hasn't changed much, except for the hair,' she said. She went on: 'He was a bit sweet on you if I remember rightly. It's a very long time ago – did you see the others?'

She sounded elaborately casual but that could be my suspicious mind. I swallowed. Now it had come to the point I was nervous.

'No,' I said. 'Marco – the one who was married – lives in Milan. I believe Mario sees him from time to time. And I'm afraid that Sandro – the artist – died in 1981.'

'Oh? You were mad about him, weren't you?'

'I find it hard to recall how I used to feel,' I said. 'I don't suppose he ever knew what I felt – after we got back to England I couldn't stop thinking about him – it went on for several months. How silly one used to be.'

'Oh Vivien,' she said affectionately. 'You were always in love with someone or something. They never lasted, did they?'

'Sometimes they did,' I said a little indignantly. 'Three years, one of them – and the way I feel about Cusio – I've been very faithful to my idea of it, haven't I? You can be in love with places as well as people.'

'Can you remember your actual first feelings though, for a place or a person?'

'I can with my mind – and even enjoy the memory – but I can't understand why a particular person affected me so much, can't feel the feelings again for that person – I suppose the feelings must be there still somewhere but with nobody now to attach them to. Perhaps places last longer in one's mind.'

'How did you feel about Mario? – he was always the studious one – just right for you, I always thought!'

'Still much as I did. Do you remember—' I had started – I might as well get this over – 'Do you remember that Sandro ... did sketches of us both?'

Now was the moment.

'Yes—'

'As a matter of fact I saw a book of some of his drawings and paintings. Mario had it in his shop – it's out of print though.'

She said nothing but held out her glass to be refilled, a sufficiently uncharacteristically gesture for me to be wary.

'There were none of the sketches he did of us at the café or at that restaurant in Stresa. I was disappointed. What was so surprising was that one of the other sketches – a nude life drawing as a matter of fact – looked very like you.' I emphasized the words to make my meaning clear.

Now it was out. I waited, took a gulp of wine myself.

'Really?' she exclaimed. 'You mean, in the altogether?'

'Yes.'

'Well, well, when can he have done that?'

'I don't know. I suppose he could have imagined what you looked like. He must have been more interested in you than we thought.' I remembered that Sandro had 'liked English girls'.

'He liked English women,' said Lizzie, echoing my own thought.

'Mario hinted he was a bit of a *coureur de femmes*,' I said. 'He married twice. In fact his daughter from his first marriage – she's called Chiara – now lives in Cusio. She's a photographer. I actually met her when I was looking for the old studio and the old shop gallery, but it's all changed now.'

Lizzie cleared her throat and then she said, looking away: 'I *did* sit for him once, but I didn't tell you. You'd have been hurt that he wanted to draw me like that.'

Yes, I supposed I would have been. Terribly jealous in fact. I'd forgotten those feelings that go with infatuation.

'You were really crazy about him!' Lizzie went on. She seemed to want to talk about me, not herself.

'I know – I do remember. Mario is much nicer.'

'I imagined you might have gone back there to relive your youthful passions,' she said.

'Well, if I took a holiday in every place where I'd once fallen in love it would be an expensive itinerary. Nothing happened anyway, either then or last month. Sandro was never interested, even if he did kiss me once. And Mario was, and is, the sort of man you can be friends with – not that I had enough sense when I was thirty to see how rare that is . . . .'

'Sandro kissed you then? You never told me that!'

'Well, you didn't tell me you had sat for him, did you? When was that? I can't remember you were ever with him in his studio except that day Mario and I went to Zermatt—'

'Yes, I believe it *was* that day—'

'You told me you went to the studio but he was so busy he couldn't do any drawings of you.'

'Fancy your remembering after all this time! When did he kiss you?'

'Oh, it was the time you were going to meet him by the lake – one morning right at the end of our holiday. Don't you remember I went up alone to the Sacro Monte and came upon him sketching there. I told him you were expecting him by the lake, and he said he'd forgotten, or it didn't matter. It was on the way back he gave me a very chaste kiss.'

'Chaste?'

'Yes, on the forehead.'

'Good grief!'

'Well, I knew he didn't find me sexually attractive. I think he liked me. I found him terribly sexy though – an awful waste that these things aren't arranged better. If he'd seduced me then and there I don't think I could have resisted.'

'Well, he stood *me* up that very morning!' Lizzie exclaimed.

'He always put his painting first, I think,' I said, as I measured out some coffee. Lizzie cleared away the plates.

'Do you think Emma's Guido is like that?' she asked me. 'I mean, I see he is quite attractive but is he really suitable?'

I tried not to smile. She sounded so exactly as her mother had once. Not that Adrian Hill had not been eminently 'suitable' but it was the epithet that had hounded me in my own childhood and youth and doubtless many more people of my generation: 'unsuitable' opinions on sex; 'unsuitable' clothes; 'unsuitable' attachments . . . .

I said: 'She loves him and you can see that he loves her.'

'Do you really think he loves her? I trust your judgement.'

'I'm sure he does – he's more of a Mario, I'd think,' I replied. I added: 'He seems an awfully nice steady sort of young man – entirely suitable for Em. I wish he were going to be *my* son in law.'

'It's always possible they'll eventually live abroad when they're married,' said Lizzie.

We went into my sitting room to drink the coffee. Now we had done the serious bit, I felt relieved. I hoped the matter of posing for Sandro would not come up again.

I changed the subject. We talked about Lizzie's sons and their jobs. Then I mentioned I was thinking about going back to live in Dorset.

'You've been saying you might ever since Roland died,' said Lizzie, rather brutally, I thought. 'But I don't think you will!'

I hadn't realized I had been thinking about it for so long – but trust an old friend to tell you when you repeat yourself!

'Well, I don't *have* to live here,' I said. 'I like London less and less. All right if you're young, I suppose. Or if you have a family.'

Lizzie was eminently practical. 'What would you do for transport in Dorset? Does Eleanor drive?'

'Yes, she does, but I wouldn't be dependent on her,' I replied, trying to convince myself. I knew that to live in the nicest parts of England you have to like driving, unless you are very rich and can afford a chauffeur. 'Well, there's a reasonable bus service into Dorchester,' I went on, 'and a taxi always available in the village. Just imagine – a beautiful place and not much traffic on the roads and no horrible London pollution . . . .'

'Oh, Vivien you are such a romantic! There are just as many problems in the countryside as here – drugs are everywhere and they say crime is just as bad in market towns. Don't you think it's a *time* you want to go back to, not a *place*?'

I was surprised at her perspicacity. 'I know, Lizzie,' I replied humbly. 'Perhaps it's only a pipe-dream. I begin to wonder whether Dr Johnson was wrong when he said a man who was tired of London was tired of life. Tired of a certain kind of life perhaps? But I don't *have* to live in London, do I? I could even go to Italy – "away from it all" . . . ' I had visions of an old-fashioned 'organic' community but I knew Italy was no answer really.

'There's nowhere ideal, is there?' said Lizzie. 'I mean nowhere absolutely secure, unless you live behind an electronic fence with guard dogs!'

But I was not to be deflected. I had to have my dream. 'There could be work for me in Dorset! There's an Evening Institute that needs people to teach adults – and I might start to go to classes myself. I'd like to learn how to paint in oils—'

'You could do that here.'

I sighed. 'The trouble is I'm not sure what I want,' I said. 'It would be different if I had a job – or children who were moving somewhere.' I thought, my 'freedom' somehow made it harder to decide what I wanted.

'Our boys may very well find better jobs in the provinces – nothing is for ever, but I don't think we'd follow them. I'd miss *you* though, Vivien, if you left London.'

I was touched.

We parted amicably. I thought she looked tired. Would I miss her and all my London friends if I moved back to the country? Or if I moved abroad?

I woke twice in the night.

The first time I'd been dreaming about something clinging or pulling at me. I remembered for some reason the baby snails which as a child I'd used to detach from railings on summer holidays in Weymouth. In the dream the sensation was that of little hands plucking at *me*. I was the passive one.

I went back to sleep but I woke again at about five o'clock from the dream of a divinely beautiful church, so beautiful that in my dream I had tears in my eyes. The shreds of my dream were clinging around the idea of there being *two* churches. The particular one I had been looking at was so breathtakingly lovely that I felt: here indeed is perfection, and was uplifted by an aesthetic sensation I no longer had very often in waking life. It seemed to be in a university city abroad, but also gave the impression of Queen Anne's London. My emotion was mixed into the idea of 'more than one', the second just as beautiful even if I could not see it. There is a cathedral in Barcelona and a church – Santa Maria del Mar – that is larger than the cathedral, I believe, and I wondered whether my idea of there being 'two' arose from memories of Catalonia. The beautiful window I gazed at in the dream had bands of light in a mixture of indigo and azure.

I could not get to sleep after this. What Mario had told me kept coming into my mind. It wasn't so much what he had said about Lizzie's sitting for a life drawing as a conviction that he had not been telling me all he knew about Sandro Montani. Yet, there was no reason why he should. It was a little strange, though, that he had assumed I'd want to see him, had even told Chiara Montani to direct me to his shop . . . . There was something too that he'd not said during our last conversation, on my last evening in Cusio, before I had said goodbye and gone to pack … some nuance that had entered our conversation and made for a slight constraint between us. Perhaps he had felt nothing of the kind – I knew I was sometimes over-sensitive to nuances.

As I lay sleepless, thinking about Lizzie's confession, I wondered why her having sat for Sandro Montani in the nude should upset me. Almost half a life time had passed and I hadn't continued to nurse a youthful passion for Sandro. My return to Cusio had not been to find him, but to see a place again and remind me of my own youth. Mario had been a bonus.

I would have minded had I known at the time, but why should Lizzie have thought it mattered so much that she had never mentioned it to me over all the years? We could have laughed over it together. Maybe she wouldn't have said anything to Adrian, but she could have told *me* ... Did it matter now?

Was Sandro the reason for Lizzie being critical about Italians?

I could not get back to sleep. What had Mario said about his friend? That Sandro always had plenty fish to fry? And – when we had been talking about Chiara – that there might have been 'foreign ladies over the years coming looking for him'. Whatever he had been hinting was nothing I had not already known. Sandro had been an extremely attractive man. I – who had been acquainted with him for only two weeks – had been only one of his countless admirers. Sandro must have made numberless conquests. I still wished I had been one of them! Liz had been unimpressed by him, so why had she agreed to be immortalized in one little drawing? Should I even mention it to Mario in my next letter?

Next morning, in spite of being awake for so long in the night, I felt quite energetic. I decided to invite Emma and Guido to dinner. I didn't want to have Emma's parents there as well. They could come another day. There was a well-established convention for family or friends to invite an engaged couple without their parents as a sort or recognition of a new future unit of society, so Lizzie would not mind. I intended a different kind of gathering for the summer – I wanted to make plans for the future to keep myself busy, otherwise I might feel my life had come to some hiatus. Life hadn't stopped because I had retired, nor because I had met Mario again. As long as it went on I would have new books to read, music to listen to, things to learn, new ideas.

We all judge children too much by their parents. From its baby-hood we compare son or daughter with mother and father. We look for similarities, to begin with in physical attributes, and easily find them: 'He has the Montmorency nose . . . . She's the image of her grandmother.' Or we find small differences and blame them on some familial missing link. Whereas in reality, having inherited some distant genes, or made a new and never before created cocktail of a double inheritance, a child is completely new, completely its own person, completely 'other'. Of course there will be certain similarities, usually from having inherited a particular environment, but people are mysteries. If they were not, nobody would ever have bothered discussing character either in life or novels or biographies. I used to think this when I taught children and it occurred to me again as I observed Emma when she came to my house and saw how she was her own different and delightful person.

She and Guido were easy with each other; there was none of that tension you sometimes find when a woman is in love with a man who does not wear his heart on his sleeve. They were not the sort of very young lovers who embarrass older people when they can't keep their hands off each other. How grown up Emma was! Then I mocked myself for not having quite believed she was grown up before. She was certainly more mature than I had been at the same age.

I had made another effort to organize the rest of my possessions, and I had managed – at last – to find more of the old snaps I'd taken on my first holiday in Cusio, mostly of the lake and the houses. Search as I might, previously I had not been able to find them, but now they had turned up in the middle of an old school register that had been lying in a bottom drawer. I must have taken them to school to show colleagues and then kept them along with that term's notes. Now I could compare the Cusio of thirty years ago with its present manifestation. I bought a new album and put them in it along with my more recent snaps.

Before we ate our dinner Emma had been looking at Chiara's book of photographs and had much admired them. After dinner I showed her and Guido both my own recent photographs of Cusio in the snow and the old snap of Lizzie.

'Here is one of the men your mother and I met years ago,' I said, handing her over a photo of Mario. I'd written Mario Sartoris on the back. 'He was a friend of the father of the young woman whose book of photographs you were looking at,' I explained.

Guido looked over her shoulder. 'I believe I've heard of Mario Sartoris,' he said. 'He's quite well known in the artistic world at home – didn't he give up his auction consultancies to run a book shop?'

'Why, yes. Fancy his being famous. He's awfully nice. Have you heard of a painter called Sandro Montani as well?'

'No I don't think so—'

'Montani – that was the name of the woman photographer?' asked Emma.

'Yes, he was her father.'

'Let me look at your other snaps. Oh, what a pretty snow scene – and here you are Vivien – looking quite at home. She could be Italian, couldn't she?' she said to her intended.

'Unless I open my mouth,' I said. 'How's your own Italian coming on, Emma?'

'Better ask Guido.'

'Her accent is very good – but the verbs need practice,' he replied.

'You must have some of these enlarged,' said Emma. 'They're really very good.'

I told them a bit about the island and about the Sacro Monte. Guido said he had once visited another Sacro Monte.

'Perhaps we could go to Piedmont for our honeymoon?' said Emma.

'Oh you'd want a warmer place, unless it was high summer,' I said. I felt suddenly that Cusio would be the wrong place for them.

'I want to take Emma to several Italian cities,' said Guido firmly. 'She doesn't know Padua or Parma – or even Bologna – never mind the Marches or the South—'

'Then you must take her there,' I said.

'I've only been to Tuscany and Rome – but I shall go to your Cusio one day, I promise,' said Emma.

After they had gone the room seemed so empty and quiet. I needed young people to cheer me up and hoped they had not found me too ancient and boring. I was still in two minds about my own life, where to live, what to do. If I left England what would I be cutting myself adrift from? I suppose I must confess that I had hopes of Mario coming to England to see me – and settling the question.

I went to stay with Eleanor for a week. I would entertain her in London later in return for her hospitality, and we made arrangements for the summer.

When I returned I had made up my mind more firmly than before. If I moved it would not be to Dorset; I would keep it for the occasional refreshment of holidays and as a place for my imagination but I did not belong there any more.

Lizzie telephoned me. They had fixed the date of the wedding, which was to be in a small Catholic church.

'Tell me about your trip to the West Country,' she ordered me. 'I need to think of something other than wedding arrangements.'

I was relieved that she didn't want to talk about Guido – or even Mario. I told her about my adventures in Dorset. 'I have made up my mind,' I said. 'Although I *could* live there quite happily, I think – I get so fed up with London – I've realized it's modern life I don't like. Just like you said. You know, when you put the radio on, all that cacophony of voices all day and even all night – the chirpy women announcers with their curious intonation, strange to anyone over fifty – and the politicians with their 'at the end of the day' and 'to be honest' and 'having said that'. Nobody ever says "yes" any more – have you noticed? They say "right" instead.'

'You don't *have* to listen to the radio,' objected Lizzie. 'They probably say exactly the same things in the West Country.'

'Yes, I know they do. That's what I mean – it's true, it's not the place but the time that is wrong for me – but it's worse in England than in Italy. I just keep feeling I need to get away from it all in a village or a small town – but it's me, not the place.'

'Stop the world I want to get off?'

'A bit. It was *so* peaceful in Cusio – mostly pedestrianized too!' Oh dear, I'd better keep off the subject of Cusio.

'And as you don't drive Dorset wouldn't be a very good idea—'

'You're quite right. If I moved at all I might just as well go abroad. Lots of people do retire in France or Italy.' I hadn't meant to stress Italy again. Now she would ask me about Mario.

She did not. Instead she said: 'Why don't you come over for a nice little lunch – I'll be all alone next Tuesday.'

She sounded as if she rather than myself was in need of cheering up. I was, however, a little wary.

Before Tuesday, yet another letter arrived from Mario. He thanked me for the photographs: 'The one of you, dear Viviana, will always remind me of a very pleasant January,' and went on to say he was planning a business trip to New York in the spring. There would be book fairs and many of his contacts to keep up with.

I wondered how long he would go on working. Till he dropped, I expected. Right at the end of the letter he added: 'I have been thinking about our mutual friends. The matter is probably better left undisturbed.'

I had not had time to tell him that Lizzie had confessed to sitting for Sandro, so that when I arrived on the Hills's Wimbledon doorstep at half past twelve on Tuesday I was determined to leave the whole thing well alone and say not one word more about it.

'Adrian's out at his West End office,' said Lizzie when she greeted me.

We went to sit in the small sitting room-cum-study where Lizzie did her accounts and typed Adrian's business correspondence. There was a comfortable sofa there too, and two chairs, all covered in a chintzy material, with matching curtains for the two long windows. It occurred to me that Lizzie's way of life was not too far removed from the one I had once dreamed of, except there was no piano and the baby had grown up. All Lizzie had done was get herself married to a successful professional man. Was that what I, who had deluded myself with romantic daydreams, had really needed when I was a young woman?

'You're looking very disapproving of something,' said Lizzie after handing me a drink of the extremely dry sherry she knew I loved.

'Me disapproving – certainly not! I was thinking how I liked the colour of your curtains,' I lied.

She twirled the stem of her own glass between her fingers. Then: 'I have something to confess,' she said softly.

My heart began to beat very quickly. 'Look, Lizzie – *don't!*'

We had managed very well to go on being friends without confessions and scenes through the years. I thought I knew what she was going to say and I did not want to hear it. No wonder she had told me meaningfully that Adrian was out.

'You told me he was dead – you're sure he's dead?' she said.

'Sandro?'

'Of course. Who else?' She cleared her throat, then looked steadily at me. 'Because I didn't just sit for him. It was more than that.'

'I thought it might be. It's years ago – and it really isn't my concern, Liz.'

'No, I have to confess to you now. Not to anyone else.'

'It's not so terrible,' I said. 'You weren't married then – you were still a free agent.'

'I thought your going back might be a sort of – sign,' she said hesitantly. She sounded so unlike herself that I was worried. 'You were mad about him – and I couldn't tell you what I was doing,' she went on.

There was a short silence between us.

'I would have done the same, I expect, if he'd asked,' I said finally with an attempt at a smile. 'If he'd been as attracted to me in the way he obviously was to you.' I thought: *I* wasn't engaged to be married.... I did not underestimate the attraction of the forbidden for a man like Sandro Montani.

'What I don't understand,' I began, but there was a lot I didn't understand, principally when and where? So I stopped. Instead, I said: 'You were just about to marry Adrian!'

'That was why.'

'Then you didn't try to resist?'

'I didn't care. It was as if I were sleep-walking. Can you understand? I was terribly attracted to him with a part of myself I'd never known before – and he was most insistent . . . . You remember how urgent it was to get married in those days. I'd decided to marry Adrian – we got on well together, and he very much wanted to marry me, to be settled and secure himself.'

'I thought you didn't even *like* Sandro?'

'I *didn't* like him – not much.'

'And you and I were nearly always together,' I went on, 'except for when you went swimming with that young Englishman. It would have been much easier to have had a flutter with *him*. Where did you meet Sandro? No, don't tell me! It's really not my business.'

'It is your business since you are the only person who knows about it. I didn't "meet" him – it was more ... primitive than that.'

The recognition of Lizzie's duplicity felt at first like a gradual thing. Like putting your foot, then your leg, then your torso, in the water for the first swim of your summer holiday. Then when the whole was immersed I felt the shock. There was no point in feeling hard done by. I'd already suspected what she had told me, but had pushed the idea away.

'I still don't see how you could have carried on an – affair – whatever it was, under my nose,' I said.

'I see I shall have to tell you all the gory details,' she said. She took a sip of her drink. 'I could see how attracted he was to me that first Sunday – do you remember – when you went to the cemetery? I saw the men quite by chance and they took me to Stresa. It didn't take me long to realize how attracted I was to him too. That's when it began.'

I thought: how ironic. I go looking at graves, thinking about the past and even about the ancestors of people like Sandro, whilst Lizzie is getting off with him in the present!

She went on, seemed determined now to tell me everything: 'Then, when we went to your "holy mountain" – that time we were all together, do you remember – Sandro and your Mario and that Marco?'

Of course I remembered.

'Well, that was the first time he—'

'But – we were all walking around – weren't we together most of the time?'

'You won't remember, but I went to look at the view. You were with Mario, I think. Sandro found me by the wall looking over the lake. I knew already what he wanted. He'd made it plain – and I wanted it too.'

'I must have been blind, deaf and dumb.'

'He was supposed to be photographing those creepy chapels – but he wasn't. He took me into one of them by a little door at the back. It was there, we . . . .'

I was silent. Then I said: 'I remember you looked pale when we went to the ladies. I thought perhaps your fair skin had given you sunstroke.' I thought, she was always having showers, washing her hair . . . . I remembered that morning at the Sacro Monte – and I remembered finding him terribly sexy.

'Well, now you know. It happened again, of course. Do you also remember that time you went to the island and I followed you, and you said you'd fallen asleep?'

'Yes, I do, as a matter of fact.'

'Well, it's a good thing you were asleep, or at least not in the basilica, because we were down in the crypt!'

'Lizzie – in a church!'

'Don't sound so horrified. I mean, I horrify myself *now* but at the time it was an urgent matter – I couldn't help myself and he certainly wasn't going to—'

'I met Sandro in the church. He'd been in the crypt, and you came in from outside – you said you'd been looking for me.'

'There was another door in the crypt that leads outside. I'd just dashed up to it because we'd heard someone – you – in the church.'

'No wonder you encouraged me to go to Zermatt!'

'That was the end of it, really. I did go to his studio that morning, and he did sketch me. he made me wait until he'd finished his sketch ... he'd just wanted a conquest, I presume.'

'You said he was busy!'

'Yes, he certainly was. We both were. Have another drink?'

'Yes, I will.' I needed one now.

'Then he stood me up!' she went on. 'He was going to meet me by the lake the next morning and instead he went to the Sacro Monte and you saw him there. *Of course* he did it on purpose. He wasn't the kind to forget "appointments".'

'Yes, I met him there by chance,' I repeated, remembering.

'And he gave you a "chaste" kiss.'

'He must have thought me a fool.'

'No, he liked you. He did know you were keen on him – men always know.'

'I suppose that put him off?'

'Well, it wouldn't be a "conquest", would it? I've forgotten most of it, Viv,' she said. 'Though I've never forgotten how he stood me up – betrayed me – the *shame* of his ignoring me that day we all went over to Stresa.'

'I didn't notice.'

'Well, obviously he couldn't be all over me – I believe he had a girlfriend the others knew about, coming over to Cusio the next week. He'd mentioned her to me even. Don't you remember how he just contradicted everything I said? As if it was my fault I'd made him stray from the straight and narrow! The soonest-over seduction in the history of womankind.'

I didn't particularly remember Sandro's manner towards Liz on that Sunday trip. He'd sulked a bit in front of us all, wanting to go over the Mottarone. Liz herself always behaved rather coolly in public.

'When he said goodbye to us that last evening after I'd taken the photos – before he went off with Raffaelo – he smiled and shook hands with you as well as me,' I said.

'I know. Butter wouldn't have melted in his mouth. I could have killed him!'

I was thinking that we had both in our different ways been rejected by Sandro Montani. I had been infatuated with him. What had been my friend's real true feelings? I couldn't believe it had been just an animal impulse.

Echoing my thoughts, she said: 'You think I was in love with him, don't you? *You* would have been. I wasn't. I assure you it was plain lust. I was quite clear about that even then.'

'That can sometimes be part of love.'

'Of your "romantic" kind of love? No, I don't think so.'

Your romantic kind. Is that what I still was, after a marriage and a bereavement? A failed romantic?

'When you said you wanted to return to Cusio, I just wished something would happen to stop you. I knew you would go in the end. You always do what you say you will. Do you think there was some force of fate operating to make you want to go there?' That didn't sound like Liz. 'But he's dead,' she added forlornly.

I looked at her, not understanding.

'What if Sandro Mantani had still lived there and – I don't know – tried to blackmail me or something? Tell Adrian? I was in agonies all the time you were away. Then you told me he'd died some time ago. You don't know how relieved I feel. Do you think your Mario knew about Sandro and me?' It was 'my' Mario now.

'He might have done – they were great friends. He's a very discreet man – and it's all long, long ago. Forget him. Sandro was never the sort of man to threaten you – he was married himself.'

I supposed it was guilt that had made her frightened. Was it that her own past instincts now revolted her?

Lizzie went on: 'It seemed like fate. You were impelled to return to Cusio. Then Emma suddenly tells me she's fallen in love with an Italian! Don't blame me for thinking history might repeat itself. I couldn't bear for her to be hurt. I know we haven't always got on too well, but I love her.'

'Lizzie, Guido is more a Mario, I'm absolutely sure of that.' She was quite clearly worried about Emma. Did I really believe that destiny had put the idea of returning in my head – something working away underground that we had no control over? I suddenly wished I'd never gone to Cusio if it was going to upset Lizzie.

I tried to lighten the tension: 'I remember a lot about that holiday and all I can say is that you were excessively discreet.'

She got up.

'Will you have something to eat?' she asked. 'I feel a bit better now. Confession does wonders for the soul.'

For the rest of my visit to Lizzie that day I was haunted by the feeling that I could never have really known her. If she had acted as she said she had, I had been completely mistaken about her character. Did I understand her any better now? I wondered whether I had been just as misled about other things. And had I been strictly truthful about my own feelings for Sandro Montani? Hadn't that probably been, deep down, a crude sexual desire dressed up in romantic finery?

When I got home I made myself a cup of tea and sat in a daze, hardly realizing I was drinking it. It revived me a bit but I went on sitting there. I said aloud: *Once upon a time two young women went on holiday together. The same man attracted them both. The first young lady was used to being passed over by the kind of man she found sexually attractive, but she continued, for the duration of the holiday and a little time after, to feel something for this man whom she hardly knew. The other young lady had not even liked him, but he had persuaded her, got what he – and it would seem she too – had wanted and had then abandoned her without so much as a word.*

Not really a pleasant story. Yet it had all ended happily. Lizzie was a long-married matron with a family, and I was – what was I? – a recently retired widow, long resigned to childlessness. It was my internal landscape that had changed, not Lizzie's.

I felt guilty. I hadn't done anything wrong, but I might, in pursuing my own dream, have made Lizzie a prey to fear and guilt. I tried to think how I would have reacted if Sandro had made a beeline for me. Alas, it had never been on the cards that I might have been the object of the desires of a man like Sandro. Of course I would have been delighted if I had been, being at the time free, not engaged to another young man.

That was the bit that worried me about Lizzie, and made me wonder how I'd have reacted if someone like Sandro had wanted to seduce me when I was already married to Roland. But I was older then by eight years, those years that make such a difference to women. In Cusio we hadn't been in the first flush of youth, Liz and I, but we'd been a sufficient number of years away from our forties, when women, they say, stop being noticed.

I pondered the enigma of young men. They were all different; Mario and Sandro represented types of masculinity that were seemingly opposed to each other, yet they'd been friends. The world – and most young women – would always have found Sandro's type more attractive. Nature was most unjust. Even so, Emma's Guido, a pleasant and well set up young man, was more of a Mario than a Sandro. Thank goodness. I thought Emma had probably had too many Sandros in her life already.

Masculine physical strength and beauty pass just as surely as women's beauty evanesces, though there are some men who never give up the chase, and who often get their woman. I didn't truly like such men very much, and although I had sometimes been attracted to them in the past, once I was married I thought I was immune. Now, I was in the fortunate – or unfortunate – position of not having to eat my heart out over any of the Sandros of this world. It would be nice though to go on liking the Marios.

I remembered the song at the hairdresser's: *'per un'ora d'amore'* indeed!

It was only the next day when there had been time enough to let Lizzie's revelations sink in that I found I was still unsettled. I wished I could have talked to Mario about love, but it would have been dishonourable to encourage gossip about the past. I had not told Lizzie yet anything further about Sandro's marriages and his general past.

I didn't contact her for a few days. I thought she'd like to be left in peace. I would wait for her to telephone me.

It was now the end of February and the days were getting appreciably longer, even if the trees were still bare and only a few straggly snowdrops were out in the garden. My heart lifted a little as it always lifts in spring. It's the lengthening of days rather than the relaxing of the grip of cold weather that makes me feel cheerful.

I received a letter from Mario at the beginning of the following week in which he told me something he had not felt able to tell me in Cusio.

He was not a man to hint but wrote quite simply: 'You asked me about your friend Elisabetta and my old friend Sandro. I thought you knew, but when you saw the drawing you did not seem to want to believe that she would even have posed for him, never mind that they were close. I know for a fact that she did pose for him and that this drawing is definitely of her. Nobody else knows, and as it is a long time ago I do not think a husband could be made angry over it. As you said to me not long ago, it is no business of ours.

'My old friend Sandro had much charm, and the sort of charisma that attracts people, not just women. His daughter is a little like him, I think. I told him at the time that I did not approve of what he was doing with your friend – with me he was quite open about it. I said he was playing with fire, but he said: "Oh it is a fire that will soon go out." Now that he has been dead for over fifteen years it is better to say no more, I think. If I am ever asked to re-edit that book I shall leave that life drawing "unattributed as to model". If you wish, you may tell your friend that I do remember her well, and convey to her my best wishes.' The rest of the letter was about his reading and his American plans. He would be away for several weeks.

I began to make my own plans for repainting my kitchen and

bathroom, something I had been wanting to have done for ages. If I wasn't going to move to Dorset, or Italy, or even Surrey, I would have to do something about my present living quarters. My neighbours, Bob and Grace, gave me the name of a young man who was said to be tidy and quick and who was free-lancing as a painter whilst he waited for a better job. Justin Bates was a graphic designer. I knew many such people were out of work, and he told me his troubles when he came to look over the job. He suggested a sort of light beige for the kitchen and pineapple for the bathroom. To all this I agreed. He was said to be very honest and perfectly capable of getting on with it if I wanted to go out, so I took the opportunity to go up to London to a few exhibitions.

I tried to forget what Lizzie had told me, but it kept coming back into my head, especially if I woke in the middle of the night. At that time of night, when resistance is low, I half entertained the notion that Mario might ask me to join him one day in a companionate 'partnership'. I missed talking to him – or just missed male company. It had been so pleasant in Cusio.

I went out to the theatre that week with Oliver Fairfax but the play irritated me and I could not tell Oliver what was on my mind. Something else kept nagging at me and I was not very good company. I did not want to reopen the subject with Mario, and he was now in any case in the States. Lizzie was the only person I could really talk to. I must see her again soon and then we could lay the whole thing to rest . . . .

I dreamed one night of Chiara Montani. In my dream she was speaking English as she stared at me. I had the idea she was going to paint my portrait. Then she exclaimed: 'Don't move! I shall take some photographs with my polaroid camera.'

Once the prints were ready she pinned them up on a beige wall, and then sat down and began to copy one of them on to her easel.

When I woke I had such a curious idea that I wondered if I was going mad. The flat was full of the smell of paint. It must be affecting my brain.

In Cusio, Chiara, with her long messy dark hair and her pale face, had looked a bit like an 'arty' English girl. She hadn't looked all that like her father as he had been when I knew him. Sandro's young face, and even Mario's and Lizzie's were difficult to remember. If we didn't have photographs I wonder if we'd remember better or worse the way people used to look? It's always difficult to remember faces. Except in dreams. Then they do return. In my dreams, anyway. I see small children I have known, as once they were, when I can no longer remember in waking life how they used to look. Even if I concentrate I can't 'see' them and yet in a dream there they are again!

My dream had made me realize something. Could I possibly be right? Had I been seeing things the wrong way round?

Could I tell Lizzie about it?

It was my turn to entertain her but I needed time to prepare myself for this. I invited her over to my flat for lunch.

'What about a week next Tuesday?' I suggested. 'All my repainting should be finished by then.'

Lizzie thanked me and said she would come.

We talked about this and that.

We talked about my new kitchen and bathroom. Neither of us mentioned her 'confession'.

My courage nearly failed me – but I must know. I could not ask her too directly.

I brought out my latest photographs of Cusio, which Lizzie had not seen. In the book I had pasted the ones of Mario old and young, and the one of Sandro and Marco at the café table.

'I showed them to Emma,' I said. 'Have they decided yet where they will go for their honeymoon? She would love Piedmont,' I added.

'They haven't decided. I believe they are thinking of going somewhere completely different,' said Lizzie. 'Greece, perhaps.'

'Cusio would be a lovely place for a honeymoon – though I can quite see why you wouldn't be too keen on the idea.' I took my courage in both hands. Now or never. I drew a deep breath, and I said: 'Perhaps your daughter *already* belongs in a way to Italy?'

There was a sharp intake of breath from Lizzie. Then she looked straight at me. She looked scared.

'Don't tell her!' she said.

'Of course not – but ought not somebody to tell her? One day?' I could see Lizzie gathering her forces:

'You can't say my marriage isn't a success. Adrian and I had slept together before I went to Cusio with you – so the baby could quite well have been Adrian's.'

'I'm sorry, Lizzie – but it just came to me. I'd been dreaming of his other daughter – of Chiara. Emma looks a bit like her. Of course she's a bit older … Originally Chiara reminded me of someone and I thought it must be her father. It's also the other way round. Emma reminded me of *Chiara* when she came over a few weeks ago.'

'I didn't think anyone would ever guess – you wouldn't have done if I hadn't told you about me and Sandro. What are you going to do?'

'Nothing, of course – as you said before, it isn't my business. I just think it might one day be Emma's.'

'I might tell her. But not Adrian!'

To have carried on such a deception for over thirty years was quite an achievement even if it was possibly more common than most people realized.

' "It's a wise child",' I said.

'I didn't really know myself until the day she was born and then – after I took one look at her . . . .' said Lizzie.

'– You know, for a day or two after they are born, babies have the imprint of their fathers . . . .'

I was silent then, but I handed her a drink which she took gratefully.

'My lips are sealed,' I said.

'Nobody else had the slightest suspicion – and Adrian was delighted with the baby. Sandro wouldn't have thanked me if I'd told him, would he?'

'No, he wouldn't have wanted to know anything about it – I feel sure of that. Perhaps he has other children as well as Emma and Chiara.'

'Oh God, I feel like getting drunk,' she said. 'I wish you had a picture of this other daughter.'

'There's a small one on the jacket of her book of photos – look.' I handed her Chiara's book. On the inside flap of the jacket at the back was a tiny photo of the photographer in the distance against the background of the lake.

'You can't tell very much from this,' said Lizzie.

'No – and the likeness is not close. It's just an impression one has – that I had. I dreamed of her the other night and called her 'Emma' though I knew she was not Emma. Do you think Emma has any idea?'

'How could she?'

'I don't know – it's just odd that she's going to marry a man from her father's country. Do you think her genes are coming out?'

'My genes too,' said Lizzie. 'Don't forget I too was powerfully attracted to an Italian!'

I poured her another glass of wine and handed her a bowl of olives.

'You've only just guessed? It wasn't the reason for your going back – to do a bit of detective work?'

'Lizzie – of course not! It was nothing to do with you or Emma that I wanted to see the place again. It was only after you told me you'd been ... intimate with him, and then with my dream, and the impression I got from Mario, I suppose my unconscious had suspicions – but they seemed outlandish. Mario knew about you and Sandro, as I told you, but Mario did not know about this.'

'Are you going to tell him?'

'No, certainly not. If he ever comes to England, though, he'd better not meet Emma! If he did, he'd guess, I'm sure, because of the resemblance to Chiara, whom I believe he knows quite well. He'd never say anything – he's not that kind of person.'

'Girls often look more like their fathers than their mothers – I've often had occasion to notice that,' said Lizzie. 'It didn't happen – of course – between Emma and Adrian.'

I marvelled as I looked at her across the table. All those years with such a secret. To have left Cusio pregnant with Sandro's child. *I* could not have carried it through. I admired her, even as I knew that *I* would not have married my fiancé. Unless I had not gone through with the pregnancy . . . . Liz had at least had the baby.

The baby I had wanted.

'Perhaps that's why I've always been so fond of Emma,' I said. 'Subconsciously I may have guessed. Just as I once thought him so attractive I always thought your daughter was lovely.'

'She *is* a lovely girl,' said Lizzie in a strangled voice. She wiped her eyes, blew her nose. After a moment she recovered and I said:

'Will she never be told then?'

'I don't know. It's too late for me to tell her now.'

'What if she ever did meet her half-sister by accident?'

'I suppose it's possible – especially if you keep telling her to go to Cusio for a holiday.'

'I won't mention it again. She's already seen Chiara Montani's book of photographs.'

'Will you show it to me again?'

I handed her the book as she sipped her coffee.

'Do you remember that picture of his I liked? The woman by the lake. Look there's a photo just like it.'

'The photographs are splendid,' she said finally. 'Another artistic girl.'

I said: 'Like Emma – who after all works for the Arts.'

'Yes – and you remember how good she was at A-level Art at school?'

I was thinking again of that light-hearted song I'd heard at the hairdresser's: 'For one hour of love...' After not more than a few hours of 'love' a child had been created – or, to put it more cogently – a human being had been created. A good and clever human being. The genesis of life was very odd.

'I wish it had been me he had wanted,' I said, when she laid down the book. '*I* was ready. I'd have loved an Emma.'

'And you wouldn't have had a wedding to get through first,' she said.

I saw there were more tears moistening her eyes. I'd never understand her.

I understood her daughter though, who was much more like me

than she was like her mother.

It was then that I told Lizzie about my long-ago abortion. She was surprised.

'I suppose that's why I was so desperate to find a father for a baby,' I said. 'Unfortunately the right man – Mario – didn't attract me in that way then.'

Lizzie spoke of the sacrifices she thought women always had to make to live permanently with anyone.

'You sound like a secret feminist, Lizzie,' I said.

'No – I don't go in for theories, only sometimes I envied you your independence. I made my bed and I had to lie on it – and I expect I'd have married someone like Adrian one day anyway, even if I had not had Emma.'

'Adrian has two fine sons too,' I said.

Her words had made me remember how I hadn't wanted to be 'free' after giving up what had turned out to be my first and only chance to be a mother. I hadn't had an Emma, but – was it meant to be a comfort? – until I met Roland I had 'lived at my own hands', as I believe they used to call it in the days when women had no power at all, either financial or over their own bodies. Unless they were widows. I was rambling . . . .

'You must tell me what I can give them for a wedding present,' I said briskly.

I puzzled more over the character of my friend Lizzie in the following days than I did over what had happened to her. That could have happened to many women, I thought.

Her never saying anything to me about her plight all those years ago, or later, was perhaps a question of discretion, rather than one of duplicity. If she had not been about to marry Adrian I supposed she would have told me. I saw that she had put her life on hold when she married Adrian in full knowledge. She gave up her 'freedom' and got Emma.

At what point had Lizzie suspected what had happened to her? It couldn't have been long after our return. That she had never confessed to her fiancé was, I suppose, only what many other women in the same quandary had omitted to do. If it had been myself who had returned pregnant – and unmarried – from Cusio what would I have done? I would have confessed, I supposed. Would Adrian still have married Liz if she'd confessed? Yes, he might.

I thought about baby Emma, remembering so much from her early years. She had been a cheerful little girl but one with a strong will that had sometimes baffled, even infuriated, her mother. I remembered one occasion when we had taken her to a matinée at the ballet – she must have been about four or five years old, and she had been thrilled. The amusing thing was that she had said nothing about the dancing or even the costumes of the dancers but had kept saying how pretty the trees were and the lake. The backdrop had interested her more than the dancers. When she was a little older I had sometimes taken her and her brother Simon to the Children's Arts Theatre to give Lizzie and Adrian a rest. Unless there was a fight on stage Simon had been politely bored, but Emma had loved the whole afternoon. She had been tactful even then, had told her brother that if he wanted to go to sleep she would wake him up for the tea that we had ordered as a special treat. I had really enjoyed taking her out, even when she was in her early teens and not getting on too well with her mother. I had explained to Lizzie that I was well aware it was easy for me to get on with Emma – I didn't have to *live* with an adolescent. I didn't want her mother to think me disloyal if I occasionally took Emma's side, or at least tried to listen to her side of things. Emma never had boyfriends until she went to university, and I believe her mother was relieved about that – when she wasn't worrying in case her daughter was not popular. Sussex University sorted all that out and when I met Emma again she looked slimmer, had grown up. Lizzie said she was 'in love'. That had been with the first of the 'unsuitable' ones.

As I remembered Emma's childhood and thought about Lizzie and her past predicament, I was rather dreading when I should see Emma again for the first time after her mother's revelations. There was nothing to forgive Lizzie for, but I felt I'd rather see Emma next time with Guido than at home with her parents.

Adrian was the one I felt a bit sorry for, but as he knew nothing, there was no point in my vicarious sympathy. He'd always left the upbringing of his children to his wife. He had been a good provider who got on well with his sons, but, as far as I knew, he and Emma had not had that special bond of sympathy which fathers and daughters are so often said to have. I think he was a bit baffled by her and could not see what all the fuss had been about when Lizzie had moaned about the dreadful men her daughter fell for.

Now at least Emma seemed happy, and Lizzie had told me Adrian liked young Guido, though he was still at a loss over what to talk about with him.

I need not have worried about meeting Emma again after being burdened with my new knowledge. I came across her quite by chance one Saturday afternoon in Cecil Court where I was browsing in the second-hand bookshops and print shops.

I was perusing some fascinating old postcards crammed in a box marked 'Continental'. As usual I could not resist such things and was even less able to resist reading the long-ago messages on their backs in faded ink from Como or Pisa. When I looked up for a moment I saw Emma come into the shop.

'Emma!' I exclaimed. 'Look at these lovely pictures.'

'What have you got there, Vivien?'

I told her, and she said she was looking for a flower print to frame and give her mother for her birthday. She looked so well and happy it was a pleasure to see her. I could not help smiling. All the past seemed to melt away. What did it matter who the girl's father had been? Here she was, real and alive.

'You look very pleased with yourself, Vivien,' she said.

As she went on to speak to the owner of the shop, who was telling her that a neighbouring shop on the Court might just have what she wanted, I was looking at her profile. This time the resemblance to Sandro struck me. I wondered why I had never noticed all those years before how unlike Adrian Hill she was. But it was Chiara whom Emma really resembled, Chiara whom I'd seen not long ago.

'We've more or less fixed the date,' Emma said, as she prepared to leave the shop. 'It's to be in June – your invitation will soon be in the post.'

'Oh – lovely. I'm looking forward to it,' I said.

In only three or four months, she'd be married. She hadn't known Guido all that long, but I knew couples who had married within six weeks of meeting and who were still together. Lizzie on the other hand had known Adrian Hill for years before she married him.

'Must dash – have to meet Guido at four . . . .'

After our goodbyes it did cross my mind that she was a lucky young woman. Thank goodness I had not felt in any way embarrassed, or heavy with the knowledge I must never reveal to her.

That was all past and gone.

I thought when I got back home of how so many little girls change in their prime of life from small scraps of humanity with sticking-out ears and draggly hair – little tomboys, as Emma had once been – into luscious glossy glowing young women. I'd taught plenty of girls and I knew what a surprise they sometimes gave their teachers. Sneaky adolescents became powerful merchant bankers. Sober sixth-formers became glamorous singers, and sometimes the class beauty – too early matured and married too young, with too many children, looked a drudge at thirty-five.

Emma Hills, however, was her own woman and I could not see her Guido taking any of her beauty away. Only age – and life itself would do that.

Emma was the imaginary child I'd fantasized that hot morning in the Sacro Monte, when I had felt such physical longing for Sandro. Now Emma belonged neither to Lizzie nor, even in imagination, to myself, nor to her real father, nor to Adrian nor even to her future husband Guido Taviani, but to herself. Just as the baby I had not had would have belonged to himself or herself in the end.

'The evil that men do lives after them, the good being oft interred with their bones,' is often quoted, but when Sandro Montani died, the things he left on earth were good. A double good: Emma and her half-sister Chiara. These two young women were as much his memorial as his scattered works of art. *His* good was not buried but living on. And time had left Lizzie with more than the memory of passionate lust, had left her with this new person.

The good man, Mario, had so far left nothing on earth but editions of books and some painfully acquired artistic knowledge, which I did not doubt was appreciated by specialists.

Poor old Vivien Wilson had not even left that! The actions she had taken in her youth, her sins of omission, had set the course of the rest of her life. She might live on in the minds of a few friends, but no child of Peter or of Roland would carry on into the future.

As the days passed after seeing Emma in London, Emma looking so happy, I felt that I had perhaps achieved the function of laying Lizzie's ghost to rest for her. I ought to be satisfied. Had my visit to Cusio and all it had brought in its train been meant to happen?

My old Dorset compatriot Hardy writes so often about long-ago loves returning forcefully – sometimes as ghosts. Only after his first wife died could he, through writing poetry about his long-ago love, fall in love with her again, a love accompanied this time with regret for the time that had passed. Or could it have been the other way round, his regret having brought about his art? I read and reread some of these poems during the next few weeks. Love appeared to be inextricably linked with Time. Sex certainly was – through the consequence of a new generation to carry on life into the future. I remembered how poor Hardy had been frightfully sad to have had no children with *his* Emma.

People don't change much as they age; it has been my experience that character stays very much the same. Was it too late now for me to change at all, just as it was far too late for me to have a child of my own? Was my own future now destined to be one of gathering disappointment? Any disappointment life had brought me need not stop me taking arms against it, or looking for something that would help me to keep on an even keel. Life still went on whether Vivien Wilson née Butterworth was content or not. I could expect no sudden transformation, I knew, and I had already decided, as I had told Lizzie some time before, that I would not go home to live in the West Country.

I had never forgotten Sandro, though I had nothing to remember him by.

Lizzie had borne his child – and could now scarcely remember him.

I thought of the affection I had always had for Emma, which I was sure I would always feel, and I thought of my new friendship with Mario, who would soon be back from the States.

I would write to Mario again. I would not mention the past. I was not left with nothing, even if I were a little sadder and wiser. I had made my return, to settle what might have been unfinished business, from my youth, from before my marriage – but my business had been over for some time.

It was Liz's business that had been unfinished.

And somehow I felt in a curious way that Mario's too might still not be settled.

Epilogue

... 'time which none can bind,
While flowing fast away, leaves love behind.'

One night I had another strange dream to unsettle me. Not about Chiara or Emma, which I would not have minded, but an odd dream about Sandro. At the beginning of the dream I had been reliving all the passion I had once felt for him and men like him, emotions I had not forgotten but remembered only intellectually. Like the way one sees long-gone faces in dreams, one can also re-experience feelings one thought were gone for ever. Suddenly though, in this dream, the atmosphere became menacing and I knew that he was going to murder me. I struggled to escape – and then it was no longer Sandro but some faceless male creature who caught up with me. I woke in a sweat of fear.

As I lay there recovering I still remembered the force of my old romantic feelings but now they were mixed with danger. I fell asleep again eventually. When I got up in the morning I said aloud: 'Life is not a dream'. Neither had my life ever possessed the nightmarish qualities I read about in the newspapers. I had – so far – never been attacked or raped. I was alive and glad to be alive.

I thrust the dream away from me. I didn't know what it meant but there was no reason to dwell upon it.

★

Lizzie was busy planning her daughter's wedding. The exact date had not yet been fixed. She telephoned me once or twice; neither of us made any reference to the past. I knew we might have to say something to each other eventually but I put it off, and I think she felt the same.

I decided I had better do something for others and so went out every evening for a week posting envelopes for a children's charity into unsuspecting letter-boxes, and collecting them the following week. I was often tempted to put 50p into an envelope that was returned empty, or to post a second one through the letter-box of those people who were always out. I was beginning to feel quite virtuous, but I knew it really cost me nothing.

Then I telephoned the headmistress of the primary school down the road. She had occasionally used me in the past when she needed voluntary, unpaid, but qualified help to take a small group of reluctant readers. I asked if there were at present any children in desperate need of a helping hand. Yes, there were – a teacher was about to take maternity leave at Easter but they had not yet found a replacement and Mrs Phillips kept being sick. I could come in two mornings a week until Easter if I would take some of the worst readers – all boys – off her hands in a small group. It would not be for long but Mrs Rowan sounded quite relieved that she could count on me. What with inspections and the National Curriculum and constant testing they all felt beleaguered. It counted as an 'Inner City' school even though half of its intake was from our select suburb, and she knew I believed in the old tried and trusted methods that were now making a comeback. Nobody could have been keener than myself to promote a love of reading stories.

People seemed to have thought in the recent past that teaching children to sound out words militated against their enjoyment of the stories that were read to them. Unfortunately you could read aloud to a child for six months, who might even follow your finger in the book as you read, without him – it was usually a him – grasping more than the meaning of a few shapes.

Teaching not very bright children is always a slog. You have to have the patience of Job, but in a small group it is just possible. Well, I did my bit. As I already knew, primary school children were much more gruelling to teach than they had been when I started teaching in the East End of London. I remembered those years long ago when similar children from a deprived area had been so keen to learn. Now there were children of many different races and religions, some with parents who could not speak English. They, however, were not the real problem, for most of them wanted to learn and their families wanted them to get on. The problem lay in what people were beginning to call the 'underclass' . . . .

Perhaps I was just older and therefore more easily tired, but the work did at least for a few weeks take my mind off the past.

I still seemed to be marking time as far as my own life was concerned. I had spent so much of the first years of my retirement thinking about the past. Could I for my future old age lay down some more memories?

I decided I might enrol after Easter in a local painting class. If I did not enjoy it, or seemed to make no progress, I might switch my interests to music. I could apply to a piano teacher who *might* get my playing back to the not very elevated standard I'd reached at the age of fourteen when I had stopped practising.

The day before the art class was to begin I was just putting together a few things for the first lesson – looking for my old smock and sorting bits of charcoal, when my telephone rang.

It was Lizzie, quite breathless with the update of news about Emma's wedding.

'It's to be on a Saturday afternoon – June seventeenth – three o'clock at St Michael's – then afterwards at our house.'

A marquee in the garden, I thought. What a lot of hassle. I didn't think I'd ever have been such an efficient mother as Lizzie.

'Does Guido not mind about its not being a Catholic church then?' I asked, more because I was thinking fiercely, wondering whether to allude to anything more intimate than a wedding.

'No, he's not religious. It was Emma who wanted a church wedding. I was surprised,' replied my friend disingenuously. 'I think she wants to mark the day with some ceremony, and the Town Hall isn't very impressive – especially as his parents will be coming over from Bologna . . . .'

I did not believe that Emma wanted a church wedding to impress her in-laws. It was much more likely she wanted to please her own mother. Adrian would not have had much to do with the decision.

'And Guido has just had a promotion,' Lizzie went on. 'So they're thinking of buying a flat or a house on a mortgage – either in west London, or a house in a commuter village, probably in Surrey.'

I thought the flat sounded more like Emma.

'Anyway, Viv, your invitation will soon be in the post.'

'Oh, thank you,' I said.

'It's not going to be an enormous wedding – just a small select band,' Lizzie continued.

She sounded a bit worried. Did she think I might be going to denounce her in front of the assembled congregation as a fraud?

★

I seemed in some curious way better reconciled now to my retirement. Work had never been my entire life. I would attend the painting class and take up my piano playing again, perhaps go to classes in music appreciation? I decided I might have been a little depressed after leaving teaching, before I had gone to Cusio. I must make the effort to prove that the things I had done or left undone in my youth were not going to set the course of whatever was left to me of life. I wasn't depressed any more – maybe I felt sad, but that was a positive emotion. I was still however a little disturbed about Lizzie's secret but I tried not to allow my mind to dwell on it.

I also thought quite a lot about how people regarded a woman as a success or a failure. I had been brought up to think that only by becoming a mother did a woman really prove herself. In feminist eyes I might be regarded as a reasonable success, since I had earned my own living before I married and after Roland died, and had been independent, even if that independence might only have been a surface matter. Which of us, man or woman, is truly independent, or free? – and are these always good things? Perhaps I needed to attend a class in ethics to make me think a little better . . . .

My doubts about freedom were similar to the ones I'd had all my life and probably connected with being female. The emptiness I had felt in myself – because I would leave nothing on this earth when I died – was not an emotion most men would probably feel, though Roland had felt sad about it. Why, even my mother had left me and my brother in the world, and my brother Roger had a large family. Possibly I had been brainwashed, if not by society then by Mother Nature herself?

Mario did not reply to my letter for some time. Oh well, I

thought, I have perhaps built up too much from getting to know him again. It had been a pleasant interlude, but clearly I could never fit into his life as a companion, just as he would not fit into my London life. He had wanted us to write to each other, but that did not mean a letter a week.

If only I had valued his friendship all those years ago and realized that out of a friendship and shared tastes we might have built something more. He might once have made the perfect partner for me. I knew, even then, that he preferred women who liked talking about ideas and books and music and painting. Not a woman like Liz.

Roland had not been like Mario, but I had been what he needed at the time. He had been a man who was neither too intrusive nor in any way aggressive or bossy but quite capable of holding his own. Roland would have been a good father, just as Mario would have been, I had seen that when I was in Cusio. But love is blind, and young women are attracted to bounders, those physically compelling men with mysterious sexual allure: that charisma to which Mario had alluded.

I reflected ruefully once again that Nature had arranged things badly, or we had grown beyond her. Young women feel before they think. Young women mix up sexual romance and 'settling down', and get involved with young men who are not ready for permanence. Successful marriages are often made by the middle-aged, thus defeating Nature's purpose! I wouldn't have wished years ago to pass on the genes – though we did not call them that so much then – of a man who did not care about his future possible offspring, yet Emma's genes seemed excellent. Emma was lucky, entering the state that was once grimly called 'wedlock'.

I considered I had now come to an age of enlightenment. Was it because I could no longer feel deeply? No. I might even feel again. I was sure that Roland would have wanted me to be able to do that.

I waited for Mario to reply and during that time received my invitation to Emma's wedding. I looked forward to hearing from him again. Perhaps he might have thought I had been too curious about Sandro, but he had seemed to encourage me to talk. He would reply on his return from America. It would take him some time to get back into the normal rhythm of his life on his return. I must not go on with that daydream of our getting together one day as companions, even if platonic ones.

Well, I heard from him at the end of May. He had spent longer in the States than he had intended but was now back in Cusio in the best season. He wrote that everything was now covered in blossom, but there were as yet few tourists around.

What he then went on to tell me was, I must admit, surprising – at least to me. It even made me attend Emma's wedding with mixed feelings.

I have read and reread that letter many times, but I have not told Lizzie – or anyone – its contents. It has made me consider my life once again, and think about the good husband I had once had. I thought too about the fate that had impelled me to revisit Cusio in January. I felt now that it had been something outside myself that had told me to revisit the place. It had been a good idea, in spite of everything; as though the gods had spoken and led me to that art gallery with its photographs of the place.

I thought: 'Things are in the saddle and ride us.'

I thought about all I had learned of the way Sandro had treated Lizzie, and the whole truth about that long-ago summer.

I thought about the new perspective it had all given me on my godchild Emma.

I had learned how wrong one can be about people, as I had certainly been wrong in my estimate of Lizzie.

I thought it had all made me more understanding.

I thought about how I had also acquired a new 'old friend' in Mario Sartoris, and how I had possibly allowed myself to daydream a little about our meeting again in the future.

What else was there for me to learn?

Something else was to shift the kaleidoscope again. Once it had shifted I began to wonder what was left for me.

I'd underestimated Mario Sartoris. In his letter Mario confessed to being madly in love with Chiara Montani, and to have been in love with her for the past three years. After a few paragraphs about Cusio and his travels in the States he started on a new sheet of paper.

...Ever since your visit to Italy I have been asking myself whether I should tell you what I am now going to write. As you know, I am not normally a superstitious person, but when you came here in January I thought it was like a sign. You wanted to know all about Sandro – and you are not the first woman who has asked for news of him, I assure you. I remembered so well your friend Liz. Sandro told me she was one of his 'conquests'. He did not only draw her – but I expect you had come already to that conclusion before I told you?

I have often thought about Sandro in the years since he died. I got to know Chiara when as an adolescent she was living with her grandparents. I found her even then mysterious and attractive. It was strange that she was Sandro's own

248

flesh and blood. I think that what had attracted me to Sandro as a friend was always in the back of my mind. Indeed at first I believe I fooled myself into thinking I was keeping an eye on her for him!

Chiara is no fool. Three years ago when I began to see more of her I fell deeply in love. She immediately acknowledged that she knew.

It seemed to me then and still seems to me that she deserves better than I – but who could love her as much as I do? It is not even what you call an 'affair', or I believe the Americans call a 'relationship'.

It is just that I am made happy to know she is in the world. I asked her to marry me last year but she refused. She says she will never marry anybody, that she wants to get on with her work. She won't live with me – and I would not have asked her to do so, for that would destroy her reputation in what is still a small place where people judge by the old standards.

I had to tell you about the situation, Viviana. I thought you ought to know. I want everything to be above board between us for it is as true that I was meant to see you again as that I love Chiara. I value your friendship and want to go on writing to you, if you will. You may tell your friend Elisabetta about it if you wish.

Indeed I would have told you earlier when you were in Cusio, had it not seemed an intrusion on your own preoccupations. Chiara does not love me – she puts up with me, sees me, listens to me and I believe quite enjoys my company. To her I am a sort of uncle, but her indifference only spurs on my passion – you of all people will understand that.

Forgive me if you believe I have written what I should not, and please continue to write to your old friend,

Mario

My first reactions surprised me. Hadn't I just come to the conclusion that I had reached a philosophical old age? That the past was over and could not be changed and that I – and Lizzie – would live on in the present with no more decisions to make, no more emotional wounds to bathe? That I was now above the fray? In the past I had been a sort of conduit for impossible feelings, but now all that was over.

It was patently untrue, for I was furiously angry and upset.

I realized that the emotions roused in me were those of jealousy! Deep down I must have continued with my only half formulated hope, that Mario might one day have thought of me as a companion, if not a lover. Then I cried, out of self-pity and fury and, finally, sadness. What *was* I left with? Why had Roland, who had truly loved me had to die? Had I not loved him enough?

Over several days I pulled myself together, but I could not trust myself to reply just yet.

The things I had done or not done long ago had indeed set the course of the rest of my life.

Knowledge of the real past had nothing to do with the rest of my future. Neither would it affect Emma's. I did not believe Lizzie would ever tell her who her real father was. Even if Emma had Italian-looking children she would have, after all, an Italian husband.

With Mario, though, it was not an old story but a situation with vibrations in the present. I had dallied with the idea of Emma meeting Chiara one day, with such silly thoughts as: 'Wouldn't she like to have a sister?'

Now all I could think of was, should I tell Mario about Emma? Of course I couldn't, but I wished he knew. Even this was an ignoble thought, for if Sandro was known to have two daughters it might take the spotlight off the one with whom Mario was at present so clearly besotted.

The whole thing was another example of what I have always considered masculine luck. Chiara might very well one day decide to marry her elderly swain. Women often do accept older men, though maybe not those who are at least thirty-five years older than themselves. I suppose what hurt me was that I finally had to come to terms with the fact that old men do not usually prefer women of their own generation. Their sexual urges may diminish but enough of them remain to fan the flames of passion.

Like me, Mario was a romantic. But he was a man and for men perhaps the idea of romance continues into old age. He might appear sensible, and he was certainly a man who considered women as equals, but he adored beauty, and Chiara – come to think of it – was, like Emma, a beautiful young woman. I did not begrudge either of them their beauty. If I were a man I'd have fallen in love with one of them. If I had possessed more common sense when I was Emma's age, and if Mario had pursued me a little more passionately, I might very well have ended up married to him, not to Roland. *If* only I had realized thirty years ago how very suited we were, and *if* he had been less shy, I could have got over my infatuation with Sandro and begun to appreciate Mario's solid worth. That would have been a partnership of equals. I might have had children, and if Roland had met a woman he wished to marry a little earlier than he did, he too might have become a father. But one cannot alter the past; that is why it is the past.

If life were a romantic fiction Mario and I, having so much in common, might still have got together to embark on the marriage of an Indian Summer.

Except he was in love with someone else. I believe he is the faithful type. He will be faithful to his Chiara whether he marries her or no.

I ought to be honoured by his confidences. That was the only attitude I could take when I did reply to his letter.

In the meantime Emma's wedding loomed nearer. I thought I might be tempted afterwards to send Mario one of the wedding photographs of Emma and her Guido for him to come to his own conclusions. Would I be able to resist that temptation? I knew him as the soul of discretion.

Another strange effect of his letter was to make me reluctant for a time to try my hand again at painting and piano playing. I cancelled my attendance at the painting class until the autumn and realized that what I needed was not to force myself to drag out my own feelings into paint or musical notes, but to learn from others.

I enrolled in that class for musical appreciation. I knew I did not always listen well. Some music I find so dense and difficult that I cannot understand how a composer might even imagine one bar, never mind a symphony. Brahms had always made me feel inadequate, but I often listen to music in my dreams.

I have always puzzled over the difference between listening to music one has heard before and listening to it for the first time. There seems to be a sort of strangeness about listening to notes in an order one has never heard before. As one listens, one asks oneself what will happen next? Almost as if one is creating the music as one listens to it.

A bit like life as it is lived.

What can I say about Emma's wedding? It was a great success, if weddings can ever be otherwise. It did not rain and the bride looked as brides are supposed to look, quietly radiant. Adrian gave her away with aplomb. The guests were all closely connected with the family or were friends of long-standing, of all generations. Many of them greeted me. There were also several young friends of Emma's, already married and accompanied by tiny offspring who reposed in their parents' arms or were rushing up and down and falling on the grass in toddler fashion.

Champagne flowed before the lunch that was held in a marquee in the Hills's garden – I suppose one ought to call it a wedding breakfast. I was put on the other side of Guido's father – I expect Lizzie hoped I would converse in Italian as his English was fractured.

Afterwards in the garden we all sat and chatted and the children rushed about. The sun shone and there was even birdsong. It was all a tribute to Lizzie's management skills, what is called a beautiful occasion.

I gathered there was to be a party for the younger people in London when the couple returned from their honeymoon.

'Where are they going?' I asked Lizzie, who looked resplendent in a dress the colour of moonlight. 'Or is it a secret?'

'Not really a secret,' she replied, looking at me speculatively. 'It's not to be Greece after all, but Italy! All arranged by Guido, though I'm not sure exactly where – the Veneto, I believe.' Now she was avoiding looking in my eyes. 'They'll end up on a visit to his parents,' she added. Then she looked at me. 'You liked them?'

'I thought them extremely civilized,' I replied.

She moved away and then Emma suddenly appeared in a shocking pink silk suit. But soon afterwards she left, with her husband, who looked both proud and contented.

As I sat on there for a little while, chatting amiably to ancient relatives, or catching up with acquaintances, I seemed to see, far away, Emma's shadow, Chiara Montani.

I have not wasted my life, even if Mario Sartoris is still hopelessly in love with Chiara Montani. I think I am too set in my ways now to make once more all the adjustments and compromises the married state needs, or that even living with someone requires. If I had met a Mario-like lonely widower I suppose it just might have been different, but I don't think so.

We correspond regularly. Friendship is better, and perhaps rarer, I now believe.

I am writing at almost the end of yet another year, 1996. In September, three months after the wedding, Lizzie telephoned me excitedly. Emma was pregnant, and Lizzie was looking forward to being a grandmother.

The baby, a boy, was born a year after her marriage, in June this year.

'Will you please be one of our little boy's godmothers, Vivien?' Emma wrote. They were living in the Surrey village, not the Notting Hill flat. I supposed it would be healthier for a young family. I replied that I should be delighted.

Just to be going on with I bought him a silver rattle similar to the one I'd bought my great-nephew in Cusio. Somehow, I feel that in future I shall be seeing more of Emma than of her mother.

It is late autumn, but who says that November must always be dull and dreary? A dazzling sun is shining through a dark sky.

I have been retired now for over four years but I am keeping myself busy. Mario has asked if I'd like to revisit Cusio next summer but I don't think I shall. It's true that I'd like to meet Chiara, but I don't think it would be a very good idea, even though I now feel quite detached from the past. I'll write to him now and again.

I know I have to find myself a life, become the main character in my own story.

My long ago holiday in Cusio – and my return there – had never been about *me* at all! My own real life had been in England, teaching, and being married to Roland, and retiring, and being widowed – and teaching again, and retiring again. The story was never mine, and I had not been responsible for those to whom it did belong. To Liz, and now to Emma and her husband. And, just as Cusio once belonged to Liz and Sandro, it now belongs to Mario and Chiara.

Whether in England or in Italy Emma and Guido will have a different sort of life. Like relay runners they will take up the baton from the tired old runner who brought it up to them . . . .

I shall probably go to stay with Eleanor again soon for a few days. But I shall return to London.

Yesterday I saw Adrian and Lizzie Hill's grandson, my five months old great godson, Jack Alexander Taviani at his christening.

Yes, Alexander is one of his names.

I suppose you can't always tell with a small baby but I feel sure he is going to look very like his natural grandfather: Alessandro – 'Sandro' – Montani.